The Ruins Out of Time

By

ALYSIA S. KNIGHT

Heart Dreams PRESS

The Ruins – Out of Time
By Alysia S. Knight
Published by Heart Dreams Press
Copyright © 2015 Alysia S. Knight
Cover design: by Kelli Ann Morgan @
www.inspirecreativeservices.com

The views expressed within this work are the sole responsibility of the author and do not represent Heart Dreams Press or any of its affiliates.

This is a work of fiction. Names, characters, place and events are product of the author's imagination. Any similarities to actual persons, living or dead, business establishments or events are purely coincidental.

ISBN:194200009X
ISBN-13:978-1-942000-09-9

Also available from Alysia S. Knight

Letting Love Win

☙❧

Past To Die For

☙❧

Temperature Rising

☙❧

Kare for Me

☙❧

Blind Witness

☙❧

Beauty and the Chief

☙❧

Trail to Her Heart

☙❧

His Governess

☙❧

Her Brand of Trouble

Hope you have a great day.
Happy reading.

Alysia S. Knight

Connected by destiny, brought together out of time.

Chapter One

Destruction to all.

Fear pierced Leeza's heart. She forced down the panic, backed up and started the translation again knowing it wouldn't change. Even accounting for the variants in words, the meaning was clear.

The console under her fingers picked up a chill, but it was just her imagination. Buried under the sand, the ship's temperature was constant. She knew now that was what it was, not a long-forgotten city from an advanced, ancient civilization, but a spaceship that had crashed and been abandoned centuries before.

Curious, she scrolled to the next page. It only took a second to understand the schematic for shutting down the engines. She returned to the log where it talked about the inhabitants leaving the ship, resigned to the fact that they had to make a new life on this planet since any attempt to restart the engines would bring destruction to the sky.

Destruction to all. The warning came again. She glanced at the time. It was near morning. She'd worked through the night.

Aggravation burst from her. How could they be so stupid to want to start the engines before they knew what they were dealing with? But, it wasn't stupidity. It was greed, Zareck's greed, not for scientific or historical knowledge, but to get his hands on the technology.

Leeza longed to keep reading, but another glance at the timepiece told her that time was something she didn't have. She had to alert the council. They couldn't reactivate the engines. She had to stop it.

Her frustration peaked. She'd told them they were moving too fast. They needed to give her time to translate. Two and a half months, they'd only given her two and a half months. Even though she was the top linguist with the ability to read thirty-two languages, it took time to decipher a new one. First, she had to break the coding then work it into a language. She'd been making incredible progress, but the only reason she'd been able to do it as quickly as she did, was the similarities she had found in root words.

The problem was Zareck, the man who funded the expedition. After complaining from afar for a month, he'd shown up and demanded they try to start what was figured to be the main energy system. What they didn't know was that in doing so it would cause a back flash of energy. She wasn't quite certain of the exact translation, but she got that it would cause a reaction in the particles of the air around the ship, something linked to the propulsion.

Leeza turned from the console, hurrying down the hall. The dim orange glow that filled the ship reflected off the metal walls giving her a new ominous feeling of warning. It wasn't the coolness from the interior that caused her to shiver.

She hurried faster, pulling the hood up on her cloak as the tails flowed out behind her. Coming around the corner, she ran full force into the tall, sinewy form of the man she'd just been cursing.

Zareck caught her shoulders, steadying her. "I didn't think anyone would be here yet this morning." His voice was smooth. It was always smooth as was his manner, but he didn't fool her. "Leeza Jaeff, isn't it? Linguist?"

"Mr. Zareck." She tilted her head down in acknowledgement. Leeza knew he was aware of exactly who she was. He had tried to get her taken off the expedition when she first raised caution about letting her complete her translation before they pressed experimentation with any devices they found.

"What's the hurry?"

"I," Leeza paused to catch her breath and think. She didn't trust or like the man. "I got caught up in my translation and didn't realize the time." She pulled back only to find her wrist trapped in the steel grip of his hand.

"And, just what has you all panicked, I wonder?"

"Nothing." She managed not to stumble over the word. "Please, I need to go. It's late." She pulled back to no avail. Zareck was past middle age, and despite his thin build, he was very strong.

"Actually, it's quite early. Now, what did you find?" There was a snap to his voice, and his pale eyes bore down on her.

Leeza shook her head, fighting for calm. "Nothing. I would like to go."

"And just where are you going? The council, I presume, to raise another alarm." There was no missing the malevolence behind the words. "I really should've had you killed with your father."

Shock, terror and pain ripped through her like shards of glass. She lost what he was saying as memories of her father flooded her mind. He'd been killed in an accident just four months earlier as he was coming home from the university where he taught. He'd been so excited about this expedition that Leeza had agreed to take his place as the top remaining qualified linguist.

"My father?" She choked on the words.

Zareck broke what he was saying to glare down at her. "Yes, the interfering man with his principles. I knew he would just drag out the excavation with his cautious ways. He'd worked on other projects I've had interests in before. But I hadn't figured you'd agree to take his place so soon after his death." He pulled her down the hall.

"You killed him." Fury burst in Leeza. She struck out, slamming her free hand into the back of his head.

Zareck cursed, swinging around. Leeza had no time to block his fist. The blow caught her across the side of her cheek, dropping her to her knees.

"You are no better than him, just a hindrance." Hatred spewed in his words. All his charm gone. He grabbed her arm again and resumed dragging her down the corridor.

He turned a corner before Leeza's head cleared, and she started to fight back. Hitting at his hand gained her nothing, and at his pace, she couldn't get her feet under her as she slid across the smooth floor. Reaching out, she caught the edge of a doorway only to be ripped free. The next doorframe, she got a better hold, jerking them to a stop.

Zareck turned on her, his hand already whipping around in a striking motion, but this time Leeza was ready. She kicked out, catching him below his knee, taking his leg out from under him. He released her, slammed into the wall behind him and went down.

Leeza tried to scramble to her feet, but before she could make it, Zareck caught her ankle, pulling her feet out from under her. She landed hard but kicked out wildly. Breaking free, this time she made it up and ran. Leeza didn't know where she was going, and didn't care. She just knew she had to get away from Zareck or she was dead. His footfalls echoed down the corridor behind her.

She put on more speed and skidded around a corner almost going down. The soft soled boots she wore afforded her no traction. Ahead of her was a stairway. She ran toward it, taking the steps down two at a time, fighting to keep her balance. He was gaining on her. A whimper escaped her.

Zareck caught the ends of her cloak as it whipped out behind her, yanking her from her feet. She gagged as the ties bit into her throat. She tried to release them, but they knotted, not coming free. Changing tactics, Leeza came up swinging, hitting and scratching whatever she could. Zareck released the cloak in an effort to protect his face.

Freed, Leeza sprang up to run again, only to have Zareck's hand lock onto her long braid of pale hair, yanking her back. She cried out as pain speared through her head. He jerked her back. Wrapping the braid around his hand until he reached her neck, he snapped her head around so she looked up at him.

She saw the blow coming, but her effort to block it was feeble compared to the fury-fed power behind it. His hand caught her on the side of her head. The world hazed over as she started to slip into unconsciousness.

Leeza fought to stay alert. She was aware of being lifted and thrown over his shoulder. She wanted to hit out but couldn't get past the stupor in her mind to move her hands.

They came to another set of stairs. He took the downward direction. With each step, air was forced out of her lungs. Several times, Leeza made vain attempts to catch something to slow their progress into the bowels of the ship, but nothing slowed him, not even when they came to a rubble strewn area.

Zareck stumbled over it and stopped at a door that was partially open. He dropped her unceremoniously on the floor. As soon as he set to work shoving the opening wider, Leeza tried to stagger up, only to have Zareck grab her cloak and yank her back, slamming her head into the wall.

She sank back to the floor, her legs not able to hold her. She felt sick.

"Please." Her word sounded like a moan.

"You are not going anywhere," he snarled out. "And no one will find you here. I've waited long enough."

Leeza tilted her head to the side to look up at him, pulling on all her strength to get the words out. "The engines will explode."

With a grinding sound, the door slid open. Zareck reached down and hauled her up over his shoulder again, stepping into the room. Leeza had never been in this area of the ship before. It seemed empty, but for some kind of pod-like capsules that lined the walls. Each was taller than a man. Several stood open.

Leeza was unprepared when Zareck dropped her back into one of the pods. "What?" The word hardly made it passed her lips before he hit a button on the wall, and the panel slid closed, trapping her. Leeza threw herself at it but it didn't budge. Panic gave her strength, and she struck out with her fist. "Zareck, let me out."

Zareck's face appeared in front of the small circular portal in the covering, looking back at her. "I am afraid not." The words were muffled. "I wondered how these could be useful when I discovered them yesterday. Now, I think I know. They were to hold their dead until they could be disposed of. I'm sure you're supposed to be dead when you're placed in them. But, this should hold you most effectively until I can come back and make it so."

Was it really the morgue? Panic burst in Leeza. "You can't."

The expression on his face said differently before it disappeared.

"Zareck, this is a spaceship. If you ignite the engines, they will explode," she yelled the last words.

The face reappeared. "A spaceship, truly, what else?"

"It will explode. The message is a warning." She pressed against the portal as if she could pass the knowledge to him. It didn't work.

He smirked. "Good try, Dr. Jaeff." He turned away. "I will be back to finish with you after we have started the engines." The words faded away.

"Zareck," Leeza yelled. "Zareck. It'll explode. Listen to me. It'll explode. You can't!" She pounded on the door, but it stayed firmly in place. Zareck wouldn't be back. No one would be back. No one would survive if she didn't get out and warn them.

There was a loud bang and a rolling sound like thunder. The ground shook, and a faint cloud of dust drifted into the room. Leeza knew immediately it was an explosion and not caused by the engines. Zareck had blown up the tunnel to trap her in so no one would find her. He'd left her there to starve to death. She tried to take comfort that wouldn't happen. She'd die with everyone else.

Leeza pounded several minutes more until she slumped back, exhausted. She shut her eyes, burying her face in her hands. Tears seeped free. She couldn't help it. It all seemed too unreal to be happening.

He'd killed her father. She caught back a sob.

Her father had been a wonderful man, honest, kind, handsome with his yellowish-white hair and bright green eyes, which she'd inherited. He used to say her eyes and affinity for languages was all she got from him. The rest was her mother, from the top of her head, with her hair so pale it was almost white, down her long, thin build, to the tips of her toes.

Leeza breathed deep, just thinking of him helped her gain control. She could almost hear his words when she hit a problem. *Just back up, look at it from a different angle and think.*

Leeza took another breath. She had to stop Zarack. There was no other option. That meant she had to calm down and get out of there. She dropped her hands and started to look around.

The faint orange glow still filled the outer room so, at least, she wasn't in complete darkness, but unfortunately, the small portal didn't let much light into the capsule. She started to explore as her eyes adjusted to the dark.

The whole surface seemed to be padded in a multitude of small pillows. Leeza pressed on one, and it gave, molding to the pressure, like it was filled with water or maybe some kind of gel. She didn't know what to make of it, but it didn't remind her of anything in a morgue. It was comfortable, like maybe a sleeping chamber. The thought came to her and was comforting because, if the capsule was some kind of bed, that meant there had to be a way out.

Running her hands over the lid, she found nothing so started on the sides. She almost missed it. Hidden in the shadows, there was a solid area, tucked in the pillows. She brushed her finger over it feeling three small buttons. Figuring one had to open the door, she pushed the first button. Nothing happened. When she pressed the second, the pillows swelled and conformed to her body. The space grew tight but not uncomfortable. With more confidence, she pressed the third. For a second, there was nothing then the faint hiss of air.

Leeza pressed on the door but was hampered by the inflated pockets around her. She leaned against it. It refused to budge. A fine mist started to pour into the chamber, fogging her mind along with the interior. She reached for the buttons again, but her fingertips couldn't process feeling anymore. Her body felt like she was floating, drifting off into space, everything around her fading. She tried to pull back from oblivion.

"No," she said aloud. *Have to stop them from igniting the engines.*

Her world slipped away.

Chapter Two

"Don't touch that," Jorran Carrell's warning came a second too late. Not that he figured the brick of a man would have heeded it.

Norris's hand pressed down on the panel they'd been studying.

Jorran grabbed Norris's arm, pulling the hand away. Though the man had him on weight, Jorran looked down on him. "You've been told not to touch anything." Jorran glared at him. "If you want to stay on this expedition, you'll listen to me."

"Hey, sorry." Norris pulled his arm away, holding his hands up in mock surrender. "It was an accident. I was just trying to get a closer look and forgot." The man tried for an innocent look, but the glint of challenge in his eyes ruined it.

"Don't forget again." Jorran enunciated each word. If he had his way, Norris never would have been there, but he was the eyes and ears of their sponsor, and the committee was too concerned about upsetting Tranic Corp to go against them.

Before he could say anything more, three sharp whistles pierced the air, followed by a whirring sound. The five member team froze. Around them an orange glow, seeming to come from the walls themselves, started to illuminate the room.

"What's happening?" Azas, the only female member of the team, cried out.

"Everyone out," Jorran ordered. "Now, go."

"What are you doing?" Norris objected, blocking the exit.

"Move." Jorran met his challenge. "Until we get equipment down here to make sure whatever you," he stressed the word, "activated is safe, no one goes in." He pushed the man down the corridor after the others.

"You can't do that."

"Yes, I can. Move it." He pushed the annoying man out in front of him.

"But there's something there. We didn't see what came on," Norris complained.

And if I can manage it, you never will, Jorran said in his head as he continued to nudge Norris in front of him, keeping his body between Norris and the console.

Norris stopped, turning to face him. Jorran saw the man's fist clench and prepared himself for an attack. "Do it and you are gone."

Jorran stood up to him, wishing the man would take the swing. He thought for a moment he might, but after a tense minute, Norris finally turned and strode down the long corridor. Jorran stayed on him, making sure he didn't try to slip away, hide and remain inside.

As they got close to the exit, the mugginess of the jungle reached through the opening to them. The two other men of the team and Azas waited just outside. Anxiety showed on their faces, and Jorran was sure it wasn't because of fear from any contamination. He'd worked with them all before. Even young Rese, who was still one of his students, had been on a previous excavation with him. Jorran knew, just like him, they didn't like or trust Norris.

"All right, everyone go get cleaned off. Full scrub and dispose of clothes," Jorran said to everyone. Norris was already storming away. Jorran tipped his head to Rese then motioned to Norris with his eyes. Rese gave him a single nod back, letting him know he understood he wanted him to keep an eye on Norris.

Rese and Azas headed off down the trail. Jorran watched them go, aware of Esher standing just behind his shoulder.

"Do you think that was wise?" the older man asked once the others were out of hearing range.

Jorran shoved a hand up through his hair and sighed. "Probably not, but if he took a swing at me, it'd be grounds to get him out of here."

"Tranic would just send someone else."

"Probably, but they couldn't be as bad as Norris." Jorran didn't take his attention from the path.

"Are you certain?" Esher asked simply.

"No." Jorran hated to admit it, but he figured Norris was about as bad as they got. "At least, I have some grounds to keep him out of the site until I know a little more about what we're dealing with."

"You're concerned." It wasn't a question. Esher had been his mentor when Jorran started out in archeology and knew him well.

Jorran sighed and turned to him. "Yes. I can't put my finger on it. For one thing, how could this," he motioned to the ship, "be so close to civilization and no one knew it was here?"

"It is in a protected area." The man shrugged his bony shoulders.

"Exactly, a protected area that goes back before there were records. I've been doing some research on it. The earliest things I've found said it was a forbidden area."

"You think they knew it was here and didn't say anything about it? That's not too big of a stretch. The people of the region might have been superstitious enough to fear the area. We know, almost five hundred years ago, there was a major shift that extended over the whole continent and beyond. All civilizations in the area disappeared. It was centuries before others emerged, migrating in as the climate stabilized. Is that all that's bothering you?"

"I don't know." He turned and looked back at the ship. "I feel like I'm on some kind of a precipice, like I'm about to make the most important discovery of my life. I just wish Tranic Corp wasn't involved. They've profited big off other excavations."

"That's why they fund out the big money."

"Yeah, but you and I both know they've stolen stuff, too. We just haven't been able to prove it, and until we do, the committee is going to continue to accept their proposals." Jorran's hand ran through his hair once more in a sign of his frustration.

"Just be careful, my boy," Esher cautioned. "You might be the best archeologist there is, especially when it comes to alien artifacts, but Tranic would love to have you removed from this, and you just made it personal to Norris. You better watch your back."

Jorran didn't tell him he already was and for good reason.

"Now," Esher continued, "do you really believe there is any danger?"

"No, but no harm in being cautious, and it'll give me some time to investigate on my own." He felt a surge of excitement. "That thing actually powered up, after all this time. Even if it is minimal systems, that's amazing, and Norris was right. Something was coming up on that screen. I want to have a look and figure out what I'm dealing with before I have any intrusion."

"Come on then. We need to get some kind of restrictions put in place."

Chapter Three

Leeza's mind tried to struggle through the haze. It seemed like consciousness was a long way off. She tried to take a breath, but it was difficult. Her lungs felt tight, like she had forgotten how to breathe. She was suffocating. Panic hit her. A coffin, her mind came up with an answer. It really was a coffin. She tried to fight, to move, to escape, but she was cocooned in. The dark pressed down on her like the pillows around her.

She wanted to scream but couldn't get it out. A sob escaped her, and she drew in a breath. Startled, she opened her eyes and was greeted by the faint glow coming in the small portal in front of her face. It was comforting, but she was still trapped. "H-h," her cry didn't make it through the dryness in her throat. She tried to swallow but couldn't bring up enough moisture to manage it.

Was this what it was like to suffocate? The funny thing was that her breathing seemed to be getting easier. She inhaled deeply and felt the air rush in. Exhaling, she tried it again, filling her lungs. Her mind cleared as did her vision, though everything still had a hazy look about it. She blinked a couple times, and it seemed to help.

Struggling, she managed a swallow. It eased the tightness in her throat. Exhausted, she sagged into the cushions surrounding her body. Leeza closed her eyes and concentrated on nothing but getting the next breath of air into her chest. With each breath, the next came easier. She began to feel more alive.

After a little more time, Leeza finally realized she wasn't dying. She felt like she was waking up from a deep sleep in a dry area. Her mind was working enough that it made some sense. They were in a desert region. Funny, she'd never noticed the dryness on the ship before. As her mind brought up the word ship, her eyelids sprang back open.

She was on the ship. Zareck had tried to kill her. They were going to start the engines and it would kill everyone. She had to get out of there and stop it.

She raised her hands and found the cushioning around her had diminished. She pressed against the enclosure. Nothing happened. After several more tries, she sagged back into the padding.

Leeza reached down and let her fingers brush the three small buttons. Apprehension filled and warred within her for several minutes before she broke through the fear and pushed. She cringed. There was a slight swooshing sound, then a pop. The door opened.

A faint musty smell she'd never noticed before greeted her. She wondered if it was from the explosion Zareck had set off. She shuddered with dread.

Steeling herself, she stepped forward. Her legs felt shaky and couldn't hold her. She fell, barely catching herself on the side of the capsule, sinking back into it. Again, she forced herself to take deep breaths to steady herself. She didn't realize Zareck had hit her so hard. She raised her hand to her cheek. Funny, it didn't hurt.

Brushing back a few wayward strands of hair from her face, she tried to stand again. She made it up, leaning heavily on the frame while her legs continued to shake. As the quivering in her muscles subsided, she focused her attention on the door, and with determination, went for it. Her steps were awkward. Leeza was still a couple of feet away when her strength waned. Reaching out, she caught the doorframe to keep from going down again.

Sagging against the wall, she breathed deep, in and out, trying to still her pounding heart. She couldn't figure out what was wrong with her. She was in good physical shape, but just the few steps across the room had her heart pounding like she'd run ten kilometers. Leeza felt nauseous, and closed her eyes, tilting her head against the wall to keep from passing out. It took several minutes before she felt steady enough to try moving again.

The end of the tunnel the way they'd come, or at least what she thought was the way, was blocked off, so she went the other direction. Leeza had to hold onto the wall, but with each step, she got steadier. Still, she had to stop and rest several times before she reached the corner.

Another corridor greeted her. She had no idea where she was going, but also had no choice because she couldn't stay there. Leeza was breathing hard again when she got to the end, turned the next corner and found it a dead end.

Exhausted, she slumped against the wall and was tempted to follow it all the way down to the floor. She closed her eyes and tilted her head back against the wall, breathing in. When she opened her eyes, Leeza found herself looking into a small alcove she'd missed seeing. There were rungs placed all the way up the wall through a hole in the ceiling.

The knowledge that it led up gave her the needed strength to make the attempt. One rung at a time, she climbed. She slipped off once, barely catching herself. Leeza clung to the bar, gulping in air as her body shook from fatigue and fear a full minute before she could force her hand up to the next hold. It felt like she'd been climbing forever before she collapsed on the floor next to the opening.

Dazed, she laid there until the memory of what would happen if they started the engines filtered in once more. The corridors seemed an endless maze, but Leeza forced herself to continue, going higher until she came up several floors and thought it looked familiar.

Down two more corridors, she found the chamber with the screen she'd been reading. The text had been changed to something different. That didn't surprise her. What did surprise her was that the room was empty. She was sure that, by then, the room would've been filled with the startup team.

Leeza realized she was to be a member of the team because she was the only one with actual understanding of any of the markings. Was it possible that they had held up the time trying to locate her? Perhaps with her missing it had bought her the time she needed to get free.

Relieved, she headed down the corridor that would take her out of the ship. She wondered how Zareck had explained her absence. Well, he was going to have a lot more to explain. The thought of taking him on gave her a strong enough burst of energy that it pushed back her hunger and exhaustion.

As she neared the exit, Leeza noticed the air was fresher, but there seemed to be an array of other smells in it that she couldn't quite place. They reminded her of flowers. She also noticed tracks of dirt on the floor beside the traces of sand that occasionally blew in.

Before she could contemplate it further, she froze at the sound of birds drifting in through the open door. She shook her head as she tried to make sense of it. She hadn't heard a bird since she'd arrived at the excavation site.

Slowly, she moved forward, stopping again at the sight of the largest fern leaves she'd ever seen before. Edging to the opening, Leeza looked into a jungle of thick foliage, with trees that reached to the sky, and butterflies as bright as the blossoms that attracted them.

Wide-eyed, she looked around and realized that she had to be dreaming. It was the only explanation. She was still trapped in the capsule. She wished she could go back farther and that the warning and everything to do with Zareck was a dream too, a nightmare really, but she couldn't accept it.

Unable to quell her curiosity, she edged her way down the ramp that was fashioned at the mouth of the entrance. At the bottom, she paused a second then stepped onto packed dirt which wasn't really muddy but showed traces of a recent rain.

A brightly-colored bird took flight, startling her. She caught a good enough glimpse of it to recognize it from seeing one in a zoo. It drew her gaze to a cluster of vivid, deep-throated flowers hanging down from the trees. If she had to dream, she knew she couldn't think of anything more spectacular. She breathed in deeply, glorying in the smell of rich soil combined with the heavy floral scents.

It gave her pause. Was she really dreaming the sound of birds, the smell of flowers or, was she dead? Was this what was waiting after death. She looked around, trying to take it all in, but it was too much.

She felt dizzy again. She needed to eat. Did one need to eat if they were dead? She shook the silliness of it away, looked at the trail leading off, and followed it.

After approximately a hundred meters, the trail ran into an odd formed building. A series of clear flaps covered the opening. Leeza pushed through and found a changing room set up similar to the tent they used while on excavation of the ship. There was another set of flaps at the other end. Going through it, she was on the path again.

She'd only gone a little ways when there was the sound of an engine starting up. The pitch grew higher, to a kind of a whistle. Leeza saw something move in the trees and disappear through the canopy overhead. The sound faded away.

A second later, it was replaced by what sounded like voices but the language didn't sound familiar. Cautiously, she crept forward then pulled back as the first person came into view. It wasn't anyone she recognized.

It was a tall man with hair so dark it was black. His skin was a deep tan that had a bronze tone to it. Two more men came into view. Their hair, too, was dark, but not as dark as the first, and nothing like her Athurian pale, whitish hair. As she watched, another man came up. He was young and his hair was much lighter, a soft sun color.

Everything about them was as unfamiliar as the jungle around her. Two of the men had plain tan shirts with short sleeves which stretched over the muscles of their chests and arms when they strained to shift the crates they were placing on some kind of transport. The third, the younger man, had a similar shirt but a vest over it with a hood that at the moment hung down his back. All wore pants with an array of pockets on the legs which were tucked into sturdy boots.

In what seemed like good-natured actions, they pulled the crates into a hut with large open doors. Together they came out, closed the big doors and started to walk away. Leeza edged forward, trying to see where they were heading while keeping hidden.

She pulled back in shock, blinking to wipe away her disbelief. She leaned forward again, but the view was the same. She tried to take it in. It looked like a very small village. There were easily two dozen of the odd huts in various sizes. Several were quite large. People moved around the quad between the buildings. A few stopped to talk, others hurried from one building to the next, while others worked by several long tables set in front of one building.

For all that Leeza wanted to believe what she was seeing wasn't real, she couldn't. And, if it was real, then the jungle was too. It was no dream, nor was she dead. Where she was, or how she got there, she didn't know.

Fear flooded over her. The pounding of her heart made her dizzy again. She fought to still her breathing and calm her panic. There had to be a reasonable explanation. Tears burned her eyes as the possibilities came.

Had the capsule transported her somehow? She shook her head. No, that was impossible. The ship was here, and she knew it was the same ship. So, had they started the engines, and it brought her here, wherever here was? Her fear spiked. She felt short of breath for a whole new reason. She was hyperventilating.

Calm down, don't jump to conclusions, you can work this out. They were all things her father would've told her. For once in her life, she was afraid his words weren't going to help. She needed time to think.

She leaned forward once more, peeking under a huge leaf, watching the activity. With each passing second, a tightness spread in her chest. It was so unreal. Nothing was familiar.

Numb, she turned, making her way back down the trail to the changing hut and sank down on the bench in stunned disbelief. Waves of questions swamped her mind. Tears ran down her face as she tried to wrap her mind around the possibilities and accept the fact that she had no idea where she was.

Leeza had no notion of how long she sat there in a stupor, until the rumbling of her stomach grew persistent enough for her to realize it was getting dark, and she was starving. Food was definitely her first priority.

Going through the cupboards, she found nothing that resembled anything to eat. Mostly, there was just clothing and gear, she guessed, for exploring the ship. That meant there was only one option for food. She looked at the cupboard holding clothes then down at her own.

She debated changing for a minute but couldn't bring herself to put on someone else's clothing, and hers weren't too different but in a soft, pale blue coloring. Her boots were a light tan, not as sturdy looking as those she saw, and they came higher on her leg, almost to her knees.

Her cloak was tan like her boots, and, well, she hadn't seen anything like it, but the vest the younger man wore had a hood, so she hoped it would be okay. Besides, she would need her hood to hide her pale hair. From what she'd seen, that would be her giveaway on a single glance.

Once more, she made her way down the trail, pausing at the mouth to make sure her hood was up covering her hair, and steeled her resolve. Leeza forced herself to step out before she could lose her nerve.

There were not as many people out as before. Nobody seemed to pay her any attention as she got closer to the buildings. She kept walking through the center and all the way to the other side. Going around the last building, she slumped against the wall. Her body shook with a combination of fatigue and nerves. Still, no one had paid her any notice.

She studied the building on which she leaned. It was covered by some kind of smooth shell. It seemed to be made in one piece, like some kind of modular structure that had been placed there whole. Risking a glance back around the corner, she realized most of the other structures were similar, like formed blocks strung along, connected into small groupings.

Risking another peek, she counted only four buildings that were different in their construction. They were all bigger. The one was at the far end, where she'd seen them loading stuff, Leeza figured was some kind of storage building. Across the way, situated in the center was a large building that people occasionally went in and out of. Next to it was another building of medium size, then there was the big building she'd passed just after she came out of the jungle.

She got the feeling that the town was not a permanent settlement, but like her excavation's cluster of tents. That clicked into another strong possibility. They were there to explore the ship, just like she had been. But, if that was true, where were her people and how did she get from the desert to the jungle?

Leeza swayed on her feet with a combination of being overwhelmed and the need for food. Pushing the first back, she concentrated on the one she could do something about. Strengthening her resolve, she again stepped out on the quad, walking back the way she'd just come, more slowly this time.

Leeza watched as most people seemed to be going into two of the different buildings. Angling to the first, she got close enough to look in. Flaps, similar to the ones on the hut, covered the opening. Just inside, there was a clear door. She could see into a small entry but no farther.

Changing her direction, she headed for the other building across the way, at the end. Leeza realized it was actually set off by itself, and its construction was more – haphazard was the term that described it.

Again, flaps covered the opening, but it emptied into a large, open room. Long tables, filled with men and women, covered the floor. Ahead of Leeza, a woman pushed through the flaps, and the sound of loud music and louder voices reached out to greet her, but it was the smell that drew her in.

Without conscious thought, she stepped through. Her growling stomach wiped away all caution. Twenty-five to thirty people clustered in groups at the tables. Leeza watched as the woman walked down one of the rows, greeted a group, then sat down. The woman raised her hand and made a slight wave before entering the conversation.

A burly man, with not much hair left on his head, came down the aisle and placed a plate of food and a cup in front of the woman which matched what the others in the group had.

Someone came through the opening behind Leeza, startling her. She stepped forward, out of his way. Lowering her head to keep sheltered under her hood, she walked down the same row the woman had, settling in an open spot not far away. She raised her hand mimicking the woman's action.

The same burly man tottered down the aisle and dropped a plate and cup in front of her, paying her no more attention than he had the other woman.

Leeza sighed, and picked up the eating utensil. After watching a couple people around her spear up morsels from their plates, she did the same. She hesitated a second, smelling it before hunger won over, and she placed it in her mouth.

She tried not to wince, not sure if she liked the flavor. It was different. Still, she ate. After the fourth bite, she became accustomed to it, though she wouldn't say she liked it, especially the strange film it left in her mouth.

Leeza turned her attention to the room around her and listened to the language. She became so wrapped up in the tones and flow, she forgot everything else. With food in her, it also became harder to keep her eyes open. Her head drooped down, and she started to let the fatigue overtake her when a bellow behind her snapped her awake. Leeza turned and looked up to find the man who had brought her food, leaning over her.

He barked something at her.

Leeza shook her head trying to indicate that she didn't understand, but it just infuriated him more, and he yelled louder. Leeza tried shrugging her shoulders. That didn't help. He clamped a brawny hand down on her shoulder, pulling her up, while his other hand waved wildly at the food.

Leeza thought that it might be her lack of eating that upset him. She tried to pull back and sit back down to eat some more, though the thought of another bite of the odd tasting stuff about made her sick.

He jerked her back up, his fingers biting into her flesh. Fear began to rise in her. When he yelled again, Leeza decided she had to try to answer him. "I don't understand," she tried first in Athurian then switched to Thean, Krisk, and Gryshto.

The only reaction they had on the man was his face got redder, and he hollered loud enough for all the people to turn their focus on them. The man jerked her around for all to see.

Everyone stared at them.

Fear dug deep into Leeza. She cringed back into her cloak, thankful for it, but wishing she had never come into the place. The food was making her sick. Her head pounded, and she was afraid any minute she was going to faint. Things were getting slightly blurry when she heard another shout from across the room.

Leeza turned to see a towering man stride across the room. Anger poured from him. She longed to pull back but was trapped under the weight of the burly man's hand, then she realized the tall man's rage wasn't directed at her but the man holding her. The hand dropped from her shoulder. The burly man backed into the table behind them, words fairly babbled from his mouth.

Leeza looked to the burly man then back to the approaching one. She wondered if she should be afraid also but for some reason she wasn't. She wondered if it was the fog that seemed to be drifting in her mind, but she found him quite pleasing to look at.

Up close, she had to tilt her head back so far to see into his face, she feared her hood might slip back. Leeza tilted her face back down but not before his features were fixed firmly in her mind. His hair was dark, black looking in the dim lightening of the room. She would have guessed his eyes would have been black too but they weren't. They were a light, bright purple, similar to the hue of the cluster of blossoms in the jungle.

The rumblings from his voice gave her a sense of security. Still, she jerked when a hand appeared in front of her face. The fingers, like the rest of him, were long, clean, and slightly rough. She tilted her face up, meeting his gaze. His lips were full and tilted in a smile. She found it, too, reassuring, but it was his eyes that brought her trust. She didn't even realize she'd raised her hand until she felt the skin of his hand under her fingertips.

C3&O

For the second time that day, Jorran felt his anger rise. He couldn't believe it when he heard the slimy Tash offer the small figure beside him for the night to anyone who paid her bill. Jorran felt certain no one would take him up on it, and knew Tash was just trying to get someone to feel pity for him and pay.

Still, even though he could see nothing of the woman, he could tell she was afraid. He wasn't sure how he even knew she was a woman, she stood almost as tall as Tash, and the cloak she wore totally obliterated any hint of her shape or features, but he knew.

Jorran clenched his fist, feeling his rage burn through his veins. "What is going on here?" he demanded, heading across the room.

Tash turned to him and paled. "Professor Carrell," the man stammered.

"Do you want to tell me I didn't hear what I think I heard you yell?"

Tash shifted his bulk and looked like he was going to deny. "It was a jest," he tried then faltered.

"I don't think she thought it was a jest." Jorran didn't even try to hide his disgust that anyone would treat another person so.

"She was the one making fun of me, babbling then hooting all these weird noises."

"Now you're going to blame your actions on her?"

"She came in and ate when she couldn't pay," the man said defensively.

"So you were going to sell her."

"Just–" Tash cut off what he was going to say.

But Jorran got what was coming, 'just for the night'. He reached the pair, luckily, Tash pulled back, leaving the woman standing between them. Jorran caught a glimpse of her face before she lowered her head, and his world shifted in its alignment. There was a feeling of something right and wrong all at once in the soul tearing, almost iridescent, green eyes. Eyes like he had never seen before.

He turned on Tash. "So you were what?" Jorran demanded trying to calm himself. Not really caring about the man, wanting to get his attention back to the woman.

"She wouldn't pay then just babbled." Tash was doing some babbling himself.

Jorran looked down at the plate on the table. It looked like it had hardly been touched. "Looks like she was trying to tell you it was inedible."

"It's good," Tash objected.

"Passable from what I hear. The only thing that keeps you going is it's a place where people can go for a change of pace and be a little rowdy. If you want to remain at this site, I better not hear of any more auctioning off people like this again. And if, in the future, anyone doesn't pay, you bring it to me as site commander. Is that understood?" He waited for the man to give a nod before he continued. "Don't expect this to be the end of it." He let his threat hang.

Reaching into his pocket, he pulled out some credits and tossed them to the man, who fumbled and dropped them, but Jorran had already discounted him, turning his attention to the figure standing quietly in front of him. Her head was down, and he thought she swayed slightly, like she was unsteady.

He held out a hand to her. She jerked back, her head coming up to give him another glimpse at those strikingly beautiful eyes set in the too pale face. Jorran became lost in them until he felt the tips of her delicate fingers, long, and fine-boned, rest on his hand.

The word that came out of her mouth was totally unfamiliar, but the sound was soft and pulling. There was no missing the meaning of it as it was repeated in her light-green eyes. She was asking for help, and Jorran knew there was no way he could deny her. No matter what it cost him, even his life, he would keep her safe.

"Come with me."

She tilted her head to the side as if deciphering what he'd said, but when he took a step back, she went with him. He led her outside. She seemed to be relieved to be out in the open and glanced at the dark jungle. He wondered if she was going to make a run for it, then he felt a shiver race over her.

"Where'd you come from?" The question slipped from him. He realized that was foolish. She had to come on the last transport but why? He was always notified of anyone coming in, and there wasn't to be anyone new.

There were a couple of people coming back from break. Could she be with one of them? If so, why weren't they with her? He noticed she didn't wear a band of a Life-mate. Could she be a Tranic Corp spy? If so, she sure got to him fast. He shook the thought away to find they'd stopped walking, and she was staring at him.

Her head tilted slightly to the side again as she studied him.

"So, who are you?"

The lights from the complex caught her face. The muscles between her golden eyebrows tightened, and he could almost see her dissecting the words but she remained silent.

"I know you can talk. You made noise back in there."
He pointed back to Tash's place.

A frown appeared on her face, and she shook her head.

"Okay, so no more of that." He smiled at her reaction.
"I'm not too fond of that place either."

"Leeza."

The word from her surprised him. When he made no
reaction, it came again broken into separate sounds.

"L-ee-zz-a." She pointed to herself then to him and
waited.

Jorran got it. She was telling him her name and was
asking for his. "Leeza," he repeated, pointing at her. He
liked the sound. It was different, just like her.

She nodded and smiled.

"Jorran." He pointed to himself and was about to
repeat it slower, but she beat him to it.

"Jor-ran."

"Yes. Leeza." He returned her smile, pointing back to
her.

She nodded then the smile disappeared from her face.
She swayed. The hand on his tightened down, her other
hand came up to her forehead.

Jorran reached out with his other arm to steady her, but
before he could, she broke away, staggering to the edge of
jungle. She caught the trunk of the tree and leaned over to
be sick. It seemed to pass quickly, but as she straightened,
she weaved. Her head came up. She looked back at him and
repeated the word she'd used to plead for his help, this time
with even more urgency. It was a good thing he was
already reaching for her because she went limp against him.

He pulled her tight, then got an arm underneath her and
lifted her into his arms. Panic hit him as he caught sight of
her face. Eyelashes lay like pale-gold crescents on her
cheeks. To his relief, she seemed to be breathing evenly.
Still, he headed for the Medical hut. Jorran's determined
strides covered the ground quickly.

They were halfway across the yard when he glanced up to check their path. He shifted her higher against his chest. The feel of her hood falling back over his arm had him looking back down, and he just about stumbled.

A curtain of moonlight hair spilled over his arm.

Chapter Four

He couldn't help but stop and stare at the vision of her. Jorran realized he'd seen little wisps of the light strands against her cheeks both in Tash's place and when they exchanged names, but most of her hair had been hidden by her hood. He'd discounted the coloring then, but now it was impossible. Never had he seen coloring like that, added with her amazing eyes and language. He felt his stomach muscles tighten.

Jorran looked around the yard. Surprisingly, no one was out. He changed his direction, heading to the closest building.

Jorran pushed through the outer screen, checking that the hallway was clear before going to his chambers. He juggled Leeza in his arms to punch in the code and open the door. Though his was one of the larger modules, it only took him a couple steps to reach the sleeping area.

She didn't stir when he laid her on the bed, and he got a real good look at her. She was more beautiful than he'd first imagined. Due to the coloring of her hair, there was a touch of exoticness about her, but beyond that, she looked quite normal.

He wanted to believe that she dyed her hair but couldn't do it. His mind raced over everything, coming back to the one word she'd uttered twice, a cry for help both times he was sure, but not a word he'd ever heard before.

"Leeza." He sank to the edge of the bed, reaching out to check her pulse. It was normal. At least to him, it was normal. Running his fingers back through his hair, he took a deep breath and activated the communication link.

It was answered almost immediately by a familiar voice.

"Grab your kit, and get over to my place immediately," he barked and cut the link, hearing Chel's question, "Are you okay?" as it disconnected. Jorran wasn't really sure how to answer that. He wondered if he was losing his mind. His insides were wrapped up in a woman he'd just barely met, and he wasn't sure what to make of her.

He reached down and fingered a long lock of hair. It was incredibly soft to the touch. Now he could see it all, he could tell it had been woven into some kind of braid that hung to her waist. At some time, strands had come free to frame her face.

Before he could contemplate it any further, there was a pounding on his door. He started to open it only to have it shoved the rest of the way in by Chel, the late, middle-aged med-tech.

"What happened?" the woman demanded, eyeing him up and down, obviously looking for some type of injury on him.

"I'm fine." Jorran held up a hand trying to ease her.

"Then why'd you scare the daylights out of me?" The voice shifted from caring to aggravated, her hand going to her chest, as if to still her heart.

"Sorry, didn't mean to panic you. I was just feeling a bit panicked myself for a minute."

One of her graying eyebrows arched up. "You don't panic," she said. "You might get angry, but you don't lose your temper or panic."

"Yeah, well, I need your help. Actually, I need your promise first."

At that comment Chel's other eyebrow went up, changing her expression to one of curiosity. "On what?" she asked when he didn't continue.

Jorran waited a full minute, debating everything over in his mind. "That you won't tell anyone," he said carefully.

"What won't I tell?"

"Promise me." The silence was heavy while he waited for an answer. "Come on, Chel. You know me. I wouldn't ask if it wasn't important."

The woman waited a second longer before she nodded. "All right. Anyone else ..." she pointed a finger at him. "What do you need?"

"This way." He turned to the bedroom.

"Why, Jorran ..." Whatever else her snappy comeback was going to be petered out.

Jorran heard a catch in Chel's breathing. She paused a second then pushed past him. Running a quick hand over Leeza's face, Chel pressed her finger to Leeza's neck for a pulse. Chel turned back to him. "Where'd she come from?"

"Tash's."

The eyebrow arched again.

"Honestly, that's where I met her, found her. To make it short, I stopped to see if Rese was there. Tash was making a 'jest' of offering her because she ate and couldn't pay. I stopped it, got her outside, she got sick, then fainted."

With a nod, Chel turned back to the unconscious woman. Opening her bag, she pulled out instruments to check her over. When she lifted an eyelid to check her eyes, he noticed a slight pause.

"All I got was her name before she passed out. Leeza." He watched Chel work. He trusted Chel, both as a medic and a friend. They both taught at the same university, and Chel spent many of her off times serving as medic on his expeditions.

"So why'd you bring her here and not to me?"

Jorran knew the question was coming. Still, he wasn't sure what he wanted to say. Wasn't quite sure what he believed. He wanted to hear what Chel said first. He remained quiet while Chel took a blood sample and placed it in the small portable analyzer.

"Well, no sign of toxins. Vitals are slightly low but good. She seems fine, but she's unconscious." Chel turned back to him. "So?"

He motioned. "Her hair," he said simply.

The medic looked back at Leeza. "Yes, I noticed it, very beautiful." She glanced over her shoulder at him then turned back and lifted a strand, running the analyzer over it. "It's not been colored."

Now there was a touch of awe in her voice as she fingered it. "Unusual color, but not too strange. I've seen it before. At least close. Did you notice her eye color?" She looked back at him. "Of course you did. Observant man. I would say she's Thurian and lucked out on the gene pool. But that's not telling me why you brought her here instead of to me."

He took a deep breath. "Before she passed out, she asked for help. At least, I'm positive, she was asking for help. I didn't recognize the word. She didn't understand what I was saying either."

"I don't understand, you mean mentally slow?" she asked.

Jorran shook his head. "As in the language was unfamiliar to her. Tash said she was making fun of him, babbling at him." Jorran could see the understanding and skepticism cross Chel's face.

"Everyone on the whole planet speaks Lannish. I mean some still have dialects, but they still speak …"

"Yes," he said simply, knowing she was getting it.

"Then where do you think she came from?"

"My assumption was the transport today because I hadn't seen her before." He turned to his computer, pulling up a list as Chel spoke behind him.

"It would be impossible to miss her around here."

"No record of her on the drop," Jorran announced, confirming what he knew he'd find.

"So what are you thinking?"

"I was hoping you could tell me."

The medic's eyes widened. "You don't think she came from the ship?"

"No." He pushed his fingers back through his hair. "No," he repeated. "Everything I found so far indicates the inhabitants were taller, darker. I'd look closer to them than she does."

"She couldn't have just come out of the jungle. Look at her clothes." The woman reached out and fingered them. "They're a little different." She studied them closer. "But these are finely manufactured, not at all roughly constructed from some forgotten or missing tribe. And there haven't been any new discoveries like that for nearly two hundred years. Believe me, I know."

His hand came up to his hair again. "I know. I just don't know what I believe. That's why I want to keep quiet about her. Until she wakes up, and we can find out."

The woman nodded. "I can agree with that. I'll also run a full blood workup to compare lineage. I'm still putting my guess on Thurian though. Maybe she has a speech and language problem. It does happen, though there are few that can't be corrected."

"It would make it a lot simpler."

"I take it you're still not thinking of moving her to the med-unit."

"You said she seems all right?" There was concern in the question.

After a slight hesitation, she nodded. "Except she's unconscious, and there's nothing to indicate why. She's in a deep sleep, like her body just shut down on her. That would be my guess. I think she'll wake up when her body's ready."

"Okay, then I think I'll keep her here."

"I'm going to point this out very clearly to you. You are a single man. You could be setting yourself up for a major problem."

"I understand."

"I don't think you do. Laws are very strict when it comes to mates. You keep her here and it could be challenged whether you do anything or not," she said sternly. "You are not without standing."

"I understand," he repeated.

"She is a very beautiful young woman." Chel changed tactics. "And I don't have to be a medic to tell you're interested." The woman shook her head as if figuring out she wasn't going to change his mind. "I hope you're sure of what you're doing."

Jorran kept his gaze from going to the woman on the bed. Everything in him said that it was right to keep her with him, she was right. It was like the feeling he got right before he made a big discovery.

"I'll keep her here," he said firmly. "But I need a favor. I need to go to the ship. Norris activated some systems on it this afternoon, and I want to check it out without any interference and set up a security shield. I have Esher keeping an eye on Norris tonight so he can't get there to poke around before its set."

The woman sighed. "You want me to babysit?" It was more of a statement than a question.

"I don't want her alone if she wakes up."

"I can agree with that. Okay, I can run a few tests from here. Go." The slight scowl the older woman gave him had no bite.

Jorran smiled back. "Thanks." He grabbed up a prepared pack and headed out the door, knowing Leeza was in good hands. Maybe, hopefully, Chel would have some answers when he got back and all his apprehension would be for nothing.

Jorran paused in the gear hut to gather the set of security pylons that had arrived on the transport. He'd ordered them in after catching Norris heading toward the ship a couple days earlier. He hefted the two poles so they leaned over his shoulder and headed through the jungle.

The sounds of animals hooting and calling surrounded him. Jorran moved with silent confidence. He knew there were dangerous things out there, but few would try to bother him, and he knew he could handle any that did. His main concern was human right now.

It was no accident that Norris had pressed his hand on the spot that activated the console. Jorran had noticed the place, too, and had already come to the conclusion that was what it was for. What surprised him was that it had actually powered up.

The ship itself was hard to date, but they were able to get a firm dating from debris piled on and around it. The ship had been there at least five-hundred and sixty years, before the deluge that caused massive flooding in the area, wiping out the people on a third of the continent that couldn't get away, and turned what used to be a desert into a jungle. It had affected the climate of the whole planet before it settled down.

Once again, Jorran wondered if the ship crashing there had caused the deluge, but there were signs the ship was there a while before it happened. Unfortunately, most legend and information of the area had been washed away in the storms which hit the region so fiercely and suddenly no one had been able to escape. Over two million people were lost, most of several races.

Jorran didn't stop at the ready hut, only slowing to grab a contamination monitor off a rack before continuing right out the other side. The floodlights by the mouth of the ship illuminated the area around the gaping opening. Where before the light faded into darkness, now there was an orange glow stretching into the ship.

Jorran lowered the pylons to the ground, tempted to follow that glow inside. Instead, he got to work setting up the security shield which would keep out anyone without the code, and only he and Esher had the code. He made a mental note to give it to Chel in case of an emergency.

It only took a few minutes to have the holding rods punched deep in the ground and the pylons fastened to the rods. He ran a couple tests, making sure they worked perfectly before taking a reading on the monitor. There were no signs of harmful particles so he entered the ship, activating the barrier behind him.

The orange glow was bright enough he didn't turn on his light. Jorran took his time noticing things that hadn't been as evident when using their personal lights. The temptation of wanting to explore was strong, but he kept on his course to what seemed to be the main control room.

The only thing different there was the brightly lit screen in the console. Jorran studied the writing, picking out symbols he'd seen around the ship. He took several images of the screen. It was the lingering thought of Leeza that had him heading back down the corridor.

At the entrance, he deactivated the shield and stepped through, then reactivated it. Again, he moved quietly along the jungle path. This time at the hut he paused longer, noticing several of the cabinet doors were slightly ajar. Returning the monitor to its spot, he started to go through each space. Nothing seemed out of place, but he knew everything had been closed up when he'd left earlier that day.

It was when he stepped back on the trail he noticed the lack of sounds coming from the jungle. Jorran stopped, listened, and waited for the noises to return, but they didn't. He knew one other thing. He was not alone. Someone was out there watching. He scanned the undergrowth but saw no movement in the dark shadows.

Stepping back into the hut, he pulled out a light enhancing scope. Pushing back through the barrier, Jorran scanned the jungle. He almost missed the telltale movement, catching only a brief glimpse of a form ducking behind a tree farther down the path. At the distance, it was too far to even tell if it was a man or a woman. He took off running after the person. He could hear the soft thuds on the packed dirt as someone sprinted ahead.

When he reached the compound, the only ones in sight were a couple talking in front of Tash's. Behind him, Jorran heard the sounds of the jungle come to life. He scanned the area once more before heading toward his quarters. He could still swear he felt eyes on him and would have bet on who it was. Norris, Tranic's henchman, just thinking of the man made him anxious to get back to Leeza, which was foolish, but he couldn't help it. He wished there was some way he could get the man out of there.

Chel was sitting at the desk working on the computer when he entered.

"You're back sooner than I expected," she said in way of greeting.

"I didn't want to be gone long." He glanced toward the bedroom.

"She's still out. She didn't even stir when I removed her cloak and boots. I thought she'd be more comfortable. They're over there." She pointed to the cabinet by the door. "You might want to look at them. They're not that unusual, but they do have some markings that are kind of different."

"Thanks. I'll check them out." He shifted, wanting to go back and see Leeza but, for some reason, was a touch nervous to do so with Chel there. "I appreciate you staying with her and agreeing to keep quiet about her."

"Not that it'll make any difference. The first time she steps out of here, people are going to notice her, they're also going to be aware she's staying here."

Jorran shifted under the directness of her stare. "I'm aware of that, but it will give me some time to figure out who she is, where she came from, and a way to protect her."

The medic gave him a half smile. "I always knew you were a pushover for a woman in distress." She shook her head and gave a light chuckle at his discomfort. "I'll let you know when I get the test results. I ran a full analysis on her while you were gone. Figured it would be easier while she was unconscious and with you out of the room. The preliminary results all look normal."

Chel stood and stopped right in front of him. She raised her hand to his cheek. "You're a good man, Jorran Carrell. You just be careful. You're putting yourself up against some ruthless people. I don't like the coincidence or the timing of having your visitor drop into your lap."

Jorran understood immediately what she was saying. It really could make things difficult for him. If she was a plant, there could be all sorts of messy situations he could be pulled into. He just couldn't see how she would be a part of it. If there was a challenge to their relationship, she would be forced into being his mate forever.

He knew he should follow Chel's suggestion and move Leeza to the med-lab.

"You're right. I ..." he started, but the image of Leeza flared in his mind with those large, luminous eyes pleading for his help. He just couldn't bring himself to do it. "No, she'll stay here. It's ..." again he broke off. "It's what's right."

The woman nodded. "I figured that would be the answer. I'll be by in the morning." Moving to the door, she stopped and reached back, patting his arm. "You're a good man," she said again. "For your sake, I hope it is right."

Jorran closed the door and engaged the lock. Rethinking her words, he pushed his fingers back through his hair. Was it really coincidence? Chel was right. It definitely was bad timing. Again, the image of Leeza came to his mind. Jorran shook his head, but it didn't fade. "Who are you?" he whispered to himself, then went back to check on the actual person.

She lay eerily still in the center of his bed. Chel had covered her to her neck, but it did nothing to hide her appeal. Her white hair, free from its restraints, fanned out like a pool of moonlight around her head. Her cheekbones were sculptured high and fine. Her lips were slightly on the full side and nose a touch small. It was an intriguing combination all covered by smooth, ivory skin.

He yearned to reach down and stroke her cheek, but it wasn't his right. He didn't know anything about her, and she didn't know him. He wondered again who she was.

For a moment, he just looked at her until he forced himself to turn away. He should get some sleep but didn't feel in the least bit tired. Pacing in the cramped quarters was useless so after the fourth rotation, he stopped, and once more stared down at the woman who had shifted his world so completely with a single look and word.

She was an enigma, and he had a thing for solving puzzles. That was what led him to become an archeologist, the need to figure things out. He turned his attention from the woman who, at the moment, couldn't give him any answers and directed his focus to her cloak and boots. Chel had said they had markings on them. Jorran wondered, as he picked them up, what he would do if they matched the ones on the ship.

Jorran ran his fingers over the cloak. The feel reminded him of well-tanned leather, but on closer observation, he realized it wasn't leather, but a faux material that was nicely worked. There in the collar were the markings on a small label. He imagined they were the markings of who made it and the size, similar to his own clothing, but the symbols were different. As he studied them, there was something familiar about them, like he had seen them before.

Putting the cloak down, he picked up the light, tan-colored boots, giving them the same inspection. Once again, the symbols hit him as familiar. With a touch of foreboding, he brought up the images on his computer that he'd taken of the ship's screen. It was with a strong sense of relief after studying each individual symbol that none matched. It was not a guarantee, but still it eased some of the tightness in him.

He inspected them closer. They weren't that odd. The sole was soft with no heel. There were only faint signs of walking in the jungle. She couldn't have come far. The last transport was the obvious answer. Could she have snuck on? It was possible, but why?

A small particle embedded in the seam caught his attention. Retrieving a small pair of tweezers from his desk, he removed it and several others. Placing them on a piece of paper, he ran his fingertip over them. Sand. Where would she get sand? He leaned back in his chair and let the possibilities go through his mind.

When he caught his eyes drifting closed, he glanced at the time, surprised at how late it was. Deciding the questions would be better faced in the morning, when there was a chance that maybe she could answer them for him, he went in to check on her one last time. Leeza was still sound-asleep, showing no signs of movement besides the slight rise and fall with her gentle breaths.

Jorran took the extra pillow from the bed, opened a cabinet and pulled out a blanket. Pausing to look at her one last time before heading out to the sitting area, he again felt a rightness in her. Content, he stretched out on the couch. His last thoughts as sleep overtook him were of the very intriguing woman in his bed.

The soft beep of his com-link pulled Jorran from sleep. It took him several seconds to realize he was on the couch, then assimilate that the pillow and blanket meant he hadn't just dreamed the beautiful woman with the captivating green eyes. Jerking up, he activated the com so it wouldn't ring again and disturb Leeza.

"Yes," he snapped in greeting then winced slightly upon seeing the name of the department head for the university. "Good morning, Genis." He glanced at the time to make sure it really was morning. "What's going on?"

"That's what I'd like to know," the man said in a way of greeting. "I had Turet, from Tranic Corp, call me first thing this morning complaining that you have barred his man, Norris, from the exploration. Not allowing him access to the ship." Genis was a small built man, easily excitable but an excellent organizer and supportive to his staff.

Jorran didn't doubt Genis would back him up so went right to the facts. "Yesterday, we were in what we think was the main control room. Norris pressed a button on the control panel, activating it. He said it was an accident, but I'd been keeping an eye on him, and it wasn't."

"Wait a minute, you said activated it?" the man exclaimed.

"Yes. I sent you a report."

"I haven't made it into my office yet. Remember, there was the big social yesterday. I tried to get you to come back so you could talk about some of the things you've discovered."

Jorran rolled his eyes at the thought of being trapped in a stuffy room with several hundred people pumping him for information on the ancient and alien. It wasn't that he disliked talking about it or even minded crowds. It was the setting that had him pulling back. Give him a class or regular seminar room any day.

"The thing actually started?" Genis' curiosity came back again.

"Yes. At least, a screen activated. I went back last night and took an image of it. I'll send it this morning so you can see."

"Excellent, excellent. I can't wait. Do you know what it was?"

"Not a clue, the same kind of glyphs as on the rest of the ship."

"Basm has a team set now to start working on deciphering it. So what did you do to Norris?"

Jorran could imagine Genis' eyebrows twitching. "I didn't hit him if that's what you're thinking. Not that I haven't been tempted a few times. You know me better."

"I know, but something you did had him get his boss all stirred up."

"I sent everyone off the ship until it can be gone over with an analyzer."

"That makes perfect sense and par procedures." Genis's agreement reached him.

"Yes, well Norris wasn't happy about it when I wouldn't let him get a look at the console. Last night, I went back and put up the security shield that arrived yesterday. I figured Norris would try sneaking on." Jorran felt his aggravation burn. From the very beginning it was pressed upon Norris, that he wouldn't be allowed on the ship unless accompanied by him or Esher, no one was.

"So, evidently, Norris went to check it out and couldn't get on the ship." There was a hint of amusement in Genis's voice. "You were right getting the shield. I'd really hoped they wouldn't pull that kind of stunt but can't say I'm surprised. They make a big show about promoting what's good for knowledge, but it's really about the money line for Turet."

"Yes," Jorran had to agree. Both men were under no delusion when it came to Turet and Tranic Corp's motives for funding explorations, but they both had to bend to the will of the university and accept them.

"Well, that explains that, but they had another complaint. Something about you having an unsanctioned woman onsite and staying in your quarters?"

Jorran was shocked. How could they have known about Leeza? The obvious answer was she worked for Tranic Corp, but again, he couldn't accept it. So it left only one reasonable answer. They were monitoring him. He should've figured on that. He remembered the watcher in the jungle and felt his irritation burn.

"Jorran!" Genis's voice came back sharp.

"Sorry, I'm here. I was just going over a few things. My intended came to see my work."

"You don't have an intended."

Jorran knew that was coming. "I do now, and everyone will have to accept that. We're name-locked." Jorran couldn't believe how easy the words came out.

The funny thing was, he was comfortable with the idea. It, like Leeza, felt right. He wondered what she would think of his proclamation that they were to be mated in the near future. Then again, she might not know what it meant, but there were very few things that could break a name-lock.

Jorran became aware of the silence on the other end. "I'll let you know more on that later. For now, just trust me."

There was another second of silence before Genis spoke. "If it was anyone else … I hope you know what you are doing."

So do I. "Don't worry. Chel already went over the whole list of concerns."

"All right." The words sounded dragged out. "I'll tell them that it is cleared. What's her name?"

"Leeza." Jorran savored the slide of it from his lips. He looked up and found the object of his focus staring back at him, her cloud of white hair bellowing out around her slim body. He finally came up with the color that her eyes reminded him of, it was one of the flowers that hung in clusters from the trees with lacy petals as white as her hair, striking and soft at once.

"I've got to go," he muttered in the com. "I'll contact you later with an update." He broke the connection and stood. He wanted to step to her, but the slightly panicked look in her eyes had him holding his place.

Chapter Five

She was trapped, suffocating, frozen. Nightmares of the world exploding filled her vision. She staggered down the halls of the ship, trying to escape the demon that stocked her. She wanted to turn, to fight, but didn't know where to go.

Fear ate at her. In her mind, Leeza cried out for help. In front of her, a man appeared. He was tall with wide shoulders and handsome. His sharp cut features were covered with deeply tanned skin, topped with hair the color of the darkest night.

She froze, waiting for the fear to take her but it didn't come. Comfort spread through her. Security, she would be safe in his arms. Leeza took a step toward him when a shadow moved out of the dark.

Leeza tried to scream a warning at the blow she saw coming, but nothing came out. She was helpless to stop the destruction, and all around them, everything blew up in a burst of bright, scorching flames.

Leeza jerked up, barely keeping in the cry that fought to escape her. The blanket covering her slipped down to her lap, revealing she was clothed in her clothing but that was the only thing familiar to her. The room around her was foreign. She raised one hand to her chest to still the pounding there. She wasn't sure if it was left from the nightmare or the surprise at her surroundings. She was not in her tent or any area she'd seen on the ship, and she didn't think she was back in any city either.

The walls were kind of a soft slate blue, covered in a myriad of grayish tan cabinets. She let her gaze drift over everything. It wasn't a big room, but the space was used to the maximum efficiency.

The only thing that seemed out of proportion was the large bed in which she lay. It took up most of the floor space. Curiously, she ran her hand over the blanket. The material was thin, soft, and surprisingly warm without making her too hot, though the temperature in the room was at a comfortable level.

Stretching her arms out over her head brought protests from her muscles but felt so good. She was alive. The thought came with a touch of striking hilarity. Of course, she was alive. She dropped her hands as images flashed through her mind, the ship, Zareck, the capsule, waking up, the jungle. She started to shake, but the memories continued, people and the unfamiliar language, fear of the irate man, and the man from her dreams coming to her rescue, being ill and it all slipping away.

Again, she looked around the room, and the strangeness of it brought on a fully different connotation. Sliding her feet to the side of the bed, she discovered her boots were missing. Leeza stood. The room began to swim around her.

She reached out and caught hold of a cabinet, laying her head against the surface until she felt steady. Even then, she took a couple more deep breaths before she straightened. It was then the sound of a voice reached her, a deep, rumbling sound.

She listened for what he was saying, but nothing was familiar. She knew by the pitch it was a man, and the image of the man that came to her rescue again popped into her mind. Leeza edged along the wall to where there was an opening to another area.

Her breath caught. Sitting only a couple meters away was the man of her dreams, the man who had rescued her. She glanced around the small room. Had he rescued her?

The thought dropped away as she struggled for calm. Besides her boots and cloak missing, she was starving and feeling a touch queasy. Otherwise, she felt fine. He hadn't hurt her, and for some reason, she didn't think he would.

She listened to what he was saying, trying to make sense of it, filtering the sound combinations through all the languages she knew, and though she found an array of similarities, there were no words solid enough to lock on.

Leeza edged forward and to get a clearer view of him. As in her dreams or memories, he was tall, though at the moment he was sitting. She knew he would be very tall. His hair wasn't just black. With the light on it, it appeared to have shades of blues and purple in it. It was thick and wavy as it brushed over his ears and along his neck.

She watched, transfixed as he shifted and the muscles of his arms bunched. The hand holding something she couldn't make out tightened, bringing a lightening of color around his knuckles. He was aggravated, she realized.

Leeza shifted her gaze back to his face. The planes were so well defined, but the skin was smooth. There was a dark shadowing of a beard on his jaw. She wanted to touch it. She watched his features soften, as if what he was saying brought pleasure back to him. She jerked when she heard him say her name.

When he looked her way, she froze. His eyes locked on her and held. The edges of his lips tilted up in a smile. He continued talking into the communication device, but his focus was fixed totally on her, then he reached over and pushed a button.

When he spoke again, Leeza knew it was to her. From the tone and the look on his face, she knew it was a greeting. She tried repeating the words back at him and was rewarded with a smile and a nod.

"Leeza," he said and pointed to her.

She nodded. "Jor-ran." She pointed to him.

It was his turned to nod. "Jorran."

She repeated it more smoothly. His smile deepened. "Yes," he said then nodded.

"Yes," she copied, and she got that he knew she didn't understand but was trying to learn and he was willing to teach her.

Gradually, as if he was afraid of scaring her, he stood. He was tall, taller than she remembered, or maybe it was the small quarters. She pulled back slightly, but he didn't make any move to her. Slowly, he extended his hand toward her, palm up.

Leeza glanced down at it, back to his face then again at the hand. She understood he was offering it to her and saying he wouldn't hurt her. It was her decision to take it, to trust him. Not feeling threatened but still cautious, she raised her hand and laid it in his.

The smile he gave her this time was radiant, but it wasn't what made her breath catch, but a charge of energy that seemed to burst up her arm. Her eyes went back to his, and she could swear he felt the same reaction.

His lips twitched a little as if he found it amusing, and Leeza felt her own do the same. His fingers curled around hers. Leeza could have sworn in that motion he'd linked them together, and she knew again she would always be safe with him. When he drew her hand to him, she followed, stepping forward.

Dizziness washed over her. In the next instant, she found herself pulled against his body while his arms came around, steadying her. After a second, the world stopped spinning. The hand that had been cradling her head shifted to cup her cheek, tilting it up so she looked at him.

She didn't really understand what he was asking but saw the worry in his eyes and nodded she was okay, but she was grateful his arm stayed around her. The hand on her

THE RUINS – OUT OF TIME

face made a small stroke then he brought it to his mouth in a tapping motion, and she understood he was asking if she was hungry.

"Yes." She used the word he had used for affirmative before.

"Good, yes." Jorran gave her another nod then eased her to sit where he'd been sitting. He took a couple of steps, opened a cupboard and started bringing out food, placing it on the table next to her. To Leeza's relief, several things looked familiar. When there was quite a selection, he turned and looked at her expectantly.

Leeza reached out and pointed to one piece of fruit she recognized. She said its name.

He said a different name. When she repeated it, he nodded. He lifted it and held it to her. "Eat."

She picked it up and took a bite, sighing when the familiar succulent juices slid down her throat. She took several more bites to take the edge off her hunger.

Leeza looked up to find him watching her intently. He waved back to the table. She pointed to another thing and said the name. He said another, and she repeated it. He handed it to her, and while she ate, they went over several items on the table until it started to get too many to remember.

She was getting familiar with certain sounds. His language seemed more like a combination of many. There were even words that were similar to hers. Coming up with an idea, Leeza placed her fingers on the table and mocked writing. Jorran got it immediately, opened a drawer and pulled out a small note pad and a writing implement that was strikingly the same as she used and the name was similar too.

Leeza touched the fruit, said the name then wrote it, turning the paper to him, motioning for him to write it. He did, and when he said it again, she wrote it phonetically. They went first around the table then around the room labeling everything she recognized. The things she didn't know, she just left it at his word and moved on with a shake of her head.

He'd laugh when she stumbled over certain pronunciations, and he'd make a funny face at some of her words. They'd covered most of the room with papers when there was a knock at the door. Jorran froze, brought his finger to his lips then made a motion which she got meant stay. He went to the door and opened it slightly, and the tautness went out of his body.

"Chel," he sighed.

"I was getting worried." The woman looked passed him as he opened the door enough for her to step in. "You've been busy." Chel looked around the room at all the papers then to Leeza, who was again sitting at the table looking nervous.

"We're learning."

"So she really doesn't speak our language?"

"No, but she's smart and learns fast."

Leeza's head tilted to the side as she listened to them. Curiosity filled her face. Jorran smiled at it, coming down in front of her. "It is good," he said. "This is Chel."

"Chel." The name came easy for her. Leeza turned and looked at Chel. "Good morning, Chel." She gave the greeting he'd used earlier."

"Good morning," Chel answered and looked to him and arched an eyebrow. "She does learn fast. Are you certain?"

"Yes." Jorran cut her off before she asked him again if he was certain she wasn't faking.

Chel turned back to Leeza. "How are you?"

Concentration furrowed her brow. "Good," she got out. "I am Leeza."

"Nice to meet you, Leeza."

This time there was confusion, and she looked to him.

"It's okay," Jorran said automatically and had to back up. "Good. It is good."

"It's okay," Leeza answered and turned back to Chel. "N-ice to meet you."

He smiled and nodded. "Leeza, Chel is a medic." He paused to think. "A ..." He put his fingers on her wrist to feel her pulse, then pointed to his head, ear, mouth, opening it and saying "aw", then thinking of something else pulled up a picture of the internal body on the computer screen.

Leeza nodded and said "yes" and a word he didn't quite get then pointed to Chel. "Mettic."

"Close enough." Chel said, shifting her attention back to Jorran. "So are you going to give me a report on her, since you haven't updated me yet?" Chel gave him a stern look that caused Leeza to frown.

"Sorry, we got busy." He motioned for her to sit across the table while he took the seat next to Leeza.

"I can see. So?"

"She woke up," he glanced at the time, surprised at how much time had passed, "a couple hours ago. At first, she seemed a little dizzy, but she ate several things she recognized, that's how we got naming things, and she seems to be okay."

Jorran was aware Leeza was trying to follow their conversation that was obviously about her, but her head started to droop. As he watched, her eyes closed. She jerked, forcing herself back awake.

"I'd suggest she lay back down for a nap." Chel had followed his gaze and caught the action also.

Jorran stood and extended a hand out to Leeza then pointed to the sleeping chamber.

She shook her head. "No, I okay."

"You," he pointed at her, "need sleep." He closed his eyes and tilted his head to his hand. "Sleep," he repeated when he opened his eyes and held out his hand to her again.

Reluctantly, she reached out and took it, letting him help her up. There was a noticeable shakiness about her as if all her strength had waned. Jorran slid his arm around her as he eased her back to the bedroom.

She paused in the doorway looking back at him.

"It's all right." He smiled reassuringly. "Rest, sleep." He motioned with his hands again.

This time, she nodded. "Yes, need rest."

He watched while she climbed into bed, giving her one last smile when she looked up at him before closing her eyes. He still waited a second before turning back to Chel.

The medic's eyebrow was arched in its familiar questioning way. "You know, I really think you have a thing for her."

Jorran's first instinct was to deny it but then he thought why, it was true. "There is still something right about her. And, after this morning, if anything it's stronger. It is amazing how fast she's learning. It's like learning the language comes naturally to her."

"So you still really don't think she's faking it?"

"No, definitely not. See." He pointed to one of the papers sitting by a piece of fruit. "This is her word for it. You'll notice on some things there are actually similarities. No one could make up that many names that fast."

"Maybe that is why there are some similarities?" Chel challenged.

"No," he said firmly. "See here, this is her writing out in sound how to pronounce what I'm saying, sounds that make sense to her." He turned a pad around. "This is the alphabet. And I swear I've seen some of those symbols before. I just haven't had time to think of where. It's amazing what she's done."

"Sounds like she's a linguist. But how can you be sure she's not a plant?"

Jorran stiffened then forced himself to relax. He knew the question would be coming up again. He'd even asked it himself that morning. "I don't know why, but I'm positive."

"I wouldn't put it past Tranic to try to do something to undermine you," Chel cautioned.

"You're right. Genis called first thing this morning. Tranic doesn't like that I put up a security grid."

"So you got it up."

He nodded. "Last night, when I went back to the ship. By the way," he picked up a blank slip of paper, wrote on it and handed it to her, "this is the code."

She glanced down. He knew she was memorizing it. "Didn't take them long to discover it," she said amused. "I'll bet it sure burned them."

"Yeah." He took a deep breath. "They also know about Leeza." He didn't have to wait long for a reaction.

"What?"

"They know I have a woman here."

"You may want to rethink about her being sent here for subterfuge. Okay." She raised her hand in surrender when he started to shake his head. "I'm just saying, take care."

"I will." It was an easy promise to make. He didn't trust Norris or Tranic at all. And he really didn't like them knowing or being interested in Leeza. "Did your tests turn up anything on her?"

The medic sighed. "Not really, that's why I'm here. They're still running, and I don't know what the hang up is. They haven't found anything wrong. In fact, she is surprisingly free from anything. I'd almost swear her system has been cleansed of contaminants. That brings me to the point. You don't think she's here to set you up, and my tests are coming up with nothing but questions. Then there's the question of where do you think she came from?"

Chel waved her hand around the room. "Add this to it. It's impossible for her not to know the base language when it was adopted and has been taught to everyone for over a hundred years. You're saying she learns fast, then why doesn't she already know it?"

All of her points hit hard, but they weren't anything he hadn't already thought of himself. He'd come to accept the answer sometime before. He just hadn't been prepared to say it aloud yet.

He shoved a hand back through his hair and let out a breath. "I think she came from the ship." The impossibility of it struck him again, but in saying it out loud, he knew it was right.

Chel on the other hand was stunned silent for a minute. "I thought you said she wasn't," she finally stammered out. Though, she'd been pushing toward that answer, having it come clearly disturbed her.

"I know, and I still don't think she was an occupant on the ship on its travel here." He held up a hand to forestall her question. "She doesn't fit any of the evidence I've found. I still think we," he pointed between them, "need to look closer. I'd say the average male would have had me by twenty to twenty-five centimeters, and I'm considered over average height. And again, images found, they all had darker hair and skin. Nothing fits Leeza. And, I can't see her coming in unknown on the last transport. Then there's her boots."

He picked one up and turned it over in his hand so the bottom edges of the light-colored leather were directly under the light. "It doesn't show hardly any sign of walking in a damp jungle." He ran his finger along the edge. "I also found particles of sand on them."

"The transport came from Kesler." Chel got the significance. It was just on the other side of the jungle, a rich, fertile area, not sandy. "Okay, so what are you saying?"

"I don't know." He ran his hand back through his hair. "And, until I get Leeza to tell me, I won't know. But somehow, I think she might actually have come from that ship." He shook his head. "It sounds so odd, but for now, I'm going to work under that hypothesis." When he looked at Chel, he was surprised not to find any of the skepticism he expected to see.

"One of the tests I'm running is a genetic scan. Unfortunately, it will take a couple days. So how do we keep Tranic from making problems with her?"

"That's taken care of."

"How?" She cocked her head to the side and eyed him suspiciously.

"I told Genis to tell them she was my name-lock." He was ready for the explosion, and it came abruptly.

"You what? Are you serious? Jorran, that is very binding."

"I think you made that clear last night. But, I'm not going to let anything happen to her."

"Even if that means you have to become bound to her?"

"Yes." It was simple to say the word after spending the last several hours with Leeza. He wondered just what Chel would say if she knew he was seriously considering on life binding to her and not just so he could keep her safe, but because he felt she was who he was looking for in his life. "Chel, keep it down. Leeza is trying to sleep."

She looked at him like he was crazy but didn't get to answer as there was a knock on his door. Jorran glanced at the bedroom to make sure Leeza was out of sight before he stood to go answer it.

For some reason, he wasn't surprised to see Norris standing there. The man wore a frown with his perpetual smug look. "I want to know when we are going back on the ship?" the man demanded without preamble.

"When the scans are done I'll take a team back in," Jorran said dismissively. Not that he expected it to work on getting rid of the man.

"And why aren't you doing the scans?"

"I'm following procedures for the normal cool-off period before I go in."

The man glared. "Are you sure you aren't playing with your woman." There was no mistaking the sneer at the end of the sentence. Norris leaned in as far as he could, obviously trying to get a better look inside. Jorran held his ground cutting off his view. Norris' lips tightened when he saw only Chel but no one else. His brows creased when he noticed the papers strung around. Instead of asking about them, he went right on with his next attack.

"Where is your name-lock?"

"Resting. She had quite a trip yesterday."

"I heard she made a disturbance at Tash's yesterday."

There was a challenge in the statement, but Jorran was ready for it. "Tash was being his normal crude self. He scared her, and she was already not feeling well. The medicine she took for the flight here made her groggy and sick." Jorran nodded to Chel.

"She'll be fine." Chel stood, joining the conversation. She laid a hand on Jorran's arm as if to reassure him. "I suggested she stay in and rest for a couple days."

Norris looked to her and glared. Challenge brewed from him. "She better not slow up the excavation." The threat was strong, but before Jorran could react to it, a quiet voice floated over the air.

"Jorran." All eyes turned toward Leeza as she stepped into the room.

Jorran heard the intake of air from the man behind him. He understood the feeling. With her hair in cascades of wavy light around her, Leeza was a vision, but it was her gentle smile that trapped him. Jorran could swear he saw comprehension in her eyes as if she was reading the situation.

She stepped closer. "Good morning," she greeted Norris. "I am Leeza." The words were pronounced with care but had very good fluidity.

The man was clearly taken back and just stared at her in shocked silence.

Jorran caught the tensing in her, and the nervous look she sent his way. He extended his hand to her. She took it, sidling up to him.

Chel took over the uncomfortable silence. "Men." She snorted. "What are you staring at? You've seen a Thruian before."

There was no missing Leeza's jerk. She spun to face Chel. Puzzlement showed on her face.

Chel, too, was taken back but recovered fast. "It's okay, Leeza," she said deliberately to her. "You have to forgive the men out here. Get them out of the city for a month, and they forget their manners."

Norris pushed in farther, looking from Leeza to the papers strung around the room, back to Leeza. "What's going on here?"

This time, Jorran came up with the explanations that hit him earlier. "Leeza is a linguist. She volunteered to come see if she could help me figure out some of the language from the ship. She was showing how we create a base for understanding language." Saying it reaffirmed that was indeed what she was doing, but for her language not from the ship because the symbols were different.

The man took his gaze from her long enough to look around the room again before coming back to her.

Jorran didn't like the intensity in Norris' gaze. Leeza must have felt the same because she pressed tighter against his side. Jorran broke her hold on his arm to slide his arm around her, tucking her into his body. She stiffened slightly but turned into him, pressing her head into his shoulder in what Jorran figured looked like a shy movement.

Her head barely reached his shoulder, but she felt perfect there. Then he forgot about everything as the soft strands of her hair brushed his chin, bringing with it the warm fragrance that was only Leeza. Jorran wasn't sure when he'd come to recognize the scent, but he knew it would always remain with him.

"If that's everything?" Jorran forced his attention back to the man as Norris tried again to push in for a better look. "We need to get back to work. I will make the first sweep of the ship this afternoon when the twenty-four hour cool off time has passed, then the next sweep tomorrow and I will decide if it's safe to restart the exploration."

Dark fury flashed over the man's face, leaving little doubt he didn't like the answer, but Jorran knew there was little in the way of argument he could put up because that was par procedure. "I'll let you know how everything goes." Jorran started shutting the door, forcing him back.

Norris' gaze shifted once more to the papers then back to Leeza. His look was intense.

Jorran stomach tightened, afraid the expression wasn't only related to his snooping. He closed the door firmly in the man's face, cutting him out before Norris could think of anything else to ask. Tension hummed in his body. Jorran didn't like any of the instincts flashing through his body. Norris was dangerous, and he was now focused on Leeza. As if knowing his thoughts were on her, a hand touched his cheek, breaking his focus.

He looked down to find her staring up at him, concern showed on her face. He forced a smile. "It is okay." Jorran wished he could believe his words.

"I would say it was more interesting," Chel said behind them. "I still say you'd better be careful. He is trouble, maybe dangerous."

Jorran could only nod in agreement, his attention again shifting to Leeza. She moved from his side, taking a couple steps across the room. Her head was tilted away, and Jorran could make out a distinctive pink on her cheek. She was blushing. The thought took him by surprised and heated something in him at the same time. Before he could figure out how to react on it, Chel spoke up again.

"I think we may have found out something about our mystery lady."

Jorran turned to the medic.

"Leeza," Chel looked to her. "Are you Thurian?" she said the words and pointed to her.

Jorran looked back in time to see the recognition of the word cross Leeza's face, and she nodded. "Athurian." She pointed to herself. "I Athurian."

Chapter Six

"Well, I guess she didn't come from the ship after all," Chel said behind him.

Jorran felt like he'd suffered a blow. He'd been certain she'd come from the ship. He tried to wrap his mind around what she'd said and just couldn't get it to work out, though he didn't doubt her either. Leeza had known the name, reacted to it, and looking at her was a testament to that lineage. Still, it wouldn't line up with what his gut told him. Not that he'd never been wrong before on his speculations, but this time, he was so certain.

He caught a slight shift of movement from Leeza and realized she was watching him expectantly. He nodded and smiled at her, and she seemed to relax.

"So, I guess we're back to figuring out where you came from, and that leaves one answer. You must have come in on the transport."

She tilted her head to the side.

He pointed to her then to the sky. "Transport?" He lowered his hand, mocking coming in for a landing.

She looked perplexed and shook her head.

He tried again adding sound. After the second time, she seemed to get what he was referring to but still shook her head. When he caught her yawning, he smiled. "Okay, enough for now. You didn't get your nap. Leeza, go rest. I'll work." He made a motion of writing.

There was a slight pause then she nodded.

"I'd better go finish the tests I've been running," Chel added. "Good-bye, Leeza." She pointed to the door.

Leeza seemed to understand immediately. "Good-bye," she repeated.

"I'll let you know if I learn anything." Chel turned to him. "Though, it looks like our mystery is solved."

"Maybe." He let the word slip out.

"Jorran?" Chel studied him.

He forced a smile. "Nothing. I'm just being contrary. Anyway, I need to work off some energy. I'm going to go start the scans on the ship while she's sleeping."

"Do you want me to stay with her?"

He thought about it a moment, tempted, but brushed his unease away as if being over apprehensive. "No, I think she'll be okay. I'll set the locks on the doors so she can't get out and wander off, though I doubt she'll try."

"Okay, it's up to you. See you later."

"Bye."

"See you later," Leeza repeated that salutation also, bringing a smile to Chel as she turned to leave.

Jorran turned to her as the door closed. "Rest," Jorran encouraged.

She nodded and headed back to the bedroom.

Jorran watched her go then turned his attention to the computer, bringing up information on Thurians. The physical information sure fit Leeza, though he figured she had to be a perfect specimen. He brushed over the history of the people, re-familiarizing himself with it. Thurians were almost wiped out in the storms and flooding during the Great Deluge. As a race, they had totally intermingled with others, so their distinctive traits were diluted.

He scrolled down to where it talked about language. It was almost considered a forgotten language with only a few people who could actually speak it. He brought up the script. Jorran looked at it then at the notes strung around the room. Even with the more curvy flow of Leeza's writing, it was easy to tell it was the same, and it hit him it looked slightly familiar because of his studies on ancient Thurians.

He stood, looking into the sleep chamber. Leeza was curled up on her side. Her eyelashes were a pale crescent on her high cheekbone. Her skin had picked up a healthy, warm, honey color that grew deeper as the day went on. With her white hair, it was striking.

What was most stirring about her, though, was when she looked at him. He closed his eyes and brought back the image, wondering how he would ever describe how it made him feel. He wasn't sure if he could even begin to. It was like he was looking at his destiny, and she was still a mystery.

He stared at her for a moment longer before he pulled himself away. He had things he had to do and while she was asleep was the best. With another quick look, he headed out the door to his office in the main building.

ᏟᎦᎪᎠ

Leeza woke slowly, feeling good. She sighed, burrowing deeper into the pillow. It held a scent that seemed to wrap around her and make her feel safe and alive.

Alive! Her eyelids popped open, and she was greeted with the same blue walls from her dream. But, they weren't a dream, which meant Jorran wasn't a dream either. The flash of panic that hit her faded at his name. She slid from the bed. The dizziness she experienced earlier was no longer there. Nor was any sight of the man she was thinking of.

"Jorran."

There was no answer, but evidence of their time together was still all over the room in labeling. Stepping into the grooming alcove, she washed her face and ran the straightener through her hair. Coming back out, she figured Jorran must have been called away to work so decided to spend her time going over the words. Leeza worked her way around the room.

She was halfway through when it hit her that this was one of the ways her father taught her to learn a new language. Pain slashed through her. Zareck had killed her father. He'd imprisoned her and sent her here, wherever here was. She had no idea how to get back to make him pay for his crimes.

First step, she had to learn the language to figure out where she was. One thing she'd learned is they did know of Athurians. That would help – she hoped. Strengthening her resolve, she poured herself into learning, amazed at some of the similarities she picked up.

She was going over the words on the desk when her hand bumped the computer. The screen came to life, filled with the familiar script of Athurian. Leeza sank to the chair and stared at the screen. She went over the alphabet. There were word groupings, and some pictures that looked like they were taken from some very old documents.

After several attempts, she figured out how to enlarge the pictures so she could read them. The first two were poems. One was lyrics to a song. The next was a missive sent out from the governing council.

Leeza started to read it and froze. Her lungs tightened. She forced herself to continue reading, starting over at the beginning, going over every word. It was an encouragement to all those who survived the catastrophe that wiped out what they figured was ninety to ninety-five percent of their people. It was cautioned, that for their continued survival, they needed to use common sense and work together until the storms faded, and they could begin to rebuild their great nation.

Leeza brushed back tears and looked at the top of the document for a date. She clamped a hand over her mouth to keep back the cry as what she feared appeared before her eyes. Still, she read the date over and over again, trying to deny the possibility. It was four months from then – correction, four months after Zareck sealed her in the capsule.

Surely, she couldn't have been trapped that long. She would have starved. But the evidence was all around her. Even the computer she was looking at was far beyond anything she'd ever seen except on the ship.

Tears swam in her eyes as she read the missive again. When she reached ninety percent of the people were gone, she couldn't see to go on. Pain wrenched its way from her as the words came to her mind.

'Destruction to all.'

"No!" Agony built within her. She knew what had happened. "No," she choked out again. They had started the engines, and it had done something to the atmosphere and thousands, no, millions of people had died.

Leeza pushed away from the desk, stumbling to the grooming alcove, barely making it before she was sick. After, she sank to the floor in a stupor, unable to do anything but cry. She hadn't been able to stop it, and all were gone.

She thought of the couple that lived next to her with the twin boys and the little, chubby-cheeked girl. She wondered if they were among the survivors or her friends at the university. She didn't have any other family. It had just been her and her father for a long time. It didn't make it any easier.

She'd failed. Leeza wrapped her arms around her legs and cried. *Destruction to all. She hadn't stopped it. She'd failed.*

CRBO

Jorran walked at a slow pace down the trail, listening for sounds of being followed. He didn't hear anything, but he didn't doubt Norris would be watching him. At the staging hut, he put on full protective gear, though he doubted he needed it. Taking both radiation and chemical detectors, he strapped them into place and headed to the ship.

The security pillions were just as he'd left them. He smiled at the perverse thought of Norris finding them. He knew it would have aggravated the man. Humming to counter the sound, he took care deactivating them, so anyone watching couldn't see the code or hear the code. He'd learned tricks over the years. Stepping through the portal, he reset the security shield with the same care.

Turning, he activated the scanners. Again, it was more for show, but there was no reason to be careless either. Everything showed clear as he made his way down the tunnel. The orange glow that filled the ship was odd, not at all disturbing to his senses. In fact, he liked the more complete view it gave him. He noticed many things he'd missed before. Jorran paused to turn on his imager and sound recorder, showing first an image of the readings off the scanners.

He gave the date. "Jorran Carrell, excavation head, Alien ship, Tascum Jungle. Security scan after some system activation, caused by a mishap instigated by Norris Tog the previous day."

He looked around. "Amazingly, the ship's lighting has come on. Speculation, the ship may have some kind of solar collection to power them because it is unreasonable that the ship could retain energy for this length of time. As there are no signs of contaminants, I am going to continue the scans."

Jorran continued toward the command room, pausing along the way for the recording of items he'd failed to notice before. His breath caught as he stepped into the room and saw the screen was still lit. He'd been half afraid it might have died or shut off again.

Forcing himself to do a thorough sweep, he started with the scanners again showing all clear. He then turned to the side of the opening, making a recording of the whole room, moving in a circular motion ending at the console. He studied everything. The flashing symbols at the top of the screen gave him a chill of dread, though he couldn't understand what they meant. Funny thing was the touch of familiarity in some of the markings.

Jorran was tempted to try to change the screen like he did on his own computer but was afraid of wiping out what was there, shutting it down, or activating something dangerous. Until they learned more, he knew he needed to leave it alone. Jorran circled the room one more time then decided to continue while he didn't have anyone there to distract him. It was his favorite way to investigate, though with the excitement on finds, he rarely got to do it that way.

He moved down the hall, forcing several doors open. Whatever powered the lights did not extend to giving power to the doors to open on their own as he figured they originally did. He covered most of the floor when the feeling of unease hit him. It took him a minute to realize it was not from the ship. There was nothing threatening there. In fact, he got the impression it'd been cleaned out – not by raiders, but by a people taking all they could to help them survive.

Jorran paused with the thought. It made sense. He found no signs of remains, which was surprising, though there was still a large portion of the ship to investigate. But there was a lack of small movable items including anything resembling clothing and furniture like chairs and tables. Some rooms looked almost totally gutted.

He was tempted to continue on when the thread of concern hit him again, and this time, it brought his thoughts to Leeza. Glancing at the time, he was surprised how much had passed. He hadn't meant to be gone that long.

Reluctantly, he turned and backtracked toward the entrance. He had a good feel of the layout on the level now. Something caught his eye and he was tempted to investigate it, but the nagging concern protested even though he tried to convince himself Leeza would be fine in his chambers. As soon as the thought crossed his mind, he picked up his pace as the unease sharpened.

☯

She'd failed. So many people had died. In a flash of vindictiveness, she hoped Zareck had died then felt a wave of guilt. It hit her. If Zareck had been wiped out, so would've been the whole excavation team. Tears again blurred her vision, but her mind brought up an answer to her previous question of how she got in a jungle. The ship must've been carried away when the land flooded.

Leeza tried to bring up in her mind where the nearest jungle was and froze. There was no way. The continent they were on was fairly arid. There were thick jungle areas in the south, closer to the coast, but there was a mountain chain between.

Visions of the document came to her. It looked old, ancient.

On shaky legs, she stood, making her way back to the computer. Looking for a date, she found it and, because of similarities in languages, was able to decipher it then decided she must've gotten it wrong. Though she knew it was right, she tried again. Leeza shook her head, unable to believe what was there.

She looked at the date again, around the room, then back at the date. It was impossible. Over four hundred and fifty years had passed. There were no more tears to come. She stared at the computer screen, just trying to breathe. She didn't know what to do.

The need for Jorran burst in her.

She dropped her head into her hands. Everyone, everything she knew was gone. She wondered if any of her people survived. After several minutes, it came to her that some must have because Chel knew she was an Athurian. Jorran seemed to recognize that also, though they both seemed to be totally unfamiliar with the language. Were her people ancient history just like the documents she was looking at? She couldn't take her eyes from the screen in front of her. Unfortunately, it couldn't give her any answers. At least, not that she could understand now.

Wrapping her arms around herself, all she could do was stare at the missive as pain, loneliness and fear rolled over her. To her surprise, tears again flowed down her cheeks.

CR⧉

Jorran forced himself to stop and store his equipment then do the precautionary clean off before running down the jungle path to the compound. He ignored the looks he was getting as he raced across the yard, dodging the few people who crossed his path. He slowed as he reached his door. He was being foolish. Leeza would be safely inside. Probably still sound asleep.

Still, as he reached for the handle his panic didn't abate. He punched in the code then turned the handle. Not that he needed the stealth. The woman sitting, staring at the computer didn't only fail to notice his presence, but he figured she really wasn't seeing what was on the screen in front of her. Despair hung heavy on her. Jorran didn't need to see the tears on her face to know they were there.

"Leeza?" He went to her, crouching down beside her. "Leeza?" he said again as he reached out and laid a hand on her arm. "Leeza?" Jorran cupped her cheek gently, turning her face toward him. "Oh, little one." The endearment slipped out, not that she would understand it. Still, it seemed to break through what held her trapped.

"Jorran." His name was whispered as she slid from the chair into his arms.

He was barely able to keep his balance. He wrapped her tightly against him and stood enough to shift into the chair she'd just dropped from, cradling her in his lap. Tears that trickled down her cheeks turned into streams. She clung to him as if he was the only thing that could stave off whatever torment assaulted her.

Jorran felt powerless to do anything but hold her. Totally at a loss as to what could be wrong. She'd been a little frightened and nervous before, but she'd seemed to get past that. But this, it was like she was being ripped apart.

He ran one hand up and down her back in soothing strokes. "Shh, my little one. It will be okay." He repeated it several times before there was any reaction in her. Her crying eased, but the pain was still on her face when she eased back enough to look at him.

She shook her head. "No." She then let out a string of words he didn't understand.

"It will be okay," he said again, cutting her off.

She moved her head from side to side. "No." The word was drawn out in agony. "Gone."

Jorran got the word. He just couldn't wrap his mind around the fact that she could be this distraught because he was gone when she woke up. Surely that was wrong, she couldn't think that he would just leave her.

He shook his head. "It's okay. I'm back. I'm here." He motioned to them. "Work." He motioned writing because he didn't know what else to do, but her head already was shaking negative.

Tears streamed again though she was in more control. She let out another rush of words then took a breath and pointed to the computer. "G-gone." Pronounced pain lined her face. "Gone. No."

Jorran followed the motion to see what she was referring to. It was what he'd brought up before he left on Thurians and their writings. The picture on the screen had been enlarged, making the text easily discernible. He understood immediately she had been reading it. She could understand it.

"Thurian." He pointed to the screen then to her.

"A … thur … ian." She got out amidst the tears.

He tightened his arms, rubbing the hand up and down again in what he hoped was a soothing motion. Her head dropped to his shoulder as she took the comfort. Jorran took a second to read the translation, so he could understand what upset her, since he now figured it was that and not his leaving.

It was one of the oldest surviving pieces of Thurian writing when they were still referred as Athurian. It was written during The Great Deluge, when all the races struggled to survive, especially those here on this continent while the land shifted, and water washed over much of it.

Being an archeologist, he understood well the destruction it reaped. What he didn't understand was why it was causing Leeza such grief. Did she think it was recent? She was the one who seemed to understand the language. Surely she understood it was the past, unless she didn't notice the date.

"Leeza." He placed his hands on her shoulders and eased her back. "Leeza." He pulled her attention to him. "It was a long," he motioned his hand as if he was stretching something out, "time ago." He pointed to the chronometer, then to the date on the document.

She nodded and the tears fell harder. She crumpled back down into his arms.

Jorran held her for several minutes before she stilled. Realizing she'd fallen asleep, he stood, carrying her back to the bed. As soon as he started to lower her down, she stirred and locked onto him. The action brought a smile to him, and he lowered with her, stretching out beside her as she snuggled into him.

He knew it wasn't a wise action. He was already pressing society's boundaries with her, but he figured she was already his name-link. He couldn't stop it, any more than he could the absolute feeling of rightness that came over him. He reached down and pulled the blanket from the bottom of the bed up over them, and he, too, fell asleep.

Jorran came awake, aware of the body pressed alongside him. Leeza. He ran his hand down over her hair enjoying the feel of her there. He caught a lock, lifting it so he could study the pale strands. On closer inspection, what appeared to be plain white was much more. There was an underlying, almost iridescent, gold tone. So soft that it wasn't really noticeable, but he knew it was what gave her hair that striking glow.

Chel was right. Leeza really had been blessed in the gene pool. He knew quite a few Thurians but none like Leeza. She was everything her race was legend to be. She had to be as pure a Thurian as there was.

The thought gave him pause. His heart raced. Athurian. That was how she'd said it several times. He had taken it for a Thurian, but no. He played her pronunciation over again in his mind.

Now he thought about it, he had taken what she said wrong. He should have picked it up earlier. Her pronunciations were too careful. But Thurians hadn't gone by Athurian for centuries. No one called them Athurians. No one but Leeza.

"Athurian." He shifted to look at the woman beside him. Logically, he knew it couldn't be, but as he looked down at her, he couldn't help but wonder if it was true. Then he forgot about it all as he stared at her. Something around his heart tightened and spread through his body. It was right to see her there.

Unable to stop himself, he leaned forward and brushed a kiss on her forehead, consciously keeping it gentle to not disturb her. It was hard, because more than anything, he wanted to wrap her in his arms and pull her to him. Never had the need been so great. He let his lips have one more caress before he forced himself to ease back, only to look down and be greeted by the palest green eyes.

He didn't know what he'd do if fear flashed there, but he didn't have to worry. A gentle smile pulled up the corners of her mouth. One delicate hand reached up and touched his cheek. His breath caught as her fingers traced over his skin.

Her eyes followed the process, studying him as intently as he'd been studying her moments earlier. She lifted a lock of his hair. It was longer than he normally wore it, but being out on the excavation, he hadn't worried about cutting it. The comparison of colors to hers was striking. He wondered what she was thinking. Did she find him as appealing as he did her?

As if in answer, her eyes came back to meet his. Jorran had never been in love before, but he could swear that was what he was looking into now. Her eyes full of wonder and softness.

"Jorran."

His name whispered its way from her lips as if it was sneaking out on its own. It pulled at him, and he leaned forward to answer it. Tugging lightly on the strand of her hair he still held, he drew her near to him. There was timidity as her lips met his but no hesitation.

Recognition and energy sparked in him. Leeza gasped as if the same hit her. Jorran tried to force himself to break the kiss, but it was impossible. He eased more of himself into the kiss, and she accepted and gave back as their hearts pounded and fused as one.

Jorran had no idea how much time passed before he finally broke the kiss and eased away. Leeza's eyes were closed, and she trembled slightly in his arms, but he knew it wasn't from fear. Still, he raised his hand to brush her cheek with the back of his knuckles in what he hoped was a comforting move. Her lashes rose, letting him see into her soul, and he found himself there.

"Jorran." The words that followed he didn't know, but the meaning behind them was clear. They were words of love or at least caring.

Then as if realizing what she'd said, she shook her head slowly. He stopped her, brushing his mouth to hers. "Yes, Leeza." He followed with another kiss. When he leaned back, he pulled her to him, wrapping his arms around her cradling her against him. After a second of hesitation, he felt her soften and mold herself into his arms.

He savored the feel of her, the yearning to make her his burned deep within him. He pressed kisses against her temple on the way back to her mouth. When he felt her shiver in reaction, his logic finally caught up with him.

It was too soon. He had to give her time to make sure she understood what their union would mean. He was Ellandish. When they mated, it was for life. He broke the kiss but continued to hold her until the need for her became almost unbearable. He released her abruptly and stood, backing up a couple feet to keep from reaching for her.

He could tell his actions startled her and maybe her own did too. Color heightened in her cheeks. One hand came up to her mouth as she took in small gasps of air.

"Sorry, I shouldn't have done that. It's too soon, but I want you for my heart-mate. I promise to take care of you. You will have my heart forever." He didn't know why he was going on. She couldn't understand. "It's okay." He turned away. He was about to bolt for the door when her hand rested on his arm. Jorran steeled himself before turning back.

He hadn't heard her stand, but she was right behind him. The shyness was back around her, but a tender smile was also on her face.

"I." She laid a hand over her chest, her eyes drifted closed again as if pulling up her nerve. She opened her eyes again, and moved her hand from her own chest to over his heart. When he could tell she was about to move it, he raised his hand to cover hers, keeping it there, sealing the promise between them.

Together, they stood in the center of the room as one, locked together as they were locked in each other's eyes, until the sound of a received transmission jerked them apart.

Leeza caught a breath and the edge of her lip between her teeth then turned her attention toward the computer.

"It's okay. Let's see who it is, but I can guess." Jorran sat down, activating the link. "Genis," he greeted the man as the image appeared. Leeza pressed closer, obviously curious.

"I've been waiting for an update." There was no anger in the words.

"Sorry, things have been busy here."

The man shifted his gaze to see past him to Leeza. His eyebrow arched up. "So that is the mystery woman." There was reverence in his voice.

"Leeza," Jorran held out a hand to her. There was no hesitation in her laying her hand in his and moving closer to his side. "Leeza, this is Genis Pravail, my boss. Genis, Leeza."

"Leeza Jaeff," she said and dipped her head toward him in way of greeting. "Hello."

"Hello," Genis greeted back. Jorran could see him holding back his curiosity then the question slipped out. "And what is your purpose for being at the excavation?"

The expression on Leeza's face showed her trying to work over what he had said but she still didn't have enough basics to decipher the sentence. She turned to him. "What mean?"

Jorran felt a touch of shock at her putting the words together. Trying to rephrase the question was another challenge. "Why are you," he pointed to her, "here?" He swept his hand around them. He was unprepared when tears filled her eyes.

"Zareck." The word erupted from her with anger and pain. She paled and started to tremble.

"Genis, I need to go."

"Wait, what was that? I need a report."

Jorran glanced back at the man. "I did a sweep of the ship. Everything showed clear. I will send you some updated images later, and I'll do another sweep tomorrow then get back to you. I'll talk to you later." He cut the connection before Genis could say anything back.

"Leeza." He stepped to her. Still, she surprised him when she dove for him, throwing her arms up around his neck. He caught her up, lifting her off the ground, not that she seemed to notice.

She clung to him, burying her face into his neck.

"Shh, my heart." The endearment flowed from him with his need to comfort her. "Shh." Once more he settled back in the chair with her in his lap, rubbing his hands up and down her back. It took some time for the tears to end, and she sagged in his lap, spent. Jorran brushed the remaining tears from her face then cupped her cheek, lifting it up to meet him. "Tell me. What?"

He watched her struggle for ways to answer. Leeza leaned forward, pointing to the computer. She said something then paused, biting the edge of her lip and frowned. She moved her hand like she was turning pages back in a book.

"You want me to go back? Back?" He made to motion.

"Yes."

She followed his motion as he backed up to the previous screen. He'd only gone back two when she grabbed his hand stopping him then pointed to the screen. He leaned forward to once again study the page she'd been looking at earlier.

"Athurian." He annunciated the word carefully. "You are Athurian."

"Yes." She nodded then pointed to the screen again. "Zareck," she said then looked at him and mimicked an explosion with her hands and sound.

"Leeza, this happened a long time ago."

"Zareck." She pointed again to the screen.

"I don't understand, but I think I finally know something that will help. I should have thought about it earlier," he said as he reactivated the communication, and Genis face appeared immediately.

"What was that? What is going on there?"

"Sorry, I'll explain in a minute. First, I need you to send me a translator as soon as you can. If there's not a delivery scheduled in tomorrow, I will cover the delivery."

"You asked for it a week ago. I sent you a translator in the last shipment." The man looked perplexed. "Didn't you get it?"

Jorran felt a wave of relief. "Things have been a bit hectic. I haven't gone over the delivery list yet."

"Jorran, what is going on?"

"It's hard to explain. Do you think it has Athurian in it?"

"Athurian? Possibly, limited. Why?"

"I need Athurian."

"You found Athurian on the ship?" There was excitement in his voice.

"No. Leeza speaks Athurian. I need the translator for her."

"If she speaks Athurian, why do you need a translator for that?" The furrows over his brows deepened.

"Because she doesn't speak Lannish."

"That's impossible." The words were almost mumbled out as he thought over the connotations. "Jorran?"

"I'll get you the answers when I get them. I need to go find that translator. Thanks." Jorran again cut the connections and brought up the list of inventory. He was surprised to see the translator had been taken to his office.

Then again, it was the logical place for it. He just hadn't been there to see it.

"Let's go." He pointed to the door. "With me." He picked up her boots. "We also need to find you more clothes."

She, at least, got the idea he wanted to take her somewhere. She stood, took her boots and pulled them on.

Chapter Seven

Leeza wasn't sure where they were going, but it didn't matter. She wanted to be outside. Suddenly, she felt as if she had been cooped up for a long time. Still, as they stepped outside, she pulled back at the shock of seeing the jungle.

Part of her had wondered if she'd dreamed it. Though, since she was with Jorran, she knew it had to be true. She looked at the man, and her insides did another flip.

She was in love with him. She wanted to deny it. But even the firm logic that she really didn't know him, and they could hardly communicate, couldn't shake the fact that, deep down within, she felt she was linked to him. Even more confusing was that he seemed as aware of the bond as she was, and he didn't doubt it either.

She tried to deny her feelings and convince herself that it was just the turmoil that she was feeling, but the bond was too strong to be ignored. So when he held his hand out to her, she confidently placed hers in it and let him lead her across the quad.

There were more people out doing various activities. Two men were down by the storage unit working on some kind of vehicle. One looked up and glanced away, then his attention snapped right back to her, and he let out a low whistle. The other man looked up and joined the first in staring at her.

Uneasy, Leeza shifted her gaze from them, gliding over the place she ate the night before, catching a glimpse of the short, pudgy man as she did. She tried to ignore him, but his eyes on her made a shiver race down her spine. Leeza edged closer to Jorran, taking comfort in his large hand wrapped around hers. Instinctively, she knew he would protect her.

He must have felt her shift because he looked down and smiled. Leeza felt her breath catch. His features seemed chiseled in powerful angles but there was something very pleasing in them.

She'd never known a man like him. He was so handsome. The sunlight caught on his hair bringing out tones of blues and purples. Leeza had an urged to reach up and finger the intriguing strands. Her focus shifted to his lips, and she remembered the feel of them on hers and almost stumbled.

She wondered what he'd say if she said she hadn't ever been kissed like that before. When it came to relationships with men, it was something there had never been time for. There was always another new language to study, and her father had always been too busy to think of arranging a marriage for her. Not that she'd been interested. Whenever she was asked when she would be paired, something always seemed wrong about the idea.

Leeza realized they had stopped walking. She raised her gaze to meet his. Intensity burned deep like violet fire in his eyes. Her heart pounded in reaction to it. The hand holding hers tugged her forward, but it was some kind of internal pull that drew her in.

Little waves of awareness prickled over her. Her breath caught, bringing with it the scent of him. His head lowered toward her. Leeza could almost feel his lips against hers when he seemed to catch himself and pull back.

"I shouldn't, we shouldn't." He stopped what he was saying. "We'd better go." The words though odd were becoming familiar and she understood the meaning as he pointed to the building she'd debated entering the evening before.

Funny, it seemed inconceivable that it was only just one day. He led her through the flaps and down the hall turning to the left. He made another turn into a short hall then stopped at a door and punched several buttons on a pad then opened the door, directing her inside.

The small room was obviously an office. Two walls of the compact space were filled with cabinets similar to those in his quarters. There was a small stack of papers on his desk. He bypassed them and opened the packing box, whatever was in it seemed to please him.

Jorran pulled out a small, thin, rectangle devise and activated it. It let out several tiny peeps. His attention was locked on the screen on the top. He slid his fingertip over it, and Leeza caught the motion of words scrolling under his touch.

He started to look perplexed. After a moment, a frown marred his features. Jorran said something that sounded like he was voicing his displeasure. He pushed one of the lines and said something, and the machine said a series of sounds in return that she knew where words. He touched the screen again and spoke. This time she picked out a distinctive difference in the tone of the words that came.

Frustration flared on Jorran's face. He tried once more, and Leeza picked up what sounded like a familiar word in the return of clipped sounds.

Jorran did whatever he'd done twice more when she again picked up another more familiar word from the machine. She reached out and stopped him before he could change the setting again. Now she felt perplexed.

Lifting the device from his hands, she turned it over, inspecting it. She could swear the machine had spoken Krisk. She wanted to think that was impossible. Before she had a chance to figure it out, the communication link on Jorran's wrist beeped.

She looked at the communication device as Chel's voice came out of it then back at the instrument in her hand as the language she was almost sure was Krisk came out of it. There were differences but so close. She was sure Chel was telling Jorran that she needed to meet with him.

Her thoughts ran over things. The technology Jorran had was more advanced than her time, and it made sense there would be a progression in technology. Leeza shook off the stab of pain at the thought. Could the devise actually translate one language into another? The thought intrigued her, but before she could experiment to see, Jorran took her hand.

"Come. We need to go see Chel." He led her from the room as the instrument translated his words. They went back down the short hall, passing the entrance and continued the other direction down the hall to the other side. He knocked at the door then opened it.

Chel sat at a desk across from the door. She looked up as they entered. This room was bigger, lined with cabinets and counter space that held an array of odd instruments. Two padded tables sat at the back of the room.

"Hello," Chel greeted.

"Hello," Leeza returned. As Chel shifted her attention to Jorran, Leeza turned her focus to the device in her hand. When she activated it, the devise started to pick up what Chel and Jorran were saying. It only took a couple phrases for Leeza to affirm it was translating their words into Krisk, though the stronger guttural sounds were not quite as pronounced. Still it was not hard to translate.

☙❧

The urgency Jorran detected in Chel's voice over the link was clearly evident in the anxiety in Chel's face. Apprehension rose in him, knowing how unflappable the woman was.

"The genetic test finished its run." Chel glanced at Leeza. "She is Thurian, but not like the Thurian we have now. I guess the only way to term it is, she's like a throwback. If we had a code of a pure Athurian, I would imagine it would look like hers."

If Chel expected shock, it didn't come. Chel waited for him to say something but he couldn't. She'd just confirmed what he already knew. It didn't make it any easier to accept. Slowly, he nodded. His mind tried to wrap around the thought that Leeza might be five hundred years old when Chel hit him with another bombshell.

"There is another problem."

"What?" He jerked his head up and looked at her.

"You know how I told you her scans had come back incredibly free from contaminants."

He thought back and answered. "Yes." He waited for her to continue.

"The test I just ran showed a shift in her antibodies." She paused a moment. "Like her body is gearing up to fight a disease attacking it."

It took a second for Jorran to assimilate the meaning, though it was plain. Beside them, they heard Leeza draw in a sharp breath. Both their attention turned to her. Leeza looked stricken.

Jorran stepped to her, his attention dropping to the translator in her hands. "Leeza, do you understand what it said?"

"Yes. Krisk."

"You can understand that," he repeated.

She nodded.

"Is that your language?"

She shook her head. "No. Athurian."

Behind him, Jorran heard Chel take in a breath. He ignored it to stay focused on Leeza.

"But you can understand that. Do you know other languages?" He waited for the machine to repeat what he said.

"Yes." She rattled off a list of what he thought sounded like a lot of other languages.

He held up his hand to stop her. "Okay, so you know several languages. We'll work on that later. Let's get back to what Chel is saying." He wasn't sure he wanted Leeza to hear it because he knew it was going to be bad news, but he also couldn't keep it from her.

"So what are you telling us?"

"It looks like Leeza's body is trying to fight off a virus. I would like to run some tests to see."

Jorran wanted to ask her if there wasn't more, but a glance at Leeza held the question. He turned to Leeza instead. "Is it all right if Chel runs some tests on you?" he asked, letting it be her decision since she understood.

There was only a touch of hesitancy when Leeza nodded. "Yes," she answered in Krisk then she beat the machine in translating it into Lannish.

Jorran had no trouble detecting the tension in Leeza as he watch Chel take a blood sample. Though he knew there was little pain involved, he still had the desire to wrap his arm around Leeza and protect her from the process. Unfortunately, what he was afraid he needed to guard her from was what was happening in her body, and there was nothing he could do about that. He didn't want to think of her getting sick. To block that out, he concentrated on figuring out what he had learned.

Chel pretty much confirmed Leeza was ancient Thurian. Athurian as Leeza called it, which it hadn't been known by for over two hundred years. Looking at the beautiful, young woman who sat on an exam table watching Chel as she worked, it seemed impossible. To take it a step farther was Leeza's reaction to the Great Deluge. He'd have to question her about it, and now with the translator he could, but it was certain from her reaction that to her it wasn't ancient history, which would make her closer to five hundred years old.

He shook his head against the thought and shoved his fingers through his hair.

As Chel finished and turned away, Jorran stepped forward and laid his hand over Leeza's hands that were clasped in her lap. He squeezed down. She looked up and smiled a slightly shaky smile. Unable to stop himself, he raised a hand to caress her cheek.

He was surprised when she slid off the table, wrapped her arms around his waist, and laid her head on his chest. He hugged her to him, marveling again at how right she felt there.

"My heart," he whispered down to her, feeling words surge within him. When she raised her head to meet his gaze, he became lost in her vivid green depths.

"My heart." She mouthed the words back at him an instant before he captured her lips, sealing the words with his mouth. He kissed her deep, full of promise – promise to love her with everything he was.

The sound of a throat clearing had him easing back. Pulling away from her was one of the hardest things he had ever done. It was like pulling away from his destiny. And as she looked up at him, the same emotion seemed to echo in her eyes. Heart and soul, they were one.

Unfortunately, the timing was not with them. The thought of time and Chel clearing her throat again behind him brought him the rest of the way back to reality. He caught the blush that snuck over Leeza, more a faint ruby color than pink.

He slid his hand down her arm to interlock their fingers. He didn't know if Leeza understood the context in his civilization, the action spoke of commitment, that their lives were intertwined. He squeezed down, and she returned the motion.

He shifted his attention to Chel in time to catch her glance at their hands. She definitely did not miss the connotation. "I'm done here. Why don't we get some dinner while this starts to run."

Jorran got the message that Chel was trying to slow things down. Though he didn't want to, he could see the wisdom. Besides, as hungry as he was, he knew Leeza had to be also, especially after being sick, and with her body fighting off some kind of virus.

"Come on." He drew her with him, following Chel from the med-lab. Jorran didn't question going to the commons for dinner. News of Leeza's presence would have already made the rounds. People would be curious about her, and if he kept her hidden, speculation would only grow.

Leeza seemed to understand because she went with him, in sync, and so close that every once in a while she brushed against him as they moved. The commons was a large room that buzzed with the noise of people talking at a series of round tables when they entered.

They hadn't even made it a few feet inside when a hush fell over the room. All attention turned to them, particularly, Leeza. Jorran felt her edge closer, but a glance her way showed no signs of fear on her. She studied the others in the room as much as they studied her. With a slight tug on her hand, she walked with him to the long serving table set along one wall.

Jorran felt a touch of concern about what she could eat, but she didn't seem to have the same reservation. She studied the array and slowly picked out certain choices. Some, she took just enough to give her a sample, and several things, which he guessed were familiar to her, she took more of.

When he noticed Esher and Rese sitting together at a table, and several seats open to the side of them, he led Leeza that way with Chel following behind them.

"Can we join you?" Jorran asked in the way of greeting.

"Sure," the older man said, his eyebrow arching in a quizzical manner.

Rese seemed to have lost the ability to speak, his attention riveted on Leeza.

"I don't think you have had the opportunity to meet my name bound, yet." Jorran decided it was best to lay the groundwork before there could be any questions.

Esher's brow rose even higher, but he didn't say anything to counter the statement for which Jorran was grateful. If Esher accepted it without question and with Chel by them, everyone else would follow suit.

"Leeza, I'd like you to meet Esher Tamar and Rese Raehumn. Esher, Rese, this is Leeza Jaeff."

"Hello," Leeza said in greeting looking first to Esher then to Rese.

"A pleasure." If Esher's greeting confused her she made no show. She accepted it before turning toward Rese who stumbled over his hello.

Jorran, not for the first time, thought how the young man reminded him of himself. At that age, he'd been so wrapped up in his learning that, what little time he had left over was taken up with athletics, so women were a mystery to him. It hadn't bothered him much, though, because until he met his mate it wasn't much of a concern. Still, as time went on, and he never felt that draw, he wondered if there really was a woman for him.

Jorran glanced at the woman beside him and felt the flare burn to life. There was no more cause to worry now. He'd found his one.

As if Leeza felt his attention, she looked over, smiled then tilted her head down in an obviously shy movement. The flames within him surged, and for a second, Jorran lost track of the conversation.

ଔଛ

Leeza felt heat flood over her when she caught the look Jorran sent her direction. Her heart pounded, once again she, wasn't sure what to make of it. The effect that Jorran had over her was disconcerting. She had never known anyone to have that kind of a draw.

With a simple look, he claimed her, and she couldn't even begin to raise an objection to it, not that she wanted to. It was as if she was destined to be with him. The thought gave her a thrill of excitement.

Jorran was totally opposite of anyone she knew. She found his dark looks appealing. But that wasn't what captivated her. She watched how he interacted with the others at the table and those on neighboring tables who called for his attention. Jorran was well liked and looked up to. Leeza realized he was a leader of some kind there.

She thought of the confrontation with the man that had come to Jorran's chambers, Norris. There was no doubt Norris wanted to challenge Jorran but years of studying people for their actions regarding how they said things beside the words they said, let her detect an underlying caution and maybe even a touch of fear in Norris's actions. Leeza felt a jab of concern. It didn't bode well. For a man like Norris, it could make him dangerous.

Pushing the unpleasant thought aside, Leeza tried to focus on what was coming through the translator. She barely caught the end of a sentence directed toward her from Rese.

She looked up at the younger man. "Sorry," she started her apology. "I–," She stopped unsure of the word in Lannish. Without thinking, she held up the translator as if it could offer her an excuse.

"An Extreme Systems Language Translator, wow." He looked interested when the machine repeated what he said. "What language is that?"

"Krisk," she answered easily.

The young man nodded. "You understand that?"

"Yes."

"Wow," the young man exclaimed again. "I've never heard it before. Though, I have studied some of the ruins." He looked at Jorran. "One of your classes."

Jorran nodded. "Leeza's a linguist. She's going to help us work up a translation of the language on the ship."

"Really." Esher looked intently at her.

"Yes." Jorran answered for her. "Right now, we're just seeing how many languages in the translator she knows."

Leeza felt a touch of fear as she got what he was saying. She forced herself to relax, knowing Jorran would remember what setting was Krisk, and she wouldn't lose the ability to communicate with him. Under the edge of the table, so only he could see, she made the motion of writing then remembered the name and said it.

Jorran pulled a thin rectangular object from an oversized pocket on the side of his pant leg. Leeza was surprised when he pushed a button, and the top lit up in a screen similar to a computer. It was amazing. She felt a touch of awe and wanted to study it, but now was not the time to ask him. It was amazing though.

Jorran smiled, noticing her interest. He tapped a symbol then made a list of numbers down the screen. Beside the number six, he touched it, and it highlighted the line and he wrote in Krisk. He handed her the pad and took the translator and started to tell Esher and Rese about going in the ship.

After a minute, Leeza wrote the word in the language she readily recognized. Jorran looked over then changed the translator to the next line down. After a minute of listening to Jorran talk and the machine repeat, she shook her head. On the pad, Jorran wrote the name then no and moved to the next. The next three were familiar. Jorran continue to talk, breaking only to write the name of the language as he knew it as she moved through the list.

Of the thirty languages on the translator, Leeza recognized nineteen. When she finished going through them all, she switched the translator back to Ferish, a language she was not only fluent in but she realized, more importantly, was similar to Lannish.

After making the connection, the more she listened to it, the easier it was getting for her to follow and understand the Lannish words directly. There seemed to be a lot of other words thrown in that had a totally different base language.

"Well, gentlemen," Chel spoke abruptly. "I don't know if you realize how much time has passed, but I think it's about time for Leeza and I to say goodnight to you."

Leeza could tell from Jorran's reaction that he was as surprised as she was by the announcement. The first words that escaped her were an objection, but being in Athurian, no one understood. Jorran's hand caught hers, intertwining their fingers. When he squeezed lightly on her fingers, she looked to him.

He gave a faint smile. "It's okay," he said softly, drawing her up. He looked at the others at the table. "I'm going to walk Leeza to your place, Chel," he announced, leaving no doubt they wanted to be alone. "Goodnight." He looked at everyone at the table then directly at Chel. "Give us a minute." His words reinforced his earlier hint.

Leeza got in a goodnight as he drew her away.

Outside, there were signs that it had been raining again. The air smelled heady of rich soil and a mixture of flowers hanging from the trees. The gentle light from the setting sun filtered through the trees giving everything a warm glow.

With his hand wrapped around hers, Jorran led them toward the building where Chel's med-lab was, but instead of going in, Jorran circled around the side to the back of the building where it nestled against the jungle. He came to a stop under a large palm leaf where a cluster of vibrant flowers hung down not far from her head. Jorran turned to her. His eyes seemed hot, almost feverish.

"Chel's right." He burst out before she had a chance to ask him what was wrong. "I don't like it though. I don't want to be separated from you, but you will be safe with Chel."

"Jorran," Leeza started, but he cut her off with the shake of his head. The smile he gave her was forced.

"It's hitting me hard. I didn't realize it would be so strong. It must be because I'm tired. Give me a minute." He stepped back abruptly and turned to face the foliage. His body was tense, back rigid, muscles bunched in his shoulders and arms. He seemed to be staring intently, but she didn't think he was actually seeing what was in front of him. He was laboring to take deep slow breaths. Worry built in her. He seemed in pain.

"Jorran." She laid a hand on his arm.

"Don't touch me." He jerked away.

Leeza pulled back, surprised and hurt by the forcefulness in his voice.

Jorran took several more breaths. "It's okay." He took another deep breath then turned to her. His eyes were still hot, but the fire in them now seemed banked. "I'm sorry. There is no reason to be afraid. I will never hurt you."

Leeza wanted to tell him she never thought he would, but before she could come up with the words, he was already talking again, and she had to rely on the translator to catch what he was saying.

"I want you with me, but it is not time yet. I need to give you time to get settled to what is happening around you and to where you are. You need to know you have choices, and that I will never take that from you no matter how much I want you."

He was going so fast she wasn't sure if she was getting the full meaning of what he was saying. His words confused her. One moment, she thought he was meaning he wanted to have her with him, as in a life mate. Yet, when she touched him, it was like he couldn't stand the contact, though he'd been holding her hand all evening.

Leeza wasn't sure how to ask him to clarify. She wondered if she was misinterpreting the translation or that maybe she'd been forcing her own interpretation. Maybe it was her desires and her own wishful thinking coming through.

Jorran was staring over into the foliage again. His shoulders were hunched away from her. She recognized the defensive stance. He didn't want contact with her.

She shook her head and tried to think. So much was happening, but she thought she understood what was going on between her and Jorran. What she felt was strong, but was it just her being foolish and forcing the thoughts in her mind to his actions.

"You need to stay at Chel's. It would be better that everyone knows you are at Chel's and not with me." His words confirmed her fears.

She was forcing feelings she was having for him into the translation and transferring emotions. She knew how some words translated but did not always carry the same meaning. And one word, taken out of context could shift so much. It could make one think someone cared for them deeply, when it was all just a sense of responsibility.

Pain hit her. She felt like crying but refused to humiliate herself anymore. After all, she'd been thinking Jorran loved her, that he'd been talking about becoming life-mates. What was happening was that she was becoming pathetic. He didn't want her with him.

Part of what she was feeling must have shown on her face when he turned back because he reached out and placed a hand over hers. He pulled back abruptly as if he'd been burned.

"It's okay," he repeated, but this time the words were harsh, slashing like a knife into her. "You have nothing to worry about. You'll be safe with Chel."

She didn't think he sounded sure. His gaze bore into her with a power that made her shudder, but it wasn't with fear. She tamped down on her runaway emotions in time to catch his next words.

"Tomorrow morning I will do another sweep of the ship, if everything checks out okay, in the afternoon I will take a team back in. I want you to come along. I want to see if you can decipher any of the writing." He shifted his gaze from her then back, staring with intensity. "It's getting dark. I better get you in now. You need your rest after all that has happened to you."

Leeza wasn't sure what she was supposed to say. A strange hoot burst from the jungle making her jerk and look around. She was surprised to see the sun had set. Dark shadows reached out of the jungle toward her, not all from the approaching night but the shattered feelings she'd been having for Jorran.

"Come on." He caught her hand and tugged her away from the foliage. Lights were on in the quad, but before she could even look to see if there was anyone around, he pulled her inside the building, down the hall to the door across from the med-lab they'd been in earlier. He rapped on the door. It opened almost instantly.

Chel motioned her inside. Leeza started to enter, but before she could, she was pulled back. She stumbled slightly. The tug left her plastered against Jorran's chest.

She tried to move back and steady herself, only to have his arm lock across her back like a steal band, keeping her there. Her eyes met his as his head came down. The kiss was powerful and then gone. She was too dazed to make a comment but his attention was already focused on Chel.

"Watch after her," he directed, then leaned forward to kiss Chel, catching only the older woman's cheek. His kiss seemed not to have the same effect on Chel, though the woman chuckled as he turned and strode away without any farewell.

Leeza watched him go, feeling more alone and confused than she did when she'd stumbled out of the ship into the strange new world that surrounded her. She wanted to shout at how fate could be so cruel to bring her here. She then realized that was exactly what spurred her silly runaway fantasy, the thought, no dream, that she could have been brought here to find the love she couldn't find in her own time.

"Well, that was interesting," Chel said behind her. "Let's get you settled for the night. In the morning, I'll find some other clothes for you."

Tucking her emotions back in as she had all her life, Leeza turned to the older woman. Chel studied her for a long moment then, with a shake of her head, closed the door and stepped by her.

"This makes up into a nice bed, and sleeping out here will allow you some privacy. Unfortunately, there are no extra quarters. They only brought in the minimal that was needed. Though, I don't think Jorran would have allowed you to stay on your own. He's feeling a touch on the protective side."

Leeza jerked at the word. Of course, Chel would understand Jorran was just protective of her out of a sense of duty. She'd been the one to place more on his actions. She tried not to bring the image of him up in her mind, but it slipped in and her heart caught before she could brush it away.

"Are you okay?" Chel studied her with a look of concern.

Leeza nodded, her throat too tight to let anything out.

The woman stood a moment more before turning. "Okay, let's get you settled for the night."

Chapter Eight

Jorran paced his chambers as tension coursed through his body. Sleep would not come. He wanted Leeza. She should be there with him. She was his name-bound. She was his to protect and love.

He sat at the computer and pulled up the last images he'd taken in the ship then stood abruptly as they were not enough to hold his attention. He was halfway out the door before he realized where he was going and forced himself to stop. Jorran shoved his hands through his hair. He tilted his head back and had to fight the urge to howl for his mate.

He felt a wave of self-mockery. He knew Ellandish felt strong connections when they found their life-mate and heard, for some, it was extremely powerful. But he never figured it could be this encompassing to his soul. He felt he could hardly breathe for needing Leeza.

Jorran wondered what Chel would do if he broke down the door to take Leeza back. Probably tranquilize him. It made him think of asking her if she could give him something. He pushed the thought aside and tried to lock down his emotions.

He had to give Leeza time. So much had happened to her. He couldn't trap her into a life with him before she had a chance to come to terms with everything. How long would that take her? Jorran thought in frustration. He hoped not long, because he wasn't sure how much time he could give her and keep his sanity. He should never have kissed her. Once he got her taste, it became a hunger eating at him.

Jorran made several passes back across the room before he forced himself to sit down at the computer and study the pictures, cataloging each detail he saw. The normally fascinating task seemed tedious. He was tempted to go to the ship and work but knew, in his frame of mind, it was not a safe idea.

Finally, when he hoped himself settled and exhausted enough, he went to bed. Laying back, the image of Leeza came to him. He held it in his heart and wished to hold her.

෬෩

He was there watching. Fear bubbled up within her. Leeza turned but all that was there were shadows. She went back to the translation, studying the schematic for shutting down the engines. She had to shut them down, or everyone would die. She couldn't let that happen, not again.

Out of the corner of her eye, she saw the shadows move and jerked. Concentrate, Leeza told herself, ignoring the uneasiness that built. Nothing was there. She looked up again as one of the shadows dislodged itself from the rest and lunged at her.

Leeza screamed, stumbling back. It kept coming. Its darkness threatened to overwhelm her. She couldn't let it get her. She couldn't lose. She had to stop the engines before everyone died. The shadow lashed out at her. She tried to stand her ground, but pain still flooded her with fear as the shadowed hand passed over her.

No, not again. She wouldn't let Zareck win. Laughter rang from the shadows, and she felt an evil menace her, but it wasn't Zareck. This one wasn't fueled by greed but hatred and evil, sick-pleasure. This one even more terrifying.

Leeza turned and ran. She had to find Jorran. He would save her. He would help her stop the beast. She screamed his name, but it echoed back to her, empty. He wasn't there. She was alone, always alone. There was no one for her no matter what time she was in, and she would always continue to fail, and everyone would die.

Leeza tripped and fell, going down, down, down into the shadows as they wrapped around her, swallowing her in their emptiness.

Leeza jerked up, panting, trembling from the lingering effect of the nightmare. It took her a minute to get accustomed to the faint glow around her, to recognize Chel's quarters. She didn't want to be there. She wanted Jorran, but he didn't want her. The thought bit into her like a knife. He didn't want her. He'd sent her away. He'd help her, she knew, because he felt responsible for her, not because he loved her.

She was so foolish expecting his love. Thinking she'd been there to find the love she couldn't find in her own time. It was a pathetic thought. It wasn't her destiny to be here. Again, pain swept over her, and she felt more devastated than when she found out she'd failed and most of her civilization had been wiped out.

Why, why had she survived? How had she survived?

She hadn't even thought to ask the question before, but so much had been happening. It was all too fast, and Jorran was there. Pain spiked within her again, and she pushed it away. She would not give into the folly of her heart any longer. She was an intelligent woman, top of her field. At least, she had been where she came from.

Not where − when. All those people dead. She dropped her head to her hands and let the tears flow. Would the knowledge of her failure ever cease to haunt her?

She wanted to escape, to get away from it all, but there was nowhere for her to go. She was trapped here in this time. Her breath caught as she thought again how she'd ended up here. It had something to do with the capsule she'd been in on the ship.

But what was it really? Had it transported her through time? She doubted it, but if indeed it had, then maybe she could go back in time, stop Zareck and the devastation. The possibility pulled at her. She wiped back the tears and stood.

The floor was chilly to her feet. The sleep gown that Chel had given her to wear hung just to her knees. Chel kept the air in her chambers cooler than Jorran had kept his. Leeza remembered the desert the ship had been in, in her time, and wondered if things were better how they were now. But the knowledge of all the people who suffered and died answered the question for her. If she could stop it – she had to.

She reached for her clothes hanging over a line, where they had been drying from being washed before she went to bed. Though lightweight, they were still damp but Leeza ignored that, sliding them on then stepping into her boots.

At the door, she paused a second, glancing back to where Chel slept. Leeza wondered if it would wake the woman when she opened the door. Knowing there was nothing for it, Leeza turned the lever. It didn't move. She tried again, pushed then pulled. Nothing. Locked.

Frustrated, she tried to remember what she'd seen Chel do. Nothing came to mind, but after a second of inspection, she pushed a button below the handle, and when she tried it again, the door opened.

Trying to be as quiet as possible, she slipped out. There was a faint light in the hallway, making it easy to move. The floodlights in the quad illuminated the exit. Leeza stopped in the opening, watching, but there was no sign of movement. Pushing through the barrier, she moved cautiously, staying close to the building then sprinted to the next.

She felt like a thief stealing her way through the night. She didn't know why she was being so cautious. Forcing herself to relax and straightening, she looked across the quad one more time before stepping out into the open and heading directly toward the path that led to the ship.

Once away from the lighted yard, the shadows swept in to surround her. She slowed her pace and wished for a light. Fear of getting lost hit her, and she had to force herself to go on.

A hiss came directly in front of her, she froze. Her heart thundered in her chest. She jumped as a shriek echoed through the night, and she barely caught her own scream. Leeza started to turn then stopped herself. She couldn't give up. She had to try. She had to save everyone – even if it meant losing Jorran.

She fought to keep in the sob that snuck up on her. Jorran wasn't hers. But what would it do to his world, this world, if she was able to go back? If she was able to stop the devastation, would he even be born? Would anyone be here now? Was it her right to change things?

Leeza buried her face in her hands and tried to think, but it was impossible over the pounding in her heart. "No," she said the word even before she thought the answer.

It wasn't her right. She couldn't sacrifice this time for the chance to save hers. Hers was the past. She knew its fate because she'd read about it. It was history here, and that was how it had to remain.

The real question was – where was she to remain? What were the answers for her? She really had no place here. Or did she? She might not be here for love or Jorran, but maybe she was here for a purpose, a destiny. And maybe it was all a foolish notion, like Jorran loving her, but she had to have the answer, and they might lie on the ship.

She took a step forward. The sound of something scampering in the dark made her pull back, but she tightened her resolve and moved on with her hands out in front of her to keep from running into anything. If her memory was right, there were no turn offs, but she'd been so confused and weak before.

Ahead of her, a light glow cut through the trees. She quickened her pace. Coming around a curve she was relieved to see the small structure that had been just a short distance from the ship. Leeza hurried forward. Pushing through the barrier, she let out a sigh. It took several deep breaths to calm her racing heart. The thought of stepping back into the darkness set her to work searching for some kind of light.

For having no idea what it would look like, it was surprisingly easy to find. The third cubby yielded several things that looked like they could be strapped to the head and had a disk-like thing that, when she pushed a button, gave off a surprising amount of illumination. There was also a slightly larger version that looked like it could be held or hung from the wrist.

Taking one of each, Leeza felt more secure as she stepped out the other side heading for the ship. The distance was a lot shorter than it had seemed when she'd left it.

The entrance looked different with foliage covering it, but the main difference was the two thin pillars on either side of the opening. A blue glow stretched the length of the poles, but Leeza didn't think it was for light.

An ominous feel had her stopping short. She noticed the jungle sounds seemed to pull away from it also. Like the animals didn't want to go near, and she didn't think it was the ship that made them nervous.

Leeza stretched out her hand. She felt no heat, but a low hum started and grew louder the closer she got. It stopped when she pulled back. Experimenting, she reached out again, the hum resumed, and Leeza could swear the hairs on the back of her neck twitched. The sensation ended when she stepped back.

Moving around the side of one pillar, the hum started again as she got closer and repeated when she tried the opposite side. Hands on her hips, she stared in frustration with tendrils of relief. Deep within, if she was honest with herself, she really didn't want to go into the ship alone.

A shiver ran over her. She spun around. Maybe it was the memory of what happened when she was alone with Zareck on the ship, but she expected to find someone there watching her.

No one was there.

Still, a feeling of unease settled over her, and she refused to think that she wanted to be in Jorran's arms, instead she changed it to she wanted to be back at Chel's. With one last glance back at the ship, she headed back down the path.

The feeling of being followed shadowed her, and she listened for any movement. Nothing came to her ears. For once, the jungle was quiet – too quiet. She froze. Turning in a circle, she studied every spot the power light landed, but again, nothing seemed to be there.

Hurrying fast, Leeza reached the hut. She replaced the head light back in its place but couldn't bring herself to leave the hand device. She'd either return it tomorrow or give it to Jorran. Before stepping out of the hut, she did a thorough search of the foliage then burst onto the path.

The feel of someone there watching compelled her to move faster and she broke into a run, not stopping until she reached the lighted quad. She slowed, picking up more stealth, but went directly across the open area to the building that housed Chel's chambers.

Reaching the door, she was relieved when the knob turned easily in her hand. A few minutes later, she was changed back into the sleep shirt, and she stretched out in the bed. Her heart thundered in her chest like it was trying to burst. Still, too wound up to sleep, Leeza decided to put the lingering surges of adrenaline to use and study the Lannish language. There was no way she wanted to ever misread what was being said, and the sooner she learned it, the better off she would be.

 beginning ornament

Jorran woke in a panic, reaching for Leeza. She wasn't there. For a moment, he was afraid he'd dreamed her before the sight of papers around the room of her learning kicked in, and he remembered she was at Chel's.

He laid back, one arm thrown over his eyes and took several deep breaths. He picked up the lingering scent of her in the room and desire hit him. He wondered how long it would be until he could see her again.

It was early. The sun hadn't even begun to lift the shadows from the jungle. Catching another deep whiff of Leeza's scent, he knew he wouldn't go back to sleep so sat up. One pass across the room told him he still had the caged animal feeling eating at him. He dressed.

The yard was quiet as he stepped out onto it. The lights pushed back the dark, but people wouldn't be out for over an hour yet. He headed for the ship. The path was dark, but he had traveled it so many times, it didn't bother him. Besides, he had excellent night vision. A movement up ahead caught his attention, but before he could make out what it was, it was gone. A tingle across his senses had him moving with more caution.

At the readying shelter, he was tempted to forgo the full gear and just go in with basics but decided to follow procedure and finish the needed sweep. Later, he would take the team and Leeza in. He was anxious to see her reaction to the ship.

Just the thought of her brought up other memories, the slight, almost floral smell of her skin, and her lively green eyes staring up at him with feelings that called to him. The cascade of her glorious hair down her back beckoned to his fingers. He stopped himself, shaking away the thoughts and pulled out the last of his gear before heading for the ship.

He was almost at the pillars when he felt a presence in the growth behind him. Jorran slowed his pace and listened, but could pick up nothing out of the darkness. Reaching the pillars, he started to whistle, raising the sound, so that there was no chance of anyone there locking onto the code. This early in the morning, his mind said it shouldn't be necessary but instinct skittering across his nerves said otherwise.

Once the security pillars deactivated, Jorran stepped through and reentered the code, and kept whistling as he entered the ship. The familiar thrill of the exploration coursed through his body, bringing with it a sigh of relief. Setting all his instruments to recording data, he moved forward, taking readings but at a faster pace. He wanted to get to the control room and see if the panel was still active. The glow of orange light from the wall gave him hope that it was.

The light from the main panel glowed in greeting as he stepped into the room. Jorran quickly did his scans, so he could turn his attention to the console. It looked like the same message as the day before displayed.

He took another image then studied the figures. It matched the other writing around the ship, but after being around Leeza for the last couple days – *had it only been that* – he started to pick out similarities in other symbols. Were there links in the language to other languages here on the planet?

It was something he'd really not believed before, but now wondered. Was it similar to Athurian? He brought up images of Athurian text on his personal data screen and didn't see any connection.

Since he'd already gone through the room pretty thoroughly, he decided to broaden his search without others there to encumber him. Down the hall, Jorran saw nothing much more interesting than he'd seen on his first cursory examination. Not that it all wasn't interesting, just nothing to demand and hold his immediate attention.

Reaching the stairs, he decided to follow them down to the next level. This one seemed a touch bigger, and Jorran got the feeling of quarters as most of the rooms were set up the same. He again got the feeling that they had been mostly emptied out. He wondered if the original occupants had done it, or if the ship had been found and cleaned out before.

Leeza came to his mind again. Now that they had the translator, he would ask her if she knew.

His mind locked on the possibility, and he wondered if she could have been part of the exploration group. A linguist would make sense if they thought she could decipher the language, and Leeza was extremely bright. He had no doubt about that after seeing the progress she was already making in his language. But how had she gotten here? The question burned in him as did his feelings for her.

He went down another level, finding things much similar to the one above. There were a scattering of objects that he recorded and continued on. The next level down, he discovered a larger room, which he speculated might have been labs by some of the remaining structures. Again they seemed fairly stripped. He would've liked to have seen it when it was full of its instruments. One room caught his attention, he was quite certain it was the med-lab.

It reminded him of Leeza back at Chel's, and he looked at the time. Again, more time had passed than he could believe. Everyone would be up and active by now. The pull to continue his exploration was strong, but the pull of Leeza was stronger, and he rapidly retraced his steps to the entrance.

Jorran paused before deactivating the pillars at the sight of the man on the other side. Norris. Jorran wondered if he should've guessed he'd been waiting but hadn't even thought of him. Starting his normal whistle, Jorran deactivated the code, stepped through then reactivated it before turning his attention back to the man.

"It's all clear," Jorran said in way of acknowledging the man. "We'll go in, in two hours."

"And what have you been doing?" There was challenge in his voice.

"Scans." Jorran lifted the device, glad he'd opted for the full gear so Norris couldn't try to cause trouble.

"It took you a long time." The man's words proved he'd been keeping tabs on him. Jorran wondered if Norris had been watching when he'd entered, if it had been him he'd felt. If so, what had Norris been doing here that early? Before he could think on it, Norris spoke again.

"And, is your name-bound," he made it sound like a slur, "going with us?"

Jorran felt his fury build and was sure that was what Norris was after. He managed to tamp his aggravation down. "Yes."

"Are you certain that is wise? Are you certain you really know her?"

"What are you getting at Norris?" Jorran met his challenge.

"It seems your … name-bound is very interested in the exploration. Are you certain of her motives?"

Before Jorran could ask what he was referring to, Norris swept his hand toward the ground. There, easily visible in the moist surface, were the signs of petite footprints with markings far different from the utilitarian boots the people here wore.

They circled in front of the entrance, clustered by the pillars as if she'd stopped to study them. And as his footprints had covered over some, it was obvious it was before he arrived, which meant during the night. Jorran pushed back the shock so Norris couldn't see his reaction.

"What are you asking, Norris?" Jorran met his gaze straight on.

"There is no record of a Leeza Jaeff."

Jorran waited, and after a second, Norris continued. "I want to know who she is."

"I have told you."

The muscles around the man's eyes tightened. "I don't believe you, and I think she's jeopardizing the exploration. She should be removed."

Jorran didn't like the man's choice of word in 'removed' but let it go. "She stays with me," Jorran said simply and started to move past the man.

Norris's hand shot out, locking on Jorran's arm, pulling him around.

Jorran glanced down at the hand. "Not a good idea."

"You think you can ignore me?" Anger poured from the man. Norris might have been shorter, but he was built like a boulder.

Jorran arched his brow. "And you think you can intimidate me? Consider this is your last warning. One more cross step and you're out of here. Your boss can scream all he wants but that is how it is." Jorran flexed his muscle, spreading the man's fingers, then ripped his arm away. He turned, heading down the path, but not before he saw hatred flash through the anger on Norris's face.

Anger of his own burned through Jorran as he shoved the gear back into the cabinets. He wasn't worried about Norris, but what ate at him was why and when Leeza had been to the ship. It had to have been after the evening rain. That meant during the night. He fought to calm himself as he made his way back through the jungle, heading straight to Chel's.

The lab door across the hall stood wide open so he stepped in there instead of knocking on her quarters. Chel was working at one of the counters, but there was no sight of Leeza.

"Morning," he said in way of greeting. "Where's Leeza?"

"Sleeping, finally." The woman looked at him. "I think she was up half the night. She fell asleep," Chel glanced at a time piece on the counter, "about two hours ago. She was working with the translator when I got up. From the energy level on it, I'd say she'd been at it for quite a while. I have it charging," she added.

"Do you know if she went out?" Jorran couldn't help but ask the question. Still he wasn't prepared for the answer. His stomach muscles tightened.

"Yes." Chel studied him quizzically until he answered.

"She went to the ship."

That brought a look of surprise to Chel's face. "Did she go in?"

Jorran shook his head. "I presume she couldn't get past the security pillars."

"Then why was she there?"

"I don't know." He shoved his fingers into his hair, frustration coursing through him.

"Do you think she was meeting someone? Norris?"

Jorran didn't know what to think but he was sure she didn't meet Norris. "No." He couldn't accept the possibility. "No," he said again firmer. "He is the one that pointed her footprints out to me. He was waiting when I came out of the ship. He wanted to know about her. They've been checking, and nothing comes up on her."

"If he wanted to throw you off ..." Chel let the sentence hang.

"No," Jorran objected firmly.

"Is that you or your emotions answering?" She cocked an eyebrow at him, as was her manner when she was waiting for an answer to a question she figured the person was unwilling to acknowledge or give.

After a second, he said, "Both. I can't believe my Heart-mate would betray me."

"You're not mated, yet."

"Not in the act, but within me, she is mine." The words burned with vehemence.

"She is not Ellandish," Chel pointed out softly.

"Still, the bond is there," Jorran said with a strength that he hoped could wipe out any of Chel's doubt—and the lingering of his own. Deep within, he knew Leeza wouldn't betray him. He'd seen the love in her eyes.

A flash of memory from the evening before came to him. Just before he'd walked her to Chel's and left her, he saw a shadow of pain come over her.

He hadn't been thinking very clearly at the time. His hunger for her was too strong, and he had to get out away from her fast or he would have done something about it. At the time, he was certain that what he saw on her face was longing, not wanting him to leave, but what if that wasn't it. What if she was being forced into betraying him? Force would be the only way she would betray him, he told himself, but before he could debate it any more, the door across the hall opened.

Jorran turned in time to see Leeza step out. She was dressed in clothes Chel had obviously found for her. They were slightly big on her. The belt was cinched tight at her waist, and they still bagged a bit. She wore her own boots, which still showed traces of mud on the toes. Jorran force his attention from them. She'd braided her hair, so it ran in a thick cord down to her waist. It was her wan appearance that drew him.

When she saw him, she stopped and looked uncertain, as if she wasn't sure if she dared step closer.

He smiled. "Good morning."

A look of confusion came over her as if she hadn't expected the greeting.

"Good morning." Her words clear without any hesitancy. "I have something." She turned back into Chel's quarters. When she came back out, she had a light in her hand. She held it out as she crossed the hall into the lab.

He took it when she motioned with it to him. He noticed she stayed at an arm's length away from him. He wanted to ask what was wrong, but she looked down at the light.

"I took it. It needs returned."

Jorran noted there was a slightly broken quality to the words, but still, her speech was amazing.

"Where did you get this?" He held up the light, though he figured he knew where it came from. When he saw her flinch, he realized the words came out sounding harsh, but he wanted answers. He tried to be patient as she seemed to think through the words.

"The jungle. The building."

"Why were you there?" His efforts to soften his tone failed.

"I went to ship." She looked at him as if she was meeting a challenge.

"Why?" he questioned, challenging her right back.

"No concern."

"Really. And why is that?" When she was too slow answering he continued, "Because you couldn't get on."

Her attention dropped from him, and he realized she studied the translator in her hand. She shook her head. "Poles. Bad feel. Afraid to contact."

"It's a good thing you didn't touch them. They would've given you quite a shock."

She looked confused then fearful.

"Not kill, just knocked you unconscious." The thought of her getting shocked ate at him. It could've been a near thing since she didn't know. "Why were you there?"

"No concern," she said again.

"Why?" he snapped, the need eating at him.

She jumped. "Answers," she mumbled.

"To what?"

She shook her head. The motion made her wobble slightly. Jorran automatically started to reach for her and was surprised when she pulled back.

She looked past him to Chel. "Food, please." There was a shakiness in the request as if she was about to cry.

"Oh, my, I should've thought." Chel stood and hurried to her. "You should've helped yourself. We'll go to the commons. That will be faster. That is if you're done with your inquisition?" Chel sent a glare back over her shoulder to him as she headed Leeza down the hall.

Frustration ran through Jorran as he was left to follow. He caught the unsteadiness of Leeza's normally fluid motion. Concern and protectiveness washed over him.

When they reached the entrance, he moved to her side, sliding his arm around her. He was shocked when he felt her stiffen and resist the pull to his side. It bothered him more that she refused to look at him. As soon as they were in the cafeteria, she stepped away from him as if just his touch brought her pain.

Chapter Nine

Leeza fought to steady the trembling of her hands as she picked up the plate. She tried to tell herself it was all the lack of food but knew a large portion was due to Jorran. His presence hurt as did the anger under his questions. She wondered what he wanted from her, what she had done, and where was the tender man that had first taken care of her and drew out her love.

Pain ate at her. She felt sick. She wanted to drop her plate and run but knew she needed food. Besides, where would she run? She had nowhere to go. She couldn't even get back onto the ship to see if she could try to return to her own time or any other time where there was no Jorran, and this pain in her could end.

It never would. The pain of loving him would never end.

They joined the same two men they sat with the night before. There was another woman at the table, a pretty dark-haired girl that was only a couple years older than the younger male. She was introduced as Azas.

After a greeting, the conversation around the table turned to going to the ship in an hour. Leeza almost missed hearing Jorran say she'd be going with them.

"I'm not sure she should if she's not feeling well," Chel said while Leeza was wrapping her mind around the fact.

"I am fine," Leeza said carefully.

Chel looked at her skeptically. "Then you'd better eat more."

Leeza looked at the food on her plate and felt her stomach roll, but forced herself to take several mouthfuls. She kept eating under Chel's watchful gaze and Jorran's unnerving attention.

Thankfully, he didn't trying to put his arm around her again. His accidental bumping her was enough to make her want to cry in frustration, and the heat in his glances added to the feeling. Just hours before, she had thought the hot looks were love and desire, now, she didn't know what they were, just that they hurt.

Leeza tried to keep her attention from him, but her foolish heart didn't seem to want to let her. She kept finding herself looking at him, mesmerized by his strong features, which beckoned to her fingers to reach out and trace them. He caught her looking one time, and the look he gave back was filled with so much fire, it took her breath before he ripped his attention away.

"Ready?" Jorran's question confused her, but everyone else at the table stood so she did too. Jorran reached for her hand. Panic burst within her at the thought of him touching her.

Leeza pulled back, clipping her kneecap on a chair. Pain of a physical kind took her breath and with a cry, she started to go down. Jorran's powerful hands caught her around the waist, lifting her up until she was settled against his chest.

For a moment all Leeza could do was take in the comfort and try to breathe through the agony. As it subsided a rush of other sensations flooded her body. The heady masculine scent of Jorran filled her, bringing with it dreams of being cared for and held by him. The feel of his hard muscles under her hands excited her fantasies of being loved by him. The soothing words slipped out of her dreams to become real in her ears. "I have you, my heart."

Leeza tried to cling to them, only reality stepped in to snatch them away as she remembered that the words of love were not real. My heart was a term he used. It wasn't what she had interpreted. He didn't love her. He didn't truly care. She was an obligation to him. He would protect her because he was responsible for her. They were name locked so he was bound by his name to look after her. With that thought, she pushed back, and he almost dropped her.

"Leeza." He groaned her name and settled her on her feet, but he still kept her tucked to his side.

"Is she okay?" Chel asked from her other side.

Leeza turned to her. "Yes. I hit." Leeza fought for the word then realized she'd dropped the translator. Panicked, she searched for it. Luckily, it had landed on the table. Still, she scooped it up but when no words showed on the screen, her fear increased. Jorran took it from her hands and pushed the button to turn it on, and with a little chirp sound, it came back to life.

Leeza sighed with relief as he handed it back to her. Though she'd picked up a great deal of the language in the short time, there was much more she didn't understand, and with the devise, it made learning so much easier.

"I am fine," she said carefully, hugging the translator to her.

"Maybe I better check it out," Chel suggested.

Leeza shook her head. "I just hit it. It is fine," she completed the full sentence on her own and as if to prove the point. She started for the door, forcing herself not to grimace. As she walked the discomfort lessened.

Chel gave her one last look of concern before she left the group to return to her lab while the rest continued their way to the path into the jungle. To Leeza's relief, Jorran didn't try to take her hand again, but she could feel his eyes on her the whole way. The heat from them seemed to scorch her already frayed nerves.

At the ready-hut, Jorran pulled out the hand light she'd given him earlier. He glared at it then extended it out to her. "You might need this." His words were clipped, lacking any of the softness he'd used when she bumped her knee.

Good, she told herself, she could handle this man. Though inside, she missed the warm timbre in his voice. She shook the thought away just as someone pushed through the barrier strips.

Norris, the man that had come to Jorran's quarters, stopped at the sight of her. "So he's bringing you after all," he spat out, seeing her. The look he gave her made Leeza shudder, then she felt Jorran's large hand on her back and was thankful for the touch as it steadied her.

"Since everyone's here, let's go. We'll divide up in groups of threes. Esher, Rese and Norris, you have the hall. Azas, Leeza and I the control room."

Leeza didn't miss the looks that were exchanged between Norris and Jorran. Jorran was daring the man to challenge him.

Hatred waved off of Norris, but the only thing he did was glare, then turned and stormed toward the ship.

The others followed after him. She and Jorran were the last ones in the hut. Unable to stop herself, Leeza reached out and touched Jorran's arm. He turned immediately to look down at her. For a minute, Leeza became lost in his gaze then remembered what she was going to say.

"He is…" she had to search for the word, "dangerous. He would hurt you."

Jorran's hand came down to rest over hers, trapping it to his arm. "I know. You must be careful around him too. He would hurt you also."

Leeza didn't realize she was shaking her head until Jorran said, "Yes."

"I know him not." She felt confused but remembered she felt fear around Norris, especially the couple times she'd seen him look at her.

"You must be careful around him," Jorran repeated her words back to her.

She nodded.

"Come on." Jorran slid his hand down her arm to take her fingers.

Leeza made no objection and let him lead her out. She couldn't help but savor the touch of him, though she tried to remind herself Jorran didn't mean anything by it, taking her hand while walking was normal to him.

They reached the others who were waiting by the entrance to the ship. Leeza noticed Norris's attention go to their hands. Jorran must've noticed it also because his hand tightened on hers.

The sight of the pillars didn't seem to surprise anyone else, and Leeza noticed they all stayed back from them. She remembered what Jorran had said, that they could render a person unconscious. He released her hand, started humming and stepped to one. It was then she noticed the buttons she'd failed to see in the dark.

Jorran moved his body so it was between the buttons and everyone else. Through his humming, Leeza picked up some tones but couldn't make them out clearly. Lights on the pillars dimmed, and Jorran stepped back.

"Everyone ready?" He looked around the group. "Remember, stick together in your groups and adhere to protocol. I don't want to lose any more time needlessly." Jorran glanced toward Norris, and Leeza saw the bulky man's nostrils flare as Norris glared back. Leeza wasn't sure what was going on but had no trouble seeing the tension between the men.

Leeza was unprepared for the apprehension that filled her when she stepped toward the ship. She had never felt it before. From the first time she'd stepped on, all there had been was excitement for the possibilities it held and the challenge of being able to figure them out. Now images of Zareck haunted the edges of her mind and all those who had perished. Reason said it wasn't the ship's fault but the greed of men that abused its power without heeding its warnings.

She looked at Norris and got that he was the same kind of man, though greed was not all that fed him. There was more underlying in him, and he believed the end justified the means. Especially if it suited him, Leeza tagged the thought on the end.

When Jorran extended his hand to her, she gratefully accepted it. Pushing back her trepidation, she stepped into the ship. The familiar glow of the walls greeted her. The farther they went nothing seemed to have changed. It looked just like it had the last time she'd entered. She didn't remember much of leaving the ship. She shivered.

Jorran looked at her. In the light of the ship, his skin picked up a coppery ruddiness that suited him. Leeza saw concern in his eyes and smiled reassuringly. To prove she was all right, she headed in the direction of the control room. She'd understood they were to work there. She also understood that he was hoping she could translate what was there.

Well, that she could do. Translation of languages was the one thing she was sure of. It was all the nuisances of emotions in them that she seemed to have trouble with, she thought with a stab of pain.

She looked down at the hand that held hers. The urge to break free was accompanied by one that wanted to cling to it forever. Never before had she been in such a muddle.

Leeza was so lost in the thought she was surprised to realize they'd reached the control room. Again, she was shocked at how much it looked the same as the last time she was there, not counting her stumbling through after awakening.

The flashing message on the console drew her forward. *Destruction to all.* Pain, fear and panic all washed over her with a wave of dizziness. She gripped the console to keep from going down.

"Careful."

Azas's warning came from somewhere off in the confusion of her mind, along with the translation. The ringing in her ears attempted to drown out the words. Then she was pressed into something, warm, hard and comforting. She closed her eyes and took in the sound of the heartbeat under her ear. It took a minute to penetrate the fog.

Life, Jorran, it all existed. She forced herself to take air into her own body. Her mind cleared. She found herself crushed to Jorran's chest. His arms were like impenetrable bands of protection around her. She felt secure, but inside, she knew even Jorran couldn't stop the destruction the ship brought. The only chance of doing that might possibly be locked in what the console behind her said.

Leeza forced herself to move away from Jorran. As she did, his hold lessened but he didn't release her. He eased her back enough to bring a hand up to cup her face.

"I am okay." She heard the tremor in her voice and drew in a deep breath. "Okay," she said more firmly.

"Can you read?" He nodded back to the console.

"Some. A warning. Destruction to all." The words seemed hollow to her ears as she said them aloud.

The word that barked out from behind them was unfamiliar to her, but the way it was said, Leeza had no problem figuring out it was a curse.

"What are you doing here, Norris?"

"Checking the levels like we're supposed to." The man met Jorran with a hostile look and challenge of his own. "What's this nonsense she saying?"

In a flash of memory of Zareck disregarding the warning and the importance in the translation, Leeza stepped toward the man. "It is not nonsense. The message, on the …" She waved her hand not able to come up with the word. "It is a warning. If the engines are started, it will bring destruction."

"Really? What kind of destruction?" Skepticism poured off the man.

"It does something, disrupts to the sky. The Great Deluge. It …" Even though in the early morning Leeza had gone over the words to describe what the warning said, she again couldn't come up with the word she needed. She slipped into Athurian. Unfortunately, that didn't translate.

"What's that?" Norris snapped, stepping toward her. "You swearing at me?"

"No." Leeza pulled back, but there was no need, Jorran stepped in front of the man cutting him off.

"Back off, Norris. You get to work or get out," Jorran ordered harshly.

"I have a right to know what's going on here. Tranic has a right to be kept up to date." Norris locked his muscles and tried pulling the funding card.

"They will be informed when we know more," Jorran countered easily.

"Know more, really. Taking feed from her." He shot his hand out to point over Jorran's shoulder. "And, why would you take her word? She just barely walked into this room, and you expect anyone to believe she can already read that." He jerked his hand to the writing. "No one can learn a language that fast."

His eyes tightened, and Leeza didn't like the speculation coming into them. She suddenly felt like a specimen he was studying.

"Leeza is an extremely talented linguist." There was no missing the conviction in Jorran's words. The trust there in his voice warmed her, wiping away some of the pain she'd been feeling. "Her depth of languages is impressive. I would dare say there is no one on the planet that has a better chance of deciphering what that says. Now, one last time, back to work."

Norris stood there for several seconds before he turned. It wasn't until then Leeza realized the others were in the room. Her whole focus had been on Norris and Jorran. She felt their gaze and speculation on her and forced herself to turn back to the screen. There was much she needed to learn, and this was the place to start for her answers, too.

There was a sound of shuffling then the sound of someone stepping behind her. She felt her pulse kick up in a way that was different than that left by the confrontation. She didn't need to look to know it was Jorran, her body already knew. His hands came down on her shoulders, and he started to massage the taunt muscles. Leeza sighed as the tension in her was released only to be replaced with a different kind.

"Don't let him frighten you."

"He will not listen. Like Zareck, he does not want to know."

"You have mentioned Zareck before. Will you tell me about him?"

Pain squeezed the air from her at just the thought of Zareck. "There is not time now. It is enough that he is like Norris. They would destroy instead of heeding the warning."

She knew he wanted to ask more, could feel it coming off him, but he pushed the questions away and turned his focus to the console in front of her.

"What does it say?"

"Destruction to all," she said again. "There is." She had to focus on the translator to get the words she needed. "Reference to the crash and damage." She skimmed her finger over the words, working out the translation in her mind, though it seemed like it was just a few days ago she'd translated them. Leeza pushed back her unease and concentrated on how she could tell Jorran to get him to understand. "To start engines, affect the … air … weather."

"Climate," he supplied for her.

"Yes. It caused The Deluge."

"You know this?" His question wasn't as strong as the curiosity.

Leeza bit her lip a second to keep back the tears then had to swallow down the lump in her throat. "Yes."

Jorran laid his hand over hers and squeezed. "Do you know what else it says?"

"I haven't had time to translate it. I just … worked it out … the base." Her hands clenched into fists, holding in the flood of frustration that washed over her. "I need more time."

"It's okay." Jorran's hands came down to rest on her shoulders again, massaging the tense muscles.

"No, not. No one more can die." She read over the warning that was already burned in her heart again then reached up to change to the next screen.

"Hey." The objection came from Azas. "Don't touch that."

"It's okay," Jorran cut her off. "I already recorded it, and Leeza knows what she's doing."

The look Azas gave him was as full of doubt as Norris's, but Jorran continued. "Just make sure you record every image she goes through."

Leeza took her attention off the screen long enough to look at him. "May I use your write pad?"

Azas gave her a quizzical look but didn't say anything as Jorran handed over the tablet. Leeza ignored the question in Azas's gaze, and after a minute, Azas shifted her attention back to the screen Leeza was focused on. "What is that? It looks like some kind of diagram."

Jorran looked over Leeza's shoulder with interest.

"It is. It shows how to shut down engines. I think they knew whoever found the ship would try to start."

"Why didn't they just disable the engines?" Azas asked.

"I do not know. It has not said." Leeza studied the screen, aware of the other woman recording it with several different devices. She went over the steps of shutting down the engines again and again, though she had already memorized them before.

It ate at her that it was something she had to do, had to know. And she knew there was no margin of error. Firmly in her mind so that when she closed her eyes she could see every small detail of the schematic and wording of the instructions, she moved on to the next page.

She had only gotten a brief glimpse of it before, in her own time, now it drew her in. With each phrase, Leeza felt her understanding of the language grow and strengthen, and it became easier. She got into the flow of making notes of what she understood and what she still couldn't figure out.

As she worked, despite her gaps in understanding, the log entry began to grow and take shape. The ship was for space exploration. A first for their people to reach so far, to a planet they thought might be habitable. The people on the ship dedicated their lives and the lives of their families to the adventure.

When they reached the planet, their observation revealed it was already inhabited by several groups of people, surprisingly similar in physiology to themselves, but with technology less advanced. Still, they were strong, growing civilizations, relatively free from contention.

After studying the planet for over a year, it was decided to leave them on their own and return to their planet. They were preparing to leave when an object, Leeza figured was a meteor, came close to the ship which caused a reaction of some kind that damaged many of the ship's instruments and affected the engines.

She wasn't sure what it was, one thing she knew, there was an explosion that killed most of the technicians over the engines. They were forced to land the ship. The best they managed was to pick an unpopulated area to bring the ship down in.

When it became apparent that there was no way to get the engines going again or even contact their home planet for rescue, they salvaged all they could from the ship and set out to build their own colony. With that, the record ended, though Leeza found a link to a log of the ship's captain that seemed more extensive.

She was just about to start on it when a hand touched her arm. She jerked and looked up to see Jorran beside her.

"It's time to go."

Leeza blinked and looked at the chronometer to which he pointed. She knew the time they had entered and was surprised to find five full time periods had passed. She looked back at the screen, longing to continue but turned to step away. As she did, the world began to spin.

Lights flashed in front of her eyes. A roar sounded in her ears. Leeza realized she was about to faint. Something wrapped around her. She got a brief image of Jorran's face before the world faded away from her.

Chapter Ten

Panic filled Jorran as Leeza swayed. Her eyes glazed over, and she went limp like someone shut down a switch in her. He barely caught her before she dropped. He pulled her up into his arms. She looked at him then her eyes closed.

"Leeza," he cried her name but got no response.

"What's wrong with her?" Azas asked pulling back from the console as if afraid it was somehow responsible.

"I don't know. Tell the others to meet us at the entry. Leeza." He jostled her, then pinning her against him with one arm, reached up to brush back her hair with his other hand. Her skin was slightly warm to his touch. "Come on, my heart, wake up," he pleaded. "Can you get me some water?" he asked without looking at Azas.

Azas stepped to him, dampening a handkerchief. Jorran reached out and took it from her and ran it over Leeza's forehead then down over her temple, along her cheek to her neck. He rubbed it up the other side and got a reaction of a faint moan.

"Leeza." He shifted her to slide an arm down behind her legs and lifted her, so she was cradled in his arms. "Come on," he said to Azas, heading down the corridor, leaving the woman to follow.

His entire attention was locked on Leeza. Even in the orange glow from the walls, he could tell she was pale. Against his chest, her breathing seemed strong but possibly a little rapid. He wanted her to wake up.

"What happened?" Esher's voice took him by surprise. He was so focused on Leeza he failed to notice the men waiting at the entrance.

"She just passed out. I want to get her right to Chel. Can you finish up here?" It wasn't much of a question as he was already moving past the group.

He didn't doubt Esher would take charge and the recording devices would be taken to the tech team for downloading. In a brief thought, he made a mental note to talk to Sanfra, the tech head, and see how things were going. With everything, he hadn't talked with the woman for several days.

His attention turned back to Leeza. He boosted her higher in his arms and lengthened his pace. Jorran wished her eyes would open and she'd look up at him, but the faint stirring of her breath on his neck was his only comfort. He passed through the hut without even slowing.

When he stepped out of the jungle, he heard a wave of reaction from the handful of people in the yard. Two men rushed to him while another turned and ran toward the building which housed the med-lab. Jorran was relieved to know Chel would be waiting when he got there.

"What happened?" the first man that reached him asked the expected question.

"I don't know. She collapsed. She wasn't feeling good before we left."

The man had been at the table next to them the evening before, so at least, he didn't question who she was. "Need a hand?"

"No, I got her." Jorran fought the urge to snap at the man who was only trying to help. There was no way Jorran was going to let another man carry her. She was his. The primitive thought was back stronger than ever.

"I think she just overdid it." He tried to soften his tone, then almost stumbled when he felt a slight movement against his body. Not breaking his pace, he looked down and saw a flutter of Leeza's eyelids. "Leeza." Her name escaped him.

Her eyes didn't open, but he saw and felt an intake of breath. Ahead, someone pulled aside the security folds for Jorran to pass through into the building. He looked up to maneuver down the hall.

Chel was waiting at the doorway to the lab. "What happened?" she asked the same question everyone else had. It made Jorran want to shout with frustration. He ground his teeth instead. "I don't know. She just collapsed."

Carefully, he laid her on the table and stayed leaning over her until Chel pushed him away. He moved around Chel to stand at the head of the table so he was out of the way but could still see Leeza.

His heart hurt and his arms felt empty. He longed to scoop her back up and hold her tight to him, where he could protect her, where she could be safe. As it was, he watched helplessly as Chel took the initial readings of her vitals, opened the collar of Leeza's shirt and placed a small pad on Leeza's neck and another on her chest over her heart.

When Chel moved away to an instrument on a counter to check the readings, Jorran reached out and ran the back of his fingers over Leeza's cheek to her temple. "Come on, my heart. Wake up for me." The words growled out of him, but he caught a slight movement as her head turned toward his fingers.

"Leeza," he called her name. This time she stirred.

"It's okay," Chel said stepping back over to them. "She's starting to come around." The medic pressed a hypodermic syringe to the side of her neck just below the pad.

"What's that?" Jorran demanded.

"Just something to boost her system," Chel answered offhandedly.

Jorran wanted to ask more, but before he could, Leeza shifted and her eyes fluttered open. "My heart," he gasped out, leaning down to press his lips to her cheek then found her mouth, kissing her thoroughly.

It took him a second to get a response. He leaned back when he felt Chel tap his arm.

"I'm trying to get her vitals to steady and you are causing havoc with them." The annoyance in her voice was ruined by the grin on her face. "Now, if you'll kindly get your large frame out of the way, I'd like to have a look at her." Chel bumped him farther out of the way with her hip.

Jorran shifted. His attention stayed on Leeza. She looked dazed, but her eyes seemed to study him as if she was thoroughly confused. The color of the warm evening sky flooded into her cheeks, and she turned from him to look around the room before her gaze came back to him.

Her mouth opened slightly, and her tongue snuck out to run over her bottom lip. Jorran fought the urge to follow the motion with his own tongue. He wondered if she could taste him there as he could still taste her. He craved her flavor.

She made a small gasp, and he shifted his attention from her mouth to her eyes. They were wide with a startled expression which testified that she caught the drift of his thoughts. He wanted to confirm them, but before he could, Chel gave him a shove toward the door.

"That's it, out of here. You have her system going all over the place."

Jorran let Chel continue to nudge him out into the hall, but when she started to close the door on him, he put his hand up stopping it. Chel glared at him a second then capitulated. "Just be good."

She turned back to Leeza. "How do you feel?"

Jorran saw her take a deep breath and look past Chel to him. "Tired."

"Do you know what happened?" Chel probed.

Leeza shook her head and said a word Jorran didn't understand, and at the puckering of Chel's brow, he figured she didn't either.

"Leeza, in Lannish."

Leeza frowned and looked down. Alarm came over her face. "Translator," she gasped and looked again passed Chel to him.

"I'll find it," he assured, seeing the panic on her face.

She'd been conversing so well, he forgot she was still relying on the translator to fill in much of the language for her, and as much as he didn't want to leave her, he needed to supply that comfort. He turned down the hall. Outside, he saw the rest of the group just coming out of the jungle. He ran toward them.

"Is she okay?" Rese called as he approached.

"She's awake. It appears she just fainted. Tired and lack of food." He supplied an answer that sounded reasonable, and he hoped would dissuade any questions. It seemed to satisfy them. "She dropped the translator and is worried about it."

"I have it." Azas held up the devise. "I grabbed it when she fainted. It was on the console, so luckily it's okay."

"Thanks." Jorran reached out and took it from her. "I better get back. When Leeza gets a little steadier, we'll go eat. We worked right through lunch."

He felt self-blame hit him. He shouldn't have allowed her to miss eating. It wasn't unusual for him and the members of the team to forget time. When they finally got into a ruin, they'd get involved forgoing meals and rest, but Leeza needed both.

He couldn't even begin to fathom the kind of shock her body had experienced in the last few days, but it had to be immense because Chel had said it was making her sick. Correction, it was a virus making her sick, and he should have kept an eye on her so she didn't overdo and her body could fight the virus.

He'd be more careful with her in the future.

ᘏᘓᘍ

"Now," Chel turned to her after Jorran left. "How do you feel?"

Leeza stayed still as Chel reached out and placed a hand on her forehead as if checking for a temperature, though she had already taken a reading. "Tired," Leeza repeated the answer she had given before, not having the strength to come up with something different. She just wanted to close her eyes for a moment to see if the colors flashing before her would fade away.

"Are you hungry?"

She shook her head and immediately regretted the action as nausea hit her. This time, she shut her eyes and prayed she wouldn't be sick. Leeza felt a touch of cool metal in her neck and a slight sting and opened her eyes to see Chel turning away from her.

"What was that?" she asked raising her hand to the spot on her neck.

"Something to help with nausea. The sickness you're feeling," Chel added in case she didn't understand what she meant. "When you feel better, I want you to go eat then go right to bed. I'd like to take another blood sample now." Chel waited for her to nod before reaching for her arm and sliding up her sleeve.

"What is wrong?" Leeza asked, her stomach and head already beginning to settle.

"I don't know. What I saw before shouldn't be doing this. Do you understand that?"

"Yes. It has you … troubled," Leeza put forth for the medic.

"Yes." Then Chel smiled. "No, don't worry. I will figure it out."

Leeza could see the tension lingering in the lines on Chel's face.

"Are you feeling better?"

131

"Yes, much." Her head was clearer, and it was easier to pull up what she figured was the appropriate word.

"Good, I'm sure Jorran will be back shortly. Why don't you close your eyes and rest until he gets here."

Leeza had no problem following those directions. Though she felt better, she was still extremely tired. She must've dozed off, but she didn't think much time had passed when she heard Jorran ask Chel how she was.

She opened her eyes and answered him. "I am better."

He reached her in two strides, his hand coming up to cup her cheek and then, to her surprise, he leaned down and kissed her again. Pleasure filled her along with a wave of confusion.

The night before, he'd turned from her as if not being able to get away from her fast enough. Today had been a combination of hot glances and cool detached gestures of professionalism and now, for the second time since waking up, he kissed her with such heat it burned away her fever.

"Are you really better?" he asked when he barely pulled back enough so his lips didn't brush hers as he talked.

"Yes." Her answer was whispered, but she couldn't help it. He took her breath away.

"She's okay, now," Chel said behind them. "Why don't you go get her something to eat, then I want her back here to go right to bed."

"You're not going to join us?" Jorran asked.

Leeza saw the small muscles around his eyes tighten as he looked back at the other woman.

"I want to get these tests started before I join you," Chel said dismissively, turning back to the counter. "I'll only be a few minutes."

Jorran watched the medic for a minute before turning back to Leeza. "Here." He handed her the translator then started to slide his hands under her.

Leeza realized he meant to carry her and caught his wrist. "I'm okay. I can walk." Still, she used his offered hand to sit up. When she slid from the table, it was to be wrapped in his arms and pressed up against his body. It felt too good to object. She savored the contact with him a moment before she moved back.

His arm stayed around her waist as they headed for the door, and she noticed his pace was slow, metered to match hers, which she was grateful because she really wasn't feeling too steady.

At the dining room, Jorran insisted on holding her plate and getting her settled before he went back to serve himself. He'd just sat down beside her when Esher, Azas and Rese came in, other people from the site flowed in right behind them. Some showed curiosity at seeing Leeza, but after a minute went on with their conversation to those around her.

Leeza had learned that there were a hundred and seventeen, eighteen with her, at the site in total. Thirty-nine were supporting the excavation of the ship. After the initial mapping and safety check had been done, groups would be allowed in for a more intense study and to catalog findings.

There were fifty-six scientists and students from the same university that Jorran worked at who were there studying the plants and animals in the area. The rest of the people were support staff. The cooks and cleaning crew catered to everyone.

They were halfway through eating when Chel finally came in and joined them. She looked at Leeza then down at her plate with a satisfied expression. "How are you doing?"

"I feel better. Thank you."

"Good. See if you can eat some more. You need to build up your strength."

Leeza nodded but she was feeling full and getting sleepy. Still, she forced herself to take a few more bites while trying to pay attention to the conversation going on around them at the table. Everyone was speaking too fast, and she just wasn't alert enough to follow what was being said, other than they were making plans about going to the ship again tomorrow. There was a lot of excitement about it.

Leeza didn't notice when Jorran slid his arm around her waist. It was just there, and she felt the gentle pressure curling her into his body. With a sigh, she let herself go lax and absorb the comfort of being sheltered by him.

"I think I'd better get you to bed. Chel, is your room open?"

"Yes," the medic answered. "I left everything all ready for her."

"Thank you," Leeza said as Jorran helped her rise then steadied her when she wobbled a little. "Goodnight," Leeza got out as he led her away, locked tightly against his side. She let her head rest against his chest, trusting him to guide them.

Outside the sounds of the jungle were as gentle music to her, lulling her closer to sleep. Their pace was slow, whether for her or to enjoy the pleasantness of the evening she didn't know but was grateful.

It was too soon for her that they reached the other building. For just a little while longer, she wanted to dream that Jorran cared for her more than just someone he felt responsible for. He'd been so attentive again as if he really cared.

Leeza knew she was setting herself up for heartbreak once more but just couldn't stop herself. Love really was a confusing, mysterious thing to her. She didn't understand how she could have lived without it for so long and now crave it so much from Jorran. Maybe whatever brought her here had warped her mind or her heart.

At Chel's room, she expected him to leave her at the door. Instead, he led her in, closing the door behind him.

The spare bed was made up, and her nightclothes were laid out on it.

Jorran removed his arm from around her but caught her hand, turning her to him. "Why don't you go change?"

Leeza felt her heart lurch at the intensity in his eyes. It took her breath, and all she could do was nod. He released her hand. She picked up the nightshirt, stepped into the changing alcove, and flinched at her reflection. She was pale, and shadows circled her eyes. Strands of hair had escaped her braid giving her an unkempt appearance that was definitely not attractive. No wonder he didn't find her appealing.

With a sigh, she changed quickly and removed the tie confining the braid. After running her fingers through her hair to loosen the heavy locks, she picked up the brush Chel had given her to use and ran it through her hair, enjoying the feel of the soothing strokes.

When she was done and ready for bed, she came out and was surprised to find Jorran still there waiting. He stood and reached for her hand when she stopped. His gaze ran over her, starting at the top of her head, traveling down her body, lingering at her legs that were bared to view, all the way to her feet before coming back up again in the same slow perusal.

Fire burned in his eyes when he met her gaze. "Let's get you in bed." The words seemed to rumble out of him. He made no motion to move. His eyes went over her once more. Finally, he took a step toward her then abruptly turned from her, pulled back the blanket and motioned for her to get in.

Leeza felt awkward as she moved beside him and slid into the bed. She could feel his eyes on her again and felt herself heat in response. She fought to dampen her reaction, but it seemed impossible. So instead, she muttered a quick, "thank you."

Steadying herself, she looked up to say goodnight, but the word never made it from her lips as his head swooped down. His mouth took over hers in a kiss that left her stunned and breathless as it continued to claim her all the way to her heart once more. His fingers tunneled into her hair, cradling her head and tilting it to give him fuller access.

Leeza cried out in pleasure as she felt the erotic brush of his tongue over hers. He drank down the sound then proceeded to draw another from her, which he echoed with a groan of his own. With what seemed almost savage force, he ripped his mouth away.

His chest rose and fell with labored breaths. "I shouldn't have kissed you like that. Not yet." The sparks in his eyes contradicted his words.

It was all too confusing to her, the desire coming off from him now, and the cold turn away the night before. She shook her head to clear it.

He sighed. "I should leave you." He settled on the bed next to her. "I didn't get much sleep last night."

"Why not?" Leeza finally managed to get words out.

"Missing you," he said then looked up at her. "I wanted you as I do now." The blatant need in him was there to see.

She shook her head again. "But, I thought … you didn't want me."

This time, he looked shocked. "What?" Disbelief was heavy in the word.

"You couldn't even stand my touch."

He stared down at her then a groan escaped him. "You thought …" He tilted back his head and ran his fingers through his hair. When he lowered his head, he stared directly at her.

"I hope you can understand all I'm going to say to you. Tell me if you need clarification, restating. I wouldn't touch you or let you touch me because I wanted you too much. I was barely hanging on to my control."

His eyes were intense with the meaning of his words. "I want you. You are my heart. But, it is not time yet. Though I wish it were. Do you understand? I care for you more than you can understand."

He stood and stepped to the door. "I'd better go now." He was through it before she even got a chance to answer.

"I love you," she said to the empty room.

Chapter Eleven

Jorran strode across the yard, his tension eating at him. He wanted to return to Leeza. How could she have thought he did not want her? She was the other part of him, the piece that completed him. He looked up at the moon rising over the jungle and felt like howling for his mate.

He turned back, staring toward the building, tempted to show her what she was to him. He just started that way when he saw Chel exit the commons. She must have seen him because she stopped and turned in his direction. Fortunately, she didn't head his way. He spun away to ward off any thoughts she might have had about talking to him. When he looked back, she was gone.

He sighed and shifted his attention to the path that headed to the ship. For a moment, he was tempted to take it. He had so many questions. But the answers weren't there, not truly. The answers he needed were with Leeza.

Slowly, he returned to his quarters, stretching out on the bed without even bothering to change. He stared up into the dark, contemplating the empty space beside him and envisioning Leeza, how she looked standing before him in Chel's quarters, with her hair a wavy cascade of shimmering moonlight, her trim bare legs and the look of sleepy innocence on her face. He wrapped the images in his heart and surprisingly enough, he slept.

ය

Leeza came awake with her heart pounding and the memory of being chased through the ship. Thirst drove her to stand up. Dizziness threatened her, and she clung to one of the chairs to keep her balance.

It was a full minute before she could bring the room, lit by a small light that Chel left glowing, into focus. It took all her strength of will to steady herself enough to make it the short distance to get a drink. The water was a blessed relief on her throat. She leaned back on the counter to build up enough strength to make it back to bed. She felt as if all her energy had been drained from her.

Images from her dream flashed back at her. She'd been running, trying to escape Zareck, then once again, it shifted to Norris. He was out to kill Jorran. Fear spiked in her. Leeza took a deep breath and forced it away.

She tried to tell herself that it was all just a dream, but she'd seen the animosity in Norris. The man hated Jorran, but that didn't mean he would try to hurt him. Unfortunately, she just couldn't make herself get past the images of the dream.

Closing her eyes, she drew a few more deep breaths until she felt she had herself steady. She opened them to head back to bed only to find herself looking into Chel's face.

The woman said nothing, just walked over to her and put a hand on her head. "You're a little hot." She studied her up and down. "Let's get you sitting back down, and I'll get you something for that. It's time again for another dose." Chel took her arm. Leeza was too relieved to object as the medic guided her back to bed.

"Couldn't sleep?" Chel questioned over her shoulder when she turned to get something from the counter.

"Ill dream." Leeza saw no reason not to be truthful.

"Well, this should help you sleep," the woman said coming back to her. "What was the dream about?"

"The ship. I am being pursued." Leeza flinched a bit when Chel gave her the shot, though it didn't really hurt. She then took a second to debate and added, "I fear Norris would hurt Jorran." She watched Chel for a reaction, hoping the woman would dispute the comment. She didn't.

"Jorran is aware of him," the woman said simply.

Leeza had to look at the translator for the word as Chel continued. "The others keep an eye on him, too."

"Why is he here?" Leeza asked, settling back against the wall. A languid feeling was beginning to come over her.

"The company he works for is funding a good portion of this expedition."

Leeza had to rely on the translator as her mind was having trouble deciphering. "Like Zareck," she said offhandedly.

"He was from your time?" Chel asked and Leeza nodded.

"I want to ask you," Chel began, and Leeza fought to keep her eyes open to look at the medic. "Do you have feelings for Jorran?"

"I love him." The words were sluggish as they came out. Leeza slid down the wall until she was lying back down. "Confused," she got out, not even conscious of what language she used. She was barely aware of Chel picking up the translator and reading the screen.

"I'll charge this while you get some more sleep. Your body needs it," Chel said kindly, pulling the blanket up over her. And Leeza slept.

⊂ঞ৶

Jorran was up early. To stave off his overpowering urge to see Leeza, he went to his office to go over the recorded information. The teams had gathered so much already that it would give them things to study for months. Normally, it would have enthralled him, but as it was, he kept looking at the chronometer every few minutes until he decided it was an acceptable time to go see Chel and Leeza.

The med-lab door was still closed, so he knocked softly on the door to Chel's quarters. Chel opened the door almost immediately.

"Morning." Jorran looked past her.

"She's just getting changed."

"How is she?" He looked back to Chel.

The medic tipped her head in a movement that suggested she was trying to decide how to answer. "She woke up once during the night with a nightmare and a slight fever, but I gave her something to help her sleep and boost her system. She seems better this morning, but if you're going to take her to the ship, I want you to keep an eye on her. Don't let her overdo it again. Hopefully, by later today, I can figure out what's making her sick then I can treat it."

"I'll watch her." He waited for her to say more. When she didn't, he asked. "Anymore precautions?"

"No," she said plainly.

He arched an eyebrow at not getting the expected lectures, but any further conversation was cut off as Leeza stepped into the room.

"There you are," Chel greeted her. "Let's go get breakfast."

Leeza glanced his way, a bit of shyness in the movement, but it was accompanied by a soft smile.

"Good morning." Jorran was aware that his voice had dropped to a low rumble.

"Morning."

The word sounded airy and stirred his soul. He caught her arm, holding her back from following Chel into the hall. Her face tilted up to him, and he took the offering, sliding an arm around her to pull her up against him as his head dipped to kiss her.

Jorran was about to break the contact when he felt her hand slide up his chest and around his neck. He took the cue and deepened the kiss, drawing out a groan from each of them. He was tempted to continue but was aware of Chel waiting just outside the door.

He broke the kiss and tilted his forehead down to rest against hers. "Good morning, again." He kissed the tip of her nose.

As he pulled away from her, he took her hand to lead her out. He seemed to need to keep some kind of contact with her all though breakfast and while walking to the ship, as if he didn't want her to misinterpret his feelings for her again. She didn't. The love she felt for him came back to her in waves. Leeza used it to steady herself as they stopped just outside the ship and waited for Jorran to deactivate the security pillars.

Once done, he turned back to the group. There were more with them. There was a group of five, one professor and two students and two people who had volunteered to come out of curiosity, who would be working on the outside of the ship. Besides those that had gone in the previous day, there were three more going inside.

"Okay so, Esher, Talis, and Norris will take the first level down." Jorran nodded to Esher and the other professor with them, ignoring Norris. "Azas, you will have Hesum and Emarella. You will be continuing to record the message on the console."

Leeza raised her head in shock when she realized he didn't have her working on deciphering the message. Jorran must have noticed her reaction because he motioned the others onto the ship and turned to her. "It's okay. Azas knows how to work the console, and the two students will be careful and follow her direction. They are very good."

He waited for her acceptance. Leeza wondered what he'd do if she objected, but she nodded.

He smiled, taking her hands in his. "Good." He let out a breath, and looked as if he were warning her that what he was going to say she wouldn't like. "I want you to show me where you were on the ship."

It was a sharp intake from Rese that had him turning away from her to look the younger man straight in the eye.

"What you're about to find out about Leeza, you mention to no one." There was a sternness in Jorran's voice, but it really didn't come out as a threat, more of a request.

His next sentence confirmed it. "It is important – for Leeza's safety," Jorran added, and Leeza got his meaning. If anyone found out she was from the past, she'd become a specimen to study just as the ship was.

"I won't say anything," Rese said then looked at her, wide-eyed. "You're from the ship?"

It was Jorran that answered him. "Not in the way you mean. Leeza was trapped on the ship for a while." He let it hang with that and turned his attention back to her. "Can you show us where you were?"

Jorran squeezed her hands as they started to tremble. "It's okay, I will be with you."

"I'm not sure if I can find the way." The first words were hard to get out then they came out in a rush. "Going there, I was running, trying to get away, and then when I came out, I was not feeling well or thinking clearly. I kind of stumbled out."

"Just try," he urged.

Leeza's chest was tight, and she raised and lowered her head in acceptance.

Jorran leaned forward and kissed her cheek. "It will be all right." The words caressed her cheek then he was drawing her to the entrance. They passed the control room, ignoring those working within. Leeza led them down the hall to where stairs went down. She could hear the team working on that level, but she turned in the opposite direction, leading to what, she guessed, would be considered the back.

With each step tightness gripped her insides. Leeza remember the feel of running, knowing Zareck was behind her. The terror she felt from him became a real thing again. The memory of being dragged helplessly down the hall was so clear in her mind. She looked at a doorway sure she would still see the prints of where she'd clawed at it in an attempt to break away from him.

She was about to the point of wanting to scream she couldn't go on when Rese broke the tension.

"You were on the ship?"

The question was so unexpected and filled with innocent curiosity, all the tension burst from her body, leaving her weak in the knees.

"Yes," her admittance was accompanied with a half-laugh.

"How?" he asked.

"I was on the ship trying to decipher the language."

"When was this?" Rese moved up beside her, so they walked three across with her in between the men.

Leeza found comfort in the position, and it steadied her. "A long time ago."

"But the ship was only detected last year."

"It was found before. Just all record must have been lost." She tried not to think of the reason why, but it was there in the back of her mind.

"How? I mean you knew about it." Rese was working through the answer, but it obviously didn't quite make sense.

"Something bad happened. I was trapped on the ship. Others that knew must have died." Leeza bit back the pain that started to rise. Again, Jorran's hand tightened down on hers.

"How'd you get trapped?" Rese persisted.

Pain spiked in her. "A man named Zareck." Leeza felt tears threaten to rise at the thought of him. So much had happened because of him. She shivered at just the thought, though he was long dead and could no longer hurt her.

"You've mentioned that name before. Who is he?" Jorran entered the conversation, obviously as curious as Rese.

Leeza knew it was time to tell him. Clamping down tight on Jorran's hand, she began. "Zareck funded the expedition to study the city."

"Kind of like Atrose?" Rese asked as they reached the next set of stairs.

"I do not know Atrose." She looked to Jorran for clarification.

"Turet Atrose, from Tranic Corp, is who gave money to the university, for us to come study the ship. Norris works for him."

Leeza listened to the translator for the full sentence before she answered. "Yes. The same."

"You said city." Rese shifted her direction almost bumping into her.

"That's what they thought it was. I had just learned it was a ship from the translation when Zareck caught me. Zareck came to the site to force them to start the ship. He wanted the power from it and to find out how things worked."

"What about the warning?" Jorran's interest peeked.

"I had just deciphered it and was going to report when he found me. I tried to tell him, but he wouldn't listen, and to keep me from telling the others, he …" Her heart started pounding again.

She pushed her fear down and concentrated on the way. Instead of going down the next flight, which she knew the way was blocked because of the explosion Zareck caused, she headed down the hall.

"I was the only one on the ship. It was early. I had worked all the night. I knew I didn't have much time. He discovered me here, and when I tried to get away, he chased me." She didn't realize she was crying until she unconsciously wiped her cheek and found the moisture. "He'd killed my father." She caught back a sob that threatened to escape.

"What?" Jorran stopped in mid-stride and pulled her around.

"He admitted he had my father killed. My father was the top linguist. Zareck was afraid of what he'd discover if he worked the translation. That it would make it hard for him to get the …" she had to look at the translator for the word, "technology."

Leeza found herself pressed into Jorran's chest. She clung to him, letting out the threads of sorrow trapped in her heart. His hands moved over her back in soothing strokes.

Time stood still for her until he spoke. "Come on. We'll go." Jorran started to turn her back down the hall.

Leeza pulled back. "No, I can do this. I need to do this," she added more firmly and knew it was true. If she didn't face this now, she didn't know if she ever could, and it would haunt her.

Jorran stared at her for several seconds while Rese stood to the side silently. Finally, Jorran nodded. "If you change your mind." He let it hang.

Leeza was grateful for the option but was determined not to take advantage of it. She started back down the hallway again, leading the way around the corner. They'd reached where she'd climbed the ladder. What had seemed such a long way when she'd been struggling for a way out now seemed short.

Leeza stopped and looked down. "Zareck caught me and dragged me through the ship to a room he'd found down here." The muscles in her stomach tightened. She wasn't sure if she could force herself to go down.

As if sensing her distress, Jorran stepped forward, gripping the rung. "I'll go first."

The moment his head dipped through the opening, Leeza reached for the rung, not giving herself time to think. She jerked and almost slipped when Jorran's hands clamped onto her waist.

"It's all right. I have you."

He lifted her down, turning her into his arms. Again, Leeza sagged into him, drinking in the feel of him. His hand came up into her hair, tilting her face up to him. "Are you okay?" he asked, studying her face.

She nodded and lowered her head to rest over his heart. His arms circled back around her.

"I shouldn't have brought you here so soon."

"I'm fine," she answered then raised her head. "We are almost there. Just around the corner." When she went to step away, he kept her tucked to his side. Leeza was almost afraid she'd gotten the way wrong until they turned the second bend, and she saw the pile of rubble blocking the hallway at the end.

"I wonder what happened there." Rese asked just behind them.

Leeza knew he wasn't really asking her but answered. "Zareck set an explosion."

"To trap you," Jorran asked.

"So no one would find me," she said, feeling the hollowness of the words bit into her. Subconsciously, she slowed her pace. Jorran matched his stride to hers.

Rese passed them. "What is this place?" He stopped in the doorway.

Part of Leeza didn't want to look in, but another part couldn't keep herself back. "Zareck, thought it was a place to keep their dead."

Chapter Twelve

Jorran looked into the chamber. Rows of doors, or lids might have been a better description, lined the walls. Several stood wide open. Leeza's eyes fixed on one, and he didn't need to ask to know that was where she'd been locked in. Fury burned in him. He wanted to lift her up into his arms and take her out of there. He wondered what he'd been thinking of bringing her there.

Answers. He knew it was his incessant need for answers. He wished he'd have ignored it for once.

"Wow," Rese exclaimed, going to the open chamber, running his hand over the interior. "Were you in here?"

"Yes." Leeza's voice cracked, but she stepped forward to look in it. "Zareck closed me in. I couldn't get out."

"How did you survive?" Rese finally looked away from the chamber to study her.

"I do not know." She reached out a hand to run over the pads inside. Jorran saw her pause by a set of buttons. "I was trying to get out and pushed these." Her voice picked up a ghostly whisper. "The—" she swallowed hard and looked at the translator for the word, "it swelled around me, and I went to sleep."

Jorran felt his insides tighten at the thought. Being locked in there must have been terrifying for her. Still, he couldn't keep from wanting to study it closer. She'd been in there for four hundred years. It seemed impossible but looking at it, he knew it was true.

At least, she hadn't been aware of the time passing while in there. He shuddered at the thought of being locked in an eternal, waking sleep.

Jorran looked up to find Rese looking from Leeza to him. He decided to tell the young man, knowing that Rese had already figured out much of it, and he wouldn't tell anyone else without permission. "Leeza was in there for over four hundred and forty years."

Rese let out a whistle and looked back at Leeza. "Really?" he let out, not really doubting.

She nodded.

He whistled again. "You're really old." He looked at her, a smile spreading over his face.

Leeza started to laugh, and Jorran felt his insides start to relax. Tears trickled down her cheeks, but she continued to smile and looked at the younger man. "Thank you."

Rese shrugged. "No problem. Just figured I'd point out to Jorran he has a thing for an old lady." He winked.

Jorran shrugged when Leeza glanced up at him. "He's right. Though, I hadn't thought of it. You are old." He nodded. "Athurian." He arched a brow.

"Athurian, really?" Again Rese studied her.

"Yes," she said smoothly. Her own lips twitched again at his mirth.

"You're an archeological find on your own," Rese continued.

"I guess I'm in the right," she again glanced at the translator, "company."

Jorran couldn't keep from reaching for her. Pulling her up against him, he kissed her. "I think so."

"Hey, do I get one of those?" Rese said in mock complaint.

"No," Jorran growled the word out. "She's my find, and I'm claiming her." He kissed her again as if proving the point before releasing her. "Let's get to work."

Jorran forced his attention on the room, but he kept an eye on Leeza. Now that she had relaxed, she seemed to be handling being there okay. He still wished he hadn't brought her here so soon. He watched for signs of tension and fatigue but couldn't detect any.

The room wasn't very yielding of information though he had strong theories. He knew it wasn't a morgue. He figured it was for long trips, so the passage of time in empty space would not take a toll on their bodies, a way to prolong their lives. Still, he hated the thought of Leeza locked in there, but it had brought her to him.

They finished in the room and were working their way down the hall when he saw Leeza stagger enough that she had to catch the wall for balance. She straightened immediately. Jorran glanced at the time, not surprised how much had passed.

"Come on, time to go," he said loud enough for Rese, who was at the end of the hall studying the area around the explosion, to hear.

"I'm okay." Leeza turned to him. There was a translucent paleness to her skin.

"It's time." He took her elbow. "Do we have everything?" He looked back at Rese.

"Yes."

When he turned back, he caught the sweep of Leeza's eyelids, and how they lingered closed a moment before she seemed to steady herself. He smiled down. "Come," he whispered in her ear, edging her down the hallway.

They went a few meters when he leaned close to her. "You know, I have no idea how old you are?"

She stopped and grinned up at him. "Close to four hundred and seventy but who's counting now."

He smiled and leaned down to kiss the end of her nose. "I won't hold it against you." He wrapped his hand around her hair and tugged her to him. "But, how many of those years were you awake for?"

Before she could answer, there was a clatter around the corner.

Jorran jerked his head up and met Rese's gaze. Together, they dashed down the hall. There was no one there when they rounded the corner. They raced for the next turn. Jorran reached the corner and slid around just in time to see a booted foot disappear through the opening at the top of the ceiling. He had no trouble figuring out who it was.

Norris.

Fury built within him, and he wondered how long the man had been following and listening to them. He didn't think it could have been too long, but he wouldn't know until he asked Esher when Norris had snuck away. He knew Esher would've been keeping an eye on Norris, so he would know precisely when he disappeared.

Jorran had to force himself to take a calm breath and think. He tried to go over what had been said recently and cringed at the thought of talking about Leeza's age. He prayed the man couldn't understand the reference behind the comments.

He'd had enough of the man, and Norris had just given him the excuse for keeping him out of the ship for several days. Everyone knew the consequences of breaking from their assigned role and wandering off on their own. It had been explained plainly to Norris. The man was now out.

"What are you going to do?" Rese asked as if reading the direction of his thoughts.

"The man knew the rules."

"Atrose won't like it," Rese said pointedly.

"He doesn't have to. It was made clear." Jorran turned when he heard Leeza coming around the corner.

He forgot all about his frustration at the sight of her. Her face was flushed, and she was breathing hard from the short run. He reached for her, and she caught his hand. Her hand trembled in his, and when he slipped an arm around her, she leaned limply against him as if she'd just run ten kilometers.

"She okay?" Rese stepped toward them.

Leeza pulled away, taking a deep breath. "Yes, of course. I just got startled and lost my breath."

Rese didn't look any more convinced than Jorran was.

"Did you see who it was?" Leeza asked, pulling herself up steady. She was still breathless.

Jorran didn't want to answer but did. "Norris."

She paled slightly.

"Don't worry." He squeezed down on her arm. "I'll take care of it."

"I don't like the man." She shivered.

"You're in good company," Rese commented. "None of us do."

"Come on." Jorran motioned to the rungs. "Rese, why don't you go first?" he suggested when he saw Leeza sway slightly.

The man nodded and hurried up the ladder.

"Are you okay?" Jorran studied Leeza's face.

"Yes, of course." From the tightness around her mouth, he knew she was not as steady as she tried to appear but nodded.

"Just take your time, and Rese is there to help you over the top." He kept his hands on her waist as she started to climb. She was three-quarters the way up when he had to release her. He watched her pull herself up two more rungs. She was almost where Rese could reach her when Jorran saw her hand miss the hold and her foot slip off.

For a moment, she clung to the bar with one hand then with a cry, she slipped free. Her fall into his arms was not far, but it was enough to have his heart beating as hard as hers was. After gasping a breath, she wrapped her arms around him and clung tight.

"I have you." He repeated the words over in his mind several times after saying them aloud. He tightened the arm that held her pressed against him and slid his other hand up into her hair at the back of her head and tilted her face up to his. Her eyes were shut tight. "Look at me," he demanded harshly.

Her eyes came open and she gasped in several breaths. "Jorran," she whispered his name as if she couldn't believe he was there.

"Shh," he pressed his lips along her cheek to her temple.

"I am sorry. I feel ill." She pressed her cheek against his and clung weakly.

His smile at her first words turned to a frown at what she said. He nuzzled her cheek. He looked up to see Rese looking at them, concern on his face. "I caught her." The words were almost as much for him as Rese. He looked at the narrow rungs built into the wall and wondered how he could carry Leeza up them. "We'll be up in a minute."

The younger man nodded but didn't leave his perch. Jorran wondered if Leeza had fallen asleep she was so still in his arms. But, when he reached around her for the rung, she spoke, surprising him so that he almost lost hold of her.

"I can do it." She leaned back a little from him, their bodies still tight together, her feet hanging several centimeters off the floor.

He wanted to say no but knew it would be tricky to get her up. "We'll go up together. I'll be right behind you." He didn't like the pallor of her skin.

"Okay." Her relief was palpable.

He wished there was another way up but didn't know of one. He set her on a rung as high up as he could then pulled his body up behind hers, pressing her tight to the wall. "As slow as you need. If you have to rest, I'll hold you on."

Her nod of acceptance was proof of her state. She almost slipped once, but he held her up with his body until she could get her grip and steady herself. He could feel her tremble with exhaustion though it was less than a two meter climb. When they finally made it up through the opening, Rese reached over and lifted her off the ladder and set her on the floor, keeping her steady.

Jorran stepped off and pulled her to him once more. She came weakly. Beads of sweat glistened on her forehead. Her breathing was deeply labored.

"Up you go." He lifted her into his arms.

Her objection faltered even before it made it out of her mouth. She lowered her head to his shoulder. He made it to the first flight of stairs when she spoke again. "I am better now."

"I'll carry you." He didn't give her an option.

"Sorry, I don't know what—"

"Shh. Chel warned me not to overtire you. I should have kept a better eye on you."

"I was okay, then I was not." She rubbed her cheek on his chest and fell quiet as they climbed to another level.

"Rese, will you find Esher, Talis and Norris? I will go settle Leeza by the entrance then get the team from the control room and meet you at the entrance." The younger man left them, and Jorran made his way straight to the entrance, sitting her down on a box just inside.

"Eat this and stay here." He handed her an energy bar from a pack that was sitting on the floor.

"I am fine," she started to object, but he ignored it.

"Stay here. I'll be right back." He turned and jogged away before she could say anything else.

೧೮೩೦

Leeza took several bites of the bar, barely managing to swallow them. She wasn't hungry. She was just so tired. She forced herself to take another bite then tilted her head back against the wall and closed her eyes. She felt herself drift away listening to the sounds of the jungle coming in the opening.

"What are you?" The harshly snapped words startled her. Leeza jerked up and opened her eyes just in time to see Norris's beefy hand descend toward her. Her scream was instinctive but cut off as his fingers tightened around her throat. He lifted her into the air. Leeza clawed at his hand and tried to kick out.

"Where are you from?" Norris fairly spit the words at her.

Leeza tried to answer, but it came out a gurgle. The fingers bit into her skin. Norris's face went hazy in front of her.

"Don't try to deny it. I know what you are. You're an alien. Tash was right when he said you were talking in strange hoots and snorts. You may have that fool Jorran under your power, but you won't get me."

A roaring built in Leeza's mind, muddling his words.

"I'll snap that beautiful long neck then we'll dissect you and find out what you really are in …"

Leeza felt the world slip away then she crashed down hard. Air rushed back into her along with the sound of flesh hitting flesh.

Chapter Thirteen

Jorran hurried down the hall with the team following behind. He wanted to get back to Leeza. He didn't like the weakness that was so evident in her. He berated himself for not keeping a better eye on her, but one moment she seemed fine and the next....

Jorran came around the corner to see Norris standing over Leeza. Norris's hand was locked around her neck. He lifted her up. She dangled in the air like a limp doll. Jorran's fury exploded.

"Norris!" he roared, bursting into a run.

Instead of just releasing Leeza, Norris flung her aside as he turned to face him. Jorran was aware of her crumpling into a heap on the ground just before he slammed into Norris. It was like hitting a rock wall, but the man staggered back.

Norris shoved an arm up between them and tried to follow it with a punch, but Jorran was faster, sending his fist into Norris's face. There was the satisfying sound of crushing cartilage, but Jorran had no time to take pride in it as he had to pull back and block the huge fist coming at his own face.

Jorran got his arm up in time to knock away the blow that would have taken his head off, but Norris's fist still skimmed along his jaw, making lights flash in front of his eyes. Jorran didn't let it slow him. He sent his other fist into Norris's stomach. The man staggered back. Jorran jabbed the next punch to Norris's chin. Norris deflected and swung again at Jorran. Jorran deflected the blow and countered, catching the man in the side.

Norris pulled back then charged with his arms out wide, crashing in on Jorran before he could sidestep. Norris hit with enough force that it slammed Jorran back up against the wall. Jorran sent a combination of his right fist, left, then right into the man, but pinned against the wall, he couldn't get as much force as he would have liked.

With a grunt, Norris drove his meaty fist into Jorran's side, which surely would have broken one his ribs if Jorran hadn't been able to cushion it by getting his arm in between them, taking some of the force. Jorran, in return drove his fist up, catching Norris just under his chin. The man stumbled back.

Jorran used the opening to push off the wall, driving his body into Norris. Jorran knew he had the man on reach and height, but Norris had him on weight and was a brawler. He had to end the fight now. Not giving Norris time to recover, Jorran stepped forward sending his other fist into Norris's face again with all of his weight behind it. This time, Norris dropped to the ground.

Jorran didn't even look at the fallen man. He staggered to Leeza, dropping to the ground beside her. His hand trembled as he reached for her.

"Leeza." He brushed back the hair from her face, and to his relief, she stirred. "My heart." He ran his fingers over her cheek, and her eyes fluttered open. She looked dazed and uncomprehending until she looked up at him, then her eyes went wide.

"Jor … ran." His name came from her raspy and with difficulty.

"Shh." He caught her as she reached for him, pulling her up into his arms. "Shh, my heart." He crooned as he heard a sob escape her. "Shh, I'm here. I have you." He ran his hands up and down her back, savoring the feel of her in his arms.

The tendrils of fear he felt when he saw Norris squeezing the life from her and cast her aside faded. The feeling was replaced with the urgent need to sweep her away from there to where she was safe and his only.

Jorran became aware of the crowd standing around him. No one said anything out of shock, but it intensified the drive to shelter her, and he cradled her close, his arms locked around her.

Finally, Esher broke the silence. "Is she okay?"

Bands of pain tightened around Jorran's heart as he looked down and eased Leeza back enough to see her face. Fear was bright in her eyes. She fought to still her crying. It was her hand which rose to touch his cheek that assured him though.

She lightly caressed the spot on his chin that he knew would show a bruise within the hour.

"Jorran." Her voice was stronger though a bit scratchy. Tears still trickled down her cheeks, but the pain faded in her eyes, leaving just a deep, lingering weariness. He turned his head and pressed a kiss into her palm and forced a smile.

At the sound of Norris shifting on the ground, regaining consciousness, she jerked. Jorran tightened his arms around her then stood, cradling her up in his arms.

"Jorran, I–" she glanced over at Norris and fell silent, pressing her face into his neck.

Jorran looked down to see Norris glaring up at them. Blood covered the man's lower face but it was the malevolence in his eyes which was disturbing. Jorran ignored it, meeting his gaze straight on. "You are out of here. Today. Even if I have to have a shuttle brought in special."

"You can't," the man growled back in a challenge, wiping a hand across his mouth.

"Wrong." Jorran looked down at Norris, daring him to object again. When Norris remained silent, Jorran shifted his gaze to the others. "See Norris to his chambers and make sure he packs. If the transport is still here, have it held for him. If not, I'll arrange to get one out here. But keep an eye on him. I don't want him anywhere near the medic unit."

"What about my nose?" Norris protested from his position on the ground.

Jorran glared down at him. "I'll have Chel come check you out after she sees to Leeza." Jorran didn't want to make the concession, but knew he didn't have a choice.

With that Jorran turned and headed through the jungle. He had no doubt his instructions would be followed. In fact, he figured there would be no shortage of volunteers to escort Norris to the transport. The man excelled in irritating people, especially the students, picking on them for their academic pursuits.

"I can walk." Leeza had been so quiet she surprised him when she spoke.

Jorran angled his head to look down at her. "You're good where you're at." He boosted her a bit higher in his arms.

Her hand came up to touch his cheek then hovered over his chin where the bruise was forming. "I am sorry."

"It was not your fault." He saw her frown as she sought for a new word. "Trouble." She'd dropped the translator again, but he wasn't worried, someone would get it back to her.

"I understand. You are wrong. He thinks I am," she paused before pulling up the word. "from the ship. An a … lien." She stumbled over the word.

"Do not worry. I will have Chel write a report. She will satisfy everyone."

When she remained silent, he looked down and saw her eyes were closed. He lengthened his stride. He was halfway to the compound when he felt her shift in his arms.

He glanced down to see her eyes were open again. "I have you. I won't drop you."

"I … trust you." Her voice sounded steadier. "I would like to walk."

Jorran took several more strides.

"I am better now, please."

He stopped, debating a moment before he lowered her feet to the ground. She wobbled, but before he could swing her back up into his arms, she laid one of her small hands on his chest for balance and wrapped an arm around his waist, effectively tucking herself into his side.

The feel of her gentle touch on his ribs made him immediately forget the blow he'd taken there. He laid his hand over hers, trapping it there. She clung to him as they moved forward at a much slower pace.

Jorran could hear the others coming up behind them as they stepped from the jungle and quickened his pace, not wanting Leeza to have to see Norris again. Jorran was relieved to see the transport was still there. He didn't bother shifting toward it. Jorran knew one of the others would go tell the pilot to delay the departure.

They were halfway to the main building when Leeza stumbled. Stopping, he caught her, pulling her tighter to his side. Her head dropped to his chest. She was breathing in quick, panting breaths. Her body trembled. When he cupped his palm to her cheek, he felt the heat radiating off her.

"We need to get you to Chel, now." Again, she made no objection when he scooped her back up into his arms. He strode across the yard, only not wanting to jar Leeza kept him from breaking into a run. The fact that it was almost an exact repeat of the day before didn't bother him as much as the weariness he felt in her body. Jorran wanted to convince himself it was solely due to Norris choking her.

Anger surged in him at the thought, but he knew it didn't account for the extreme weakness in Leeza. He wished he knew what was wrong. Chel was giving her antibiotics, but they didn't seem to be helping.

Jorran looked up to see Chel standing outside the entrance. She hurried toward him as soon as he picked Leeza up.

"Get her inside," Chel ordered.

Chel matched her pace to his and pressed a shot to Leeza neck. "It should boost her energy," Chel said in the way of explanation.

A moment later, Leeza went limp in his arms.

Panic hit Jorran. "I thought you said it was an energy boost?" he demanded.

"It is. I just added something for her to rest. She will feel better when she wakes up."

Jorran glanced at Chel, not breaking his stride. "What are you not telling me?"

The medic waved her hand, effectively waving the question away. "We'll talk later."

Jorran studied her, not liking what he was picking up from Chel. She was worried. He turned his attention back to where they were going, maneuvering into the building.

Leeza didn't even react to it or being settled on the exam table, but she did let out a small whimper when he released her and went to step out of the way for Chel to get to her.

"I'm not going anywhere." Jorran caught her fingers and brought them to his lips. He shifted to stand by her head while Chel started to take her vitals. He noticed immediately Chel didn't seem surprised at whatever she found.

It made him wonder about her standing outside. Was she waiting for them? Did she expect Leeza to have trouble again today? Jorran was just about to question her when Chel brought his attention back to Norris's attack.

"What are the marks on her neck?"

Jorran looked down at the bruises. He tried not to think about Norris's hands around her neck. Fury surged once more within him. He had to release Leeza's hand as his own instinctively fisted. With supreme effort, he swallowed down the rage along with the knot in his throat.

"Norris caught her. He was questioning where she was from, if she was an alien. He threatened to kill her."

"You can't be serious." Chel looked up in utter shock.

"Yes. And I think he might have if I hadn't gotten there. Leeza was sitting by the entrance of the ship while I let the other team know we were leaving. She was not feeling well, so I left her there. When I got back, Norris was squeezing the life out of her."

"So that is what happened to you." She reached over and turned his head to the side to look at his chin. "Anything I need to look at?"

"No, just see to Leeza."

"She will sleep. That's all I can do for now. So, I'll ask you again, anything I need to see to?"

He shook his head. "Really just bruises, but you will probably need to see to Norris before he leaves. I broke his nose."

Her eyebrow arched up. "You did? Nice of you to tell me. I assume by your reference, he's leaving on the transport?"

"Yes. I should go fill out a report." He looked back at Leeza.

"Don't worry. She'll be asleep for some time. I'll just go check out Norris, make sure he is okay for transport then I'll be right back."

ଔଃ଼ଠ

Leeza woke with a start, confused for a moment as to where she was at then she put it all together for Chel's lab. She'd passed out again. She groaned. She felt miserable and weak. Her throat hurt.

As soon as she raised her hand and touched the area, the memory of Norris strangling her returned. Leeza shuddered and rubbed a finger over the bruised flesh, and managed to force a swallow then groaned again at the discomfort.

"Well, I don't have to ask how you feel." Chel stepped into her line of sight. "Here, this will help you feel better." Chel pressed a shot to her neck before Leeza could say anything.

Leeza realized Chel was doing that a lot. "What's wrong with me?" Leeza caught the tightening around the woman's mouth and felt a twinge of fear.

"We'll talk about it in a minute when that has time to take effect."

Leeza was about to argue, but the woman turned away quickly, picking up the translator, handing it over to her. "Here, Jorran brought this for you, though you're doing quite well without it."

"Where is Jorran?" Leeza asked, accepting the device gratefully.

"He got called away on a conference call. He came back here after seeing that Norris left on the transport, but the man who funded of the expedition is not happy."

"But–" she started.

Chel cut her off. "Don't worry. Jorran won't get in trouble. Violence is not accepted in our civilization, and there were plenty of witnesses who saw Norris attack you. Jorran was clearly within his rights to come to your aid. Atrose, head of Tranic Corp, is just not happy at losing his man here. I'm guessing he'll have someone out here by tomorrow. I just hope he's better than Norris, though, I'm not counting on it. They have their own objectives if you ask me, and they're not for the good of knowledge."

Leeza got a strong feeling Chel was avoiding something, and she figured she knew what it was so she decided to ask straight out. "Chel, what is wrong with me?"

Chel flinched, stiffened, then her shoulders drooped slightly.

"Chel?"

"Why don't we wait until Jorran gets here?"

"Chel?" Jorran questioned from the doorway.

The medic looked from one to the other and sighed.

As if he too picked up on what was going to be revealed was not good, Jorran came to stand by Leeza, taking her hand in his and waited.

"I got the results from the test I was running." Chel looked at them. "Remember I mentioned her body was fighting off a virus?" Chel looked to Jorran.

Jorran nodded.

"At first, I was hoping by boosting her energy, we might be able to boost her ability to fight the virus. Her body was quite fatigued when you found her. When that didn't work, I added antibiotics to attack the viruses for her, but it is not helping. Her body seems not to be able to fight the diseases that we carry now."

Leeza gasped as the full significance of what Chel was saying hit her.

Jorran released her hand abruptly. "I'm killing her." Anguish was heavy in his voice. Leeza reached for him. He jerked back when she touched him.

"No," Chel snapped. "The planet is. Leeza." Chel turned her attention directly to her. "You have no defense for it. I have contacted several colleagues who specialize in immunity." Chel raised her hand to forestall any objections. "Don't worry. I did not reveal your origin, just your condition. It does happen every once in a while, someone will have an extreme deficiency, but what they suggested is not much different than what I'm already doing."

"So I'm dying." Tears filled her eyes. Leeza tried to blink them away and face Chel with strength, but her heart thundered within her, beating out all sound. She'd been torn out of her time to finally find love, and now, she was going to die before she could truly experience it.

Jorran's strong arms wrapped around her, pulling her into him.

She wanted to scream it was unfair to take that away from her. What had she ever done to be teased with love only to have it ripped away? She clung to him, listening to his own heart pound with hers. She concentrated on it, and it steadied her.

"We're not giving up hope yet. What I'm doing still could stimulate your system. We are also trying to find a close genetic match in all the Thurians, to see if we can get close enough to try a transfusion." Chel was saying. "But it could be tricky. Your body could reject it. Still, we are not going to give up looking for an answer."

"How much time do we have?" Jorran asked the question Leeza was too afraid to think of.

Leeza looked to Chel.

"It is hard to say how long I can keep you going with what I'm doing. Unless your body starts to build up and eventually fight, what I'm doing will lose its effectiveness." Chel shrugged her shoulders. "It is all a guess. This is something we've never dealt with before, a person from the past. I'd say a couple weeks, possibly a little longer if you went to a med-lab at the city."

"No!" Leeza found her voice. "I want to stay here."

Jorran tipped her chin up to look at him. "I would go with you."

"I do not want to become a specimen they would study." She knew if she went they would discover who she was, and she would be a specimen as much as a patient.

Obviously, he knew it too because he nodded. "I can take you anywhere you'd like to go, anything you would like to see," he said, cupping her face in his hands. His pain was as strong as hers. It tore at her and strengthened her.

"I wish to stay here, to help you here with the translation." As soon as she said it she knew it was what she had to do – what she was meant to do. She had to make sure history did not repeat itself on Jorran and this people. It was what her life was meant for. She looked to Jorran and tried to let him see how important it was to her.

He nodded slowly. "As you wish." He pressed a kiss to her forehead. The action was so tender it brought tears to her eyes, and she had to fight to keep them from escaping.

She took in a deep breath. "I need a minute." She slipped from the table and steadied herself with a hand on Jorran's arm before breaking to make her way out the door and down the hall. Her strength was back again, but she didn't feel steady enough to run like she wanted to. She stepped out into the quad and realized she had no idea where she was heading.

At the sight of someone across the way, she turned and headed around the building. There, sandwiched between the wall and the jungle, she stopped and tilted her head up to the sky. Once more she fought back the tears that wanted to rise. She lost her effort as one tear broke free to trickle down her face. Powerful arms circled around her and pulled her back into the shelter of Jorran's strong body.

For about three seconds, she held herself stiff then collapsed back into him. Her words flowed like her tears. "I dreamed that you could love me, that we would be together." She tilted her head back to rest on his shoulder. "I finally find someone to love, and I'm going to lose him before I even get a chance. I came through so much time, and now I have no time." The words cascaded from her as did the tears.

His lips found their way to her cheek, kissing away the moisture. "We'll think of something," he whispered against her skin. "I'm not going to give you up, not without a fight. Do you understand?" The words were harsh with the depth of passion behind them. "You are part of me. My life-mate.

We are together in this, and we will make the most of what we have, even if is only this day. Do you hear me, my heart?"

"Yes," she sobbed as joy pushed back the pain.

"Then say you will become mine now."

"Jorran?"

"Say it." He released her to turn her to face him. He dropped to his knees, catching her hands in his, bringing them to his mouth to kiss. "Say you will become my life-mate now." He pressed kisses on her wrists as he looked up at her. His eyes didn't hide any of the love or desire he felt for her.

It took her breath and made her heart surge.

Chapter Fourteen

"I love you," she cried out with her heart.

"Then be mine."

"I have been from the first moment we met."

"Yes," he groaned out, stood and caught her in his arms, lifting her off the ground as his lips captured hers. The kiss was deep and sealing. It lasted until they were both trembling from the effect of it.

Jorran finally broke contact with her mouth only to continue to run light caresses along her face as his hands ran up and down her back, pinning her to him. "You are mine now in the decree of my people. But we will make it in the sight of everyone this day. Will you agree?"

"Yes," she barely got out before he reclaimed her mouth.

When he broke again, it was to cradle her back into his arms and head for the quad.

"Where are we going?" Leeza asked, breathless.

"We need to make arrangements for the binding ceremony." Determination radiated off him.

"Can we? Legally?"

"Yes."

"I have no records." She pointed out, but it didn't deter him.

"It can still be done. I just need to get this in process, but it should not take long. Chel can keep an eye on you until all is set."

"Can it really be?" She couldn't help asking again.

They'd reached the quad, and he stopped in plain sight of anyone there. "Yes." He kissed her, cutting off all her worries. He turned and Leeza saw Chel standing there watching.

"Well, that was entertaining." The woman lips and one eyebrow kicked up.

Jorran walked to the medic and set Leeza on her feet, making sure she was steady before releasing her. "Watch after her, and make sure she rests. I need to see to a binding ceremony."

The woman didn't seem surprised by the announcement. "About time, I've wondered the last couple days when you were going to do it." Chel slid her arm around Leeza turning her back to the building.

Leeza resisted. "Jorran?"

"I will be back when all is set. It will not be long."

"But what about the ship?" She didn't want him to jeopardize his responsibilities. Her concern made him smile. "There is no worry. To appease Tranic about Norris being sent away, we agreed not to go in again until they can get a new representative here, which won't be until the day after tomorrow." He leaned forward and kissed her again before turning to stride away.

"Come on." Chel laid a hand on her arm. "You should get some rest. I think you'll need it. That man is swimming in his Ellandish drive and is no longer trying to fight it."

"What?" Leeza turned to Chel as they walked down the hall, curious at the comment.

"Jorran is almost pure Ellandish. The desire to mate is strong in them when they meet their chosen one. Jorran has been fighting it for days not to frighten you. Now that it is out in the open and declared, he will have to act on it or it will practically drive him insane. He will move heaven and earth to have you made his now. But have no fear, his request will not be denied if you have agreed that you are willing." She looked at her as if asking for an answer.

"Yes, I am willing." Leeza was filled with awe that Jorran really wanted her that strongly.

Chel smiled again. "I thought so, or I would've called a halt to it days ago."

"Called a halt?"

"If Jorran thought you did not have feelings for him or was not interested, he would have fought his desire for you. It would not have been easy for him, but he would have conquered it because, no Ellandish would ever force their heart mate. He would live an empty life first."

Leeza couldn't get any words out. All she could picture was Jorran alone and it hurt. Her regret of his loss overshadowed her thoughts of dying, but she knew what it was to never have love and she knew how precious it was to her to feel his love. If she could give him just a day of love and happiness like he gave her, she would make it the most incredible day ever. He would know her absolute love every minute they had.

Leeza swallowed hard. "Thank you. For all you've done and for every day you give us."

The woman looked taken back and actually blushed. "It is my pleasure. Now, I promised Jorran you would get some more rest." Chel waved her on. "I need to see to a few details myself before the ceremony." She stopped and took a wrapped bundle from a storage cupboard. "I had this brought in on the transport. Figured it might be needed. When you get up, you can clean up and change into it."

"I don't think I can sleep," Leeza said honestly.

Chel smiled compassionately. "I understand, but why don't you lie down for at least a little while before you change."

Leeza followed Chel's suggestion and actually was able to clear her mind and doze off. When she woke up, she went in to clean up and wash her hair. Wrapped in a drying cloth, she came out and opened the package Chel had left for her.

Instead of being a new set of clothes for her to wear around the excavation like she figured, Leeza found fine gauzy material in a pale green color which matched her eyes. Lifting it free, the material cascaded down to reveal a dress that made Leeza's breath catch. It was utterly feminine and more beautiful than anything she'd ever seen.

Leeza quickly put it on then turned to look at her reflection. She ran a finger over the soft, sheer material. The dress was gathered at the top of her shoulders, leaving her arms bare, and accentuating her long neck, it then flowed down over her breasts hugging the lines of her body, molding to her waist and over her hip where it draped down to end just above her knees in front and dipped to her calves in back. There was a cape made of just a single layer of silver film that was pinned at the shoulder folds with bright enameled pins and hung down, following the hem line.

In the bottom of the box was a simple pair of silver slippers with the same bright design as on the pins. There was also a matching hair clip.

Leeza brushed out her hair, dried it, and left it hanging down her back, catching just one side up in the clip. The tiny firestone earrings she'd been wearing all along made a perfect accent. She looked again at her reflection, pleased at her appearance. She felt a twinge of nerves at the thought of what Jorran would think.

There was a soft knock on the door then it opened. It was Chel who stood in the doorway. "Oh my, yes," the woman exclaimed. "Absolutely perfect."

"You like it, then?"

"Yes, and Jorran will be thrown speechless. All is ready to go. These are for you." She held out a bouquet of delicate lavender, light-green, and white flowers that cascaded down their stems. "One of the botany students made it up. Quite perfect."

Leeza took the bouquet and couldn't resist the urge to lean down and take in the scent of fragrant flowers before she followed Chel to the commons building.

It the entrance, Chel stopped her. "Stay here. Esher will come get you to escort you in." With that, Chel disappeared inside.

Leeza wondered for the first time what all the ceremony would entail. She hadn't thought to ask, not that it mattered, as long as it bound her and Jorran together. Leeza didn't get any time to contemplate it further as Esher appeared in front of her.

His face glowed with pleasure as he looked at her. "Our Jorran is a most fortunate man." He bowed to her. "Since you have no one here, I have been give the honor of escorting you in, if that is all right."

"Thank you." Leeza smiled and took his offered arm. "I don't know what to expect," she whispered to him before they stepped through the doorway.

He laid his hand over her hand that rested on his arm. "It is a very simple ceremony. Words of promise are exchanged for the witnesses and you are bound. Just follow Jorran's lead."

As they stepped into the commons, Leeza forgot all of what he said. Tables were set up all around the sides of the room. Flowers like the ones she carried were spilling over the sides of bowls in the center. Food filled the serving tables but everyone stood in a circle around the room.

People parted as they came close, and she saw Jorran standing in the very center. His eyes widened as he caught sight of her, and the smile that already crested his lips broadened.

He was dressed in his normal pants and boots but his shirt was bright white against his tanned skin. It had long sleeves that bellowed out around his arms but were tight at the wrists. The neck was open emphasizing his muscular chest, just fastened loosely with a silver cord. When he held out his hands to her it was all the encouragement she needed to come forward.

He caught her hands in his, bringing them to his lips. "My heart," his whisper was only for her to hear. He waited a moment for Esher to take his place just behind his shoulder then Jorran turned his attention to the older man, and Leeza followed the motion.

Esher cleared his voice and spoke up. "We are gathered here to give witness to the binding of this man and woman under the supervision of one of the High Ellandish."

It was then Leeza noticed the image of a noble looking older man in a viewing screen. The man on the screen nodded and Jorran spoke. "As hearts are given to join into one. Leeza Jaeff, I give my heart to you. Do you accept me?"

She had no trouble understanding the words and the strength of his declaration behind them. It left her breathless but she managed to get out a "Yes."

Jorran smiled and bowed his head to her.

She took his lead. "Jorran Carrell, I give my heart to you. Do you accept me?"

"Yes." The word was firm and possessive.

"Bind heart to heart," the man on the screen spoke. "One for all time. Each a piece of the other finally made whole to cherish and grow for eternity. She is the mate of your heart Jorran Carrell as he is yours Leeza Jaeff, now Carrell tied in name and heart. I bind you as your hearts have. Kiss and be one."

With that Jorran leaned to her, and Leeza had no problem joining the kiss. Heat swept through her body, burning in her heart, pulling her to him and she gave herself over.

The cheer that went up around them finally drew them apart but Jorran didn't pull away. He raised a hand to caress her cheek. "My heart," he said with such depth it resonated in her.

Leeza pressed her lips into his palm. "My heart, my love."

He kissed her again, bringing another cheer from the crowd. Laughing, he broke free, clamped his hands on her waist and lifted her high over his head. "My heart!" he shouted for all to hear.

Caught in the exuberance, Leeza threw back her head and laughed before placing her hands on either side of his face and leaning down to kiss him. She had no idea when her feet touched the floor again, but it seemed to signal everyone to crowd in to wish them congratulations. Finally, Esher called for attention and had Jorran lead her to the food and the banquet began.

Leeza had a hard time eating but it wasn't because of the food. The feelings pouring off Jorran were so strong it was as if she could feel every wave of desire that came from him.

∞

Jorran couldn't keep his eyes off Leeza. She was his now. They were one.

He could feel the answering longing in her. He noticed she wasn't eating as she watched him. He picked up a piece of meat and held it out to her.

She looked surprised at the action but opened her mouth to accept it. He almost groaned aloud when he felt her lips brush against his finger tip. He chose a piece of fruit. Feeling another brush of torment, he shifted to his fork. Spearing up a vegetable, he took a bite off it then extended the rest to her, which she received without pause. That got them started on feeding each other.

He tried to focus on the conversation going on around them, but as time passed, it became extremely difficult. Still, he was doing fine until he fed her an excessively juicy piece of fruit and her tongue darted out to catch the nectar before it could run onto her chin. Unable to stop himself, he leaned forward, running his tongue over her lips drawing up the last traces of the flavor.

It was the taste of her though that burned through him. "Are you ready to go?" He took her hand already easing her up.

"Yes." There was relief in the word.

Jorran led her out amid a chorus of congratulations and farewells. There were slaps to his back and hugs given to both of them from many of the women.

Leeza sighed once they stepped outside. "That was so kind of everyone. I can't believe they all came."

Jorran noticed the lights on in Tash's place. There was no noise coming from the place. He knew not everyone had come but he wasn't going to mention it to Leeza. He doubted she was anymore fond of the man than he was. "Would you like to walk around a while before we head in?"

She looked around then up at him and shook her head.

Jorran almost groaned in relief. He would be as patient as she needed but he really wanted to love her. Still, he gave her a moment to let the calm of the evening ease her before he turned her in his arms and dipped his head to meet her lips.

There was no holding back as she gave herself to him, though there was an innocence in her touch that steadied his pace. He had time to love her, he reminded himself then almost jerked back as the thought of losing her slid through his mind. Pain had him tightening his hold. She groaned under his pressure and he softened his hold, stroking his hands up and down her back. They were not out of time yet.

He felt her fingers run up his chest and shuddered at the surge they brought. Leaning over, he slipped his arm under her legs and lifted her into his arms. Their kisses continued into the building and down the hall to his chamber, breaking only long enough to get through the door.

CROSSO

Jorran came awake conscious of Leeza's feminine form beside him like he had dreamed of since he'd first seen her. She was his now. She was where she belonged, at his side. His possessive streak surprised him some, though he figured it shouldn't.

He was Ellandish and had been raised with the knowledge of their feelings for the heart-mates. It was just until he'd seen Leeza, he'd never experienced the drive. She was his life, all that was precious and important to him. He couldn't accept it any other way. He would guard her with every breath of his body, but what attacked her he had no defense for.

Thoughts of losing her again pierced his mind. He couldn't imagine her being sick. She'd been so healthy and loving in his arms. He didn't want to accept the possibility of her becoming ill and weak, just as he hadn't when Chel first told them. Jorran didn't want to accept it but he knew there was no choice.

He yearned to wake her, to love her again, but he knew she needed rest to keep up her strength, so he settled for brushing his lips to the top of her head, taking in the sweet fragrance of her and luxuriating in the feel of her next to him. He would savor every minute he got to be with her, and today it would just be them.

He thought of the small pool at the base of a waterfall that had been found not far from the ship. The botany teams worked there quite often but he'd ask if they could have a couple hours there alone.

He pictured Leeza there, sitting on the bank, her skin damp from the clear water, as flowers formed a fragrant canopy around her. He would make love to her there. His heartbeat jumped then jumped again when he felt Leeza's small hand traced its way lightly over his chest.

Tilting his head down, Jorran found her smiling up at him.

"What are you thinking?" She didn't have the translator with her but her speech flowed fluently.

"Of making love to you," he said honestly, wondering if she would blush as she had several times the night before. She did slightly, and it warmed his heart.

"Oh." Her hand on his chest paused then continued the action as she brushed her lips across his shoulder.

His heart raced. "How do you feel, my heart?"

She drew in a deep contented breath. "Good. Very, very good. Like I never want to move again."

"Really?"

At the word, she looked confused.

"Is that so?" He translated it for her, and she nodded. "I want to show you a place in the jungle later, but first …" He caught her hand bring it to his lips, kissing her fingertips before he interlocked their fingers, shifted his mouth to her shoulder and ran kisses up her neck to her mouth.

It was the need for food that finally drew them out, only to find a tray waiting just outside their door. After they ate, Jorran called over to the head of the botany team who wholeheartedly agreed to set some private time for them at the pool. Jorran then called to ask if he could have a lunch prepared.

To pass the time until they were going to leave, Jorran put on some music, and they found their tastes quite similar though it was all new to Leeza. She sat cradled in his lap as he brought up images on the computer screen of his house at the university, the home he grew up in and his family.

Leeza pulled up to look down at him on seeing a picture of him with his two brothers and parents. "Will they not be upset at missing your binding? Do they even know?"

"They know. I talked to them while I was preparing things for the ceremony. They are not upset. They understand the need for the timing. And that once Ellandish have chosen a life-mate and she has accepted, the ceremony is just a formality, the bond is already done."

"I do not know much of Ellandish culture," Leeza said, looking uncertain.

"It is not so different than any other. Our drive to find a life-mate is just a little stronger."

"Is it the same for a woman?"

"Yes, but it is different. Her drive is held in firmer check until the ceremony and kicks in when the first mating occurs. Then it is said she goes into a settling period where her drive is for family."

"I will not get to have your child." Pain choked her words.

Jorran wrapped his arms around her and pulled her tight. "We do not know that. We must not give up hope that something will work." He tried to force assurance in his words but pain ate at him too.

"Chel said that you will not find another after ..." She did not finish the sentence.

"We mate for life. My heart will hold you always. Even if we only had this one day, it would be enough." He felt dampness touch his shoulder and eased her back so he could wipe away the tears from her cheeks then kissed the moisture away, tasting the saltiness mingled with her. "No tears, my heart. This is a day for joy and togetherness. Come, let us go for our walk."

The smile she gave him was tremulous. "Tell me about where we are going?"

Even with Jorran's description, Leeza was unprepared for the beauty of the place he led her to. The small pool was surrounded with thick foliaged and trees that reached the sky, framing a waterfall that cascaded down over the rocks. A rainbow of colors glistened in the mist. Flowers draped down from the trees and clustered around the edge of the water, peeking out from under wide leafed plants.

Leeza stared at it trying to take it in. In her time, this was a barren land of sand and harsh rocky canyons. It seemed impossible that it could be the same location. At least something good seemed to come from the disaster, but it was at such a high cost, still she had to appreciate it. She felt Jorran's arms come around her pulling her back against his chest.

"It's so beautiful. It's …" she had to search for the word, "unbelievable … amazing." She laid her arms over his, not taking her eyes off the sight. "Thank you for bringing me here."

"You're welcome." His lips brushed her neck. "Would you like to go for a swim?"

"Oh yes, but," she broke off.

"Do you swim?" He continued caressing her neck with his mouth.

"Yes." The word came out as a slight groan. She had to pull away to formulate what she wanted to say. "Is it safe?"

"Yes, the water is totally safe." He took her hand leading her to the bank. "We have it all to ourselves for the afternoon."

They swam, made love, talked and ate while enjoying the beauty and time together. For Leeza it was the most magical time in her life. She still almost believed it had to be a dream and any moment she'd wake up and there would be no Jorran and her heart would break. But when she woke from dozing on a moss cover rock, it was to find Jorran leaning over her, a lock of her hair twisted around his finger and the back of his hand stroking her cheek.

Leeza didn't try to keep back the smile that blossomed from deep within her. "I love you," she whispered the words to him though inside she shouted them.

"And I love you." He kissed her taking her into his arms.

They walked back to the complex pressed together, arm in arm. Leeza's head rested on his chest but she wasn't at all fatigued. There were smiles and greetings as they strolled across the quad, but no one tried to interfere with their private time together, to which Leeza was grateful. She knew the next day when Norris's replacement got in, things would be back to business, but at least Norris would be gone. She couldn't imagine anyone being worse.

Chapter Fifteen

The cocoon of privacy they had been wrapped in burst when Jorran received the communication that the transport was coming in. He left Leeza to go out to meet it. She couldn't help but follow, though she stopped just outside the door of the building, keeping watch from across the quad. The transport awed her as it dropped out of the sky. The sleek tapered cylinder had four appendages, two extending from the top, two wings on either side, front and back, that looked like they were a combination of giant fans that gave it lift.

In her time there had been only minimal air travel, nothing like the transport. Most travel was done with land vehicles and on the water. When she mentioned this to Jorran, he started to make plans to take her up in the air, but it wouldn't be today. Today he had to deal with Norris's replacement.

From the distance, she watched the craft touchdown, and Jorran walk toward it as the doorway opened on the side. Leeza's breath caught as she saw a man duck through the opening. Leeza heard a word beside her that she didn't understand, and the translator didn't interpret. She turned to Chel who had moved up just behind her shoulder.

"That is one big brut," Chel said, her attention still on the man.

As he stepped down, Leeza had to agree. He still wasn't quite as tall as Jorran but nearly twice as wide. She had thought Norris was a block of a man, but this man would have made Norris look just average. Rese's lanky form looked diminutive next to him.

Thick, bushy eyebrows made his eyes look like a dark mask at the distance, set over a sharp nose that reminded her of a scavenger bird. What frightened Leeza though was when Jorran held out his hand in the greeting she had seen people there use, the man looked at it, then looked away.

The same word Leeza didn't recognize before slipped from Chel again, and Leeza had no trouble hearing the displeasure in her voice. Chel wasn't happy. "If we were hoping for someone better than Norris, I don't think we got it."

"Chel?"

"Sorry. Don't worry about it." Chel laid a hand on her arm.

"You think there will be more trouble?" Leeza asked as she looked back at the man, studying him.

The medic looked at her. "What is your impression?"

Leeza glanced at the woman then back at the man. She watched as he turned and reached back inside the doorway and snatched up a bag that was held out to him. Then, he yelled, loud enough to be heard where they were standing, at the men unloading a large crate.

A shudder of trepidation ran over her. She wanted to pull back. "He is gruff in his ways and doesn't care. He likes to give orders. He intimidates on purpose. He is not a nice man."

As if he heard them talking about him, he looked up across the open area directly at her. His eyes seemed to darken though Leeza knew it couldn't be true. Still, her tremor of unease turned into a full alarm.

As if Chel picked up the threat, the hand Chel had on her arm tightened. "I think it would be a good idea if you went inside and do not go anywhere where he can catch you alone. I would guess Norris told him his speculation that you were from the ship, even though I know they got my report and data that proves you are Thurian."

Leeza started to turn way and follow Chel when her gaze fell on another person that seemed to be watching her instead of the new arrival. Across the yard, the smirk on Tash's face made another shiver go down her spine. Seeing her attention, he disappeared back inside his establishment.

Leeza felt slightly nauseated as she followed Chel. She elected to stay with the woman while waiting for Jorran to come to her.

It was almost time for dinner when Jorran stepped through the doorway. Silently he went right to her, catching her up in his arms as she stood to greet him. His lips descended on hers in an almost savage need of assurance that she was there and fine. When his head finally lifted, Leeza realized that Chel must've disappeared into her quarters. Leeza raised a hand to smooth over the wrinkles that furrowed his brow.

"You are worried," she stated the obvious.

He caught her fingers bringing them to his lips to nuzzle with tender kisses before he nodded. "The man, Vesar, he is not as easy to read," he waited to make sure she understood the term, when she nodded, he continued. "Norris's hostility was out front for all to see. Vesar is plain gruff, yells orders, but there is a shell in which he hides his true thoughts. I think his outward malevolence is a cloak to hide what is inside. I have no doubt he's smarter than Norris, and craftier."

Jorran kissed her fingers again. "I don't want you anywhere alone. Even in our quarters the door stays locked, and you don't open it for any no one you don't know."

She was shocked at the vehemence in his voice. "Jorran–"

"No, I'm serious. Nowhere on your own. I can only guess what Norris reported about you."

Leeza nodded, and Jorran's arms went back around her tugging her to him in a firm embrace he showed no sign of releasing. She slid her arms around his back, stroking up and down in a calming motion and pressed her lips against his neck. A shudder ran through him as tension released to be replaced by another kind. Abruptly, he stepped back, took her hand and led her back to their quarters.

CRRO

Vesar did not come to the commons for dinner that night to which Leeza was vastly relieved. Whispers drifted through the room, attesting to the nervousness of everyone. No one was quite sure what to make of the man.

It was Esher that explained it to her. "Society has become quite stable. The planet is united in equality of races. After The Great Deluge, people had to pull together to survive. There is not much crime. Though we do have some, it tends to be from those like Turet Atrose, the head of Tranic Corp. He is compelled by greed, but even he is tempered with a code of conduct.

"There are few men like Norris," the older man continued, "I thought Atrose had hired the worst he could find. Now it looks like he has collected the worst he can find to do the dirty work he himself would never contemplate doing. Understand, Atrose has no qualms about stealing the technology from the ship as he believes it belongs to no one so it is open to him. He would never even consider it stealing. It would be claiming, and he softens his conscience by funding the exploration. The men he hires are just employees hired to obtain what he wants."

"I think he pretends to not know the means they use to acquire what he wishes." Jorran joined in. "He actually acted quite outraged when we discussed Norris's forced leaving." He looked directly at Leeza. "I sent a warning along with Chel's report on you that Vesar is not to bother you. Atrose knows you're my life-mate and one wrong move from Vesar and he's gone. And he'll not be replacing him."

Jorran looked at those around the table. "That goes for anything. The university backed me up on it. I'm hoping that will get Atrose to keep Vesar on a tighter tether. Still, use caution." He glanced back at Leeza. "You, my heart, especially."

She nodded, and the conversation turned to planning the teams going to the ship the next morning.

"Leeza, you will be with Azas and the translation team." Jorran looked across the table at Azas. "I want you and Marin to continue the recording while Leeza works on the direct translation."

Leeza now understood Jorran was trying to keep her close to him but away from Vesar. His next sentence confirmed it.

"Rese and I will have Vesar with us and continue exploring the ship. We are going to start mapping out a complete scale diagram. We will be measuring every distance and plotting it, then the teams can come in section by section and do a thorough log. That way we can start covering more ground, and I can still keep an eye on Vesar."

Rese made a sour face at the mention of Vesar's name, but Leeza knew he wasn't really displeased because of the chance to explore further.

With that, conversation turned more pleasant. As soon as Leeza finished eating, Jorran took her hand. They said goodnight to everyone, and he led her out. They walked across the quad and down the short trail to the pond. The lowering sun filtered through the trees making everything glow as they slipped into the water.

Leeza sighed as she felt Jorran's arms slip around her. She laid her head back on his shoulder and let herself drift. "I love it here."

"We'll come every evening."

"I would like that." A rush of pleasure coursed through her at the feel of his lips brushing her neck. "I like that, too."

"At my home there is a pool in the back. It is not near as big, but there are trees and flowers around it. I think you will find it beautiful."

Leeza felt a stab of pain at the thought that she might not get to see his home. She pushed it away, refusing to let anything mar their time together. Instead, she turned in his arms, kissed him fiercely, and then pushed him away, swimming out into deeper water knowing he would follow her. He caught her in five strokes, lifting her high up in the air, then instead of throwing her back into the water like she expected he lowered her down against him to continue the kiss, letting it lead them into making love.

CRRO

Over the next eight days a routine was set. Leeza worked with the recording team in the command room while Jorran mapped the ship. Jorran was extremely careful that they broke to eat lunch before continuing. In the evening, after dinner, they would walk to the pond to swim before returning to their quarters for the night.

Leeza was happy the team accepted her so well. At first, it was because she was Jorran's life-mate and that was enough, but it didn't seem to take long for them to become her friends and then colleagues when they realized she really could translate the language on the ship. Everyone took up the practice of watching over her; making sure she ate, drank and took rest breaks. They knew she was sick, but no one had guessed her origins.

With each passing day, she relied less on the translator, going long periods without needing the device at all for conversing but she found it useful in deciphering links with similar word roots she discovered. It was an easy hypothesis to reach that with all the commonalities in a large number of words that the inhabitants of the ship had integrated with the people of the planet long ago.

Leeza was working on putting one set of words into the translator to see if she could find any basic forms when Azas was drawn to what she was doing.

"What language is that?" Azas leaned over her.

"Ferses."

"Really, why are you translating it into that?" The woman looked perplexed.

"I am more familiar with it. It makes it easier to go to Ferses then Lannish."

"Is it like Ferses? Do you think it's related?"

Leeza smiled at the question, and could see where she got it. "No, if anything, it is more in common with some Lannish, though I am finding some reoccurrences in several different languages."

Leeza caught the woman's growing interest. "Would you like to see?"

"Please." Azas settled down beside her. Leeza showed her the surprising amount that matched up in base forms. "There are more now that I know what search parameters to look for, the translator makes it easier to match up similarities."

Azas caught on quickly, and they were working together on it when Jorran came to get them for the evening meal.

"This is fascinating," Azas exclaimed in delight. "Look at this. I would never have guessed." She held up the screen showing the list of links and where Leeza had spliced them into the page she was working on.

"There is a lot we don't know." Leeza cautioned through the woman's excitement as she stood.

Leeza heard a low grunt and glanced back. Vesar stood directly behind her, glaring down. The man's eyes were cold with open hostility. He reminded her so much of Zareck she took a step back then jerked when she felt

Jorran's arm slide around her. She hadn't realized he had moved beside her but she turned into him.

His body was stiff, muscles tense. He glared over her shoulder at the man there, but when she laid a hand over his, his fingers curled gently around hers. Still, he didn't relax his stance, until Vesar pulled back. Leeza caught a look of disdain in Vesar's gaze before he turned away.

It was several moments before Jorran relaxed fully and squeezed her fingers, breaking some of her own tension. Leeza was taken by surprise when his head dipped, and he claimed her lips in a hard kiss that only lasted a moment but left her breathless.

"Be careful around him," he repeated the warning he told her daily, then wrapped his arms around her pulling her tight to him as if afraid to release her.

Leeza closed her eyes and soaked up the sheltering love she felt flowing from him. His body was taut once more, but when she raised her hands to stroke over his back, his tension eased.

She felt his lips glide over her cheek to her neck in light brushing kisses that made her shudder for a whole different reason. Without thought, Leeza dug her fingers into his back muscles and tilted her head to the side, giving him better access.

He accepted the offering, running kisses up until he came around to reach her mouth which he savored thoroughly before raising his head.

"Let's go eat. I'm hungry," he growled out. The glint in his eyes had nothing to do with the anger Vesar had raised in him. It wasn't until she turned away from him that Leeza realized they were still on the ship, and there was no one else around. She felt herself blush at the thought of the display they had put on.

CR80

Most everyone was finishing eating when they finally reached the dining room. Leeza didn't miss the grins and arched eyebrows that were sent their way.

It was Esher who broached the subject. "Isn't it entertaining being around new life-mates.

"Oh, did I miss a show?" Chel joined in with a wicked grin which stated she'd heard all about it.

"Not much of one," Rese grouched. "Azas herded us out when it was just getting interesting."

Jorran sent the younger man a glare that lacked any real sting then turned to Azas. "Thank you," he said, "and, for your actions. I was wondering, if you would like to change assignments for a while and help Leeza with the translation? You seemed to be excited about it."

"I would like that very much," Azas said with enthusiasm.

"Good, then I'll shift someone else to help with recording and you and Leeza can work together."

"What do you think it will take to get us through that door?" Rese asked.

"What door?" Esher asked coming alert to the conversation.

"Jorran thinks we found the engine room today," Rese said as Jorran tried to cut him off.

"It's just a possibility. We won't know until we get through the door," Jorran said quickly, trying to counter the words but it was too late.

Leeza's chest tightened. She had to fight for breath. She felt sick, and it had nothing to do with the illness attacking her body. A ringing started in her ears and wiped out all sound around her. As the world drifted away, she heard Chel being called and recognized Jorran's voice. She tried to cling to it, but a fog seemed to roll over her mind.

Leeza felt a sharp prick on her arm. Then she was floating, the musky scent of Jorran filled her along with the feel of being cradled in his arms. She clung to the knowledge that he was there.

Time had passed. She had to fight to make sure history didn't repeat itself. Finding strength in that resolve, she drew in a deep breath and opened her eyes. She panted several more breaths but her mind began to clear.

"Can't start engines," she forced out the words.

"Shh, it's okay. We're not." Jorran brushed a hand over her cheek. "Shh. Lie still. You're all right."

"Engines." Her heart was pounding so strongly, she couldn't get anything else out.

"I understand. No one will try to start them. Just relax and breathe." His fingers continued to make light caresses over the side of her face, broken only by the occasional brush of his lips. Calmed, her breathing became more normal, and her head cleared, but it left her feeling weak and shaky. They were still in the dining room, surrounded by people.

"Sorry." She made a move to sit up, but found herself trapped against Jorran's chest.

"Just stay still until you're steadier." There was gruffness in his voice now.

She looked up at the worry etched on his face. It was Leeza's turn to raise her hand to caress his cheek. "I'm okay," she soothed. "Panic attack."

He caught her fingers in his bringing them to his lips. He nodded but didn't release her. "I think we're done for the evening. You'd better have an early night." He stood lifting her in his arms. "See everyone in the morning."

On the way out, Leeza caught the question she knew everyone had been thinking and someone finally got the nerve to ask. "What's wrong with her?"

Leeza was relieved when she heard Chel answer. "Her body has an immunity problem."

Leeza knew there would be more questions, but she was glad that much at least was out.

ﻌﻌﻌ

Jorran's heart pounded as he walked down the hall to his chambers. Three days had passed without Leeza having a fainting spell. He'd almost reached the point of hoping her body was fighting off the sickness, but even though this incident was brought on because of her fear linked to the starting of the engines, it was a blatant reminder that he was going to lose her.

He wanted to shout that it wasn't fair. He'd waited so long for her. He'd almost given up hope of finding the one he'd love forever, and now that he had her, she was going to be ripped away.

What had he done that was so bad? The thought burst within him. Logically, he knew the answer was nothing. It was not his fault or Leeza's. Just sometimes things happened that were beyond control.

He hated it. He was used to working for what he wanted, controlling his destiny, and now he felt like he was running out of time with the most important thing in his life. He would give everything for more time.

He tried to keep from squeezing her too tightly but the need to hold her to him was over powering. He reached the door to their quarters and couldn't bring himself to open it.

"Jorran?" The sound of his name on her lips brought a shiver to him, followed by another as her fingers lightly brushed his cheek. She drew up toward him and replaced her fingers with her lips. A shudder escaped him, and he lost the fight, tightened his hold, bringing her flush against him, burying his face in her glorious hair.

"I'm all right," she whispered in his ear, followed by more little kisses.

The only thing he could seem to get out in response was a groan. He held her to him with one arm and managed to open the door with the other hand. He barely took time to bump the door closed as he headed straight for their sleeping chamber, kissing her as he laid her down. He followed her down giving her the love that burned deep within him as he greedily savored having her in his arms.

CᴈᏰᎧ

Jorran lay awake with Leeza pressed to his side. Her head nestled on his shoulder. He didn't want to sleep. He didn't want to miss an instant of her with him. He wondered if he should take her and leave. They could go to his home where they could spend the remaining time alone, away from what was happening here. He just couldn't escape the feeling of danger and knew it was focused around Leeza.

The main problem was he didn't think he could get Leeza to leave. He knew she was driven to work on the translation, to make sure whatever happened, the engines were not started again. He understood her need but it didn't make it any easier for him. The last couple of days had been filled with such life and love that they were perfect.

He pulled up the image of her at their pond. He would always think of it as theirs. Leeza smiling, laughing, opening her arms to him. She came to him so open and loving. He'd never get enough of her if he had a hundred years. But they didn't. They wouldn't even have a hundred days. It ate at him. Chel couldn't tell them how long they had, but it was in the hours.

As much as he wanted to deny it, he saw the tiredness Leeza tried to hide. She not only slept more, but her eating swung from being like she was starving to not hardly able to eat at other times. That morning when she'd stood he'd seen her catch the wall until a wave of dizziness had passed.

Jorran wanted to force her to remain in their quarters, but he knew he couldn't. She was driven with the need to translate what she could. It gave her something to hold on to and he couldn't take that from her. He understood the need to fight. He would fight for her with every breath of his body. Jorran turned his head to brush his lips over her temple and was rewarded with her snuggling closer into him.

"My heart," he whispered the words, turning so he could cocoon her in his arms. He forced himself to relax and finally drifted off to sleep.

CR80

Leeza stared at the letters on the screen and everything blurred and waved. She blinked several times to clear her mind. It was getting harder to concentrate.

"Why don't we take a break?" Azas asked, stood, stretched, and then handed her a drink.

Leeza accepted it gratefully. The additives in the drink gave her a much needed boost. She knew the woman was watching out for her. Everyone had been. Five days had gone by since her fainting spell in the commons and though they were trying to keep it from being obvious, just as she tried to hide her weakness so they wouldn't worry, they watched her. The problem was, she was just so tired.

"If you want, we can call it a day," Azas suggested.

Leeza forced a smile. "I'm okay. I just need a moment."

"Sure. You know, this is really amazing. Now I see the patterns, they are starting to make some sense to me. I never would have guessed on my own."

"I have always been able to see and hear the patterns in the sounds. My father was the same way," Leeza said without thinking.

"He's no longer alive?" Azas asked.

Leeza realized no one had probed into her life but since she had brought it up the woman felt free to ask. She also realized the pain of loss was still there but it wasn't as bad, softened by the new friendships she was making and Jorran's love.

"No, he died in an accident." It was easier to accept that, though now she knew it was murder. My mother died when I was very young. There was only my father and me.

He was a linguist also, absorbed in his work. I learned from him. I have no family left now."

"Maybe you and Jorran will have a large family."

Leeza felt a pang of longing hit her. More than anything she would love to have Jorran's child. Funny, she had never really stopped to think of having a child before, maybe because she had never met a man that interested her. Now, she longed to feel life growing and moving in her, knowing that Jorran had placed it there, that it was part of him, of their love coming together. She choked down the sob that threatened to burst out and hurried to take a drink to cover it.

"Are you okay?" Azas knelt in front of her.

"Yes, swallowed wrong." She managed to get out.

The woman didn't look convinced. "Maybe I should get Jorran."

"No." Leeza reached out and caught her hand. "I'm okay. Don't worry him."

Azas eyed her, obviously trying to make up her mind if she should believe her, but before she could decide, their attention was called to the console by the pair recording there.

"I think it ended," Troth, a younger male student, said.

"What?" Azas straightened and went to the console.

Leeza took another drink and stood. The world shifted around her, but with will, she steadied herself and went to join them. They were right, the log had ended. She could make out enough to know they were signing off.

"What do we do now?" the other woman that had been working on the recording asked. "Is there more there, other stuff, and how do we bring it up?"

"I have no idea?" Azas answered and looked over. "Leeza?"

"I'll try to reach Jorran," the boy said.

Leeza was already focused on the symbols that had remained a constant at the top of the screen. She had always wondered about them but hadn't dared experiment until she got the original message translated. Now, that they'd recorded the entire message, she raised her hand selecting one of the little images, she pressed her finger to the symbol.

The screen changed and more writing came up. The recording was still going, so it followed her actions as she pressed another symbol. The screen changed again. Images of stars filled the screen. She pressed on the previous symbol, and it switched. She read enough to know that it was the same, before she moved to the star screen again then, on to a new one. Leeza heard running footsteps enter the room.

"What's she doing?" Vesar barked, and immediately quieted.

People clustered around her. Leeza felt a hand rest on her shoulder and knew it was Jorran. She moved back to the first screen then through the ones she'd already opened, giving enough time for the others to observe them before she moved on.

There was one screen that showed different locations on the ship, some with teams working. Another had more writing and diagrams. At the next one she opened, everyone drew in air. It was images, not of stars but people. Tall, dark haired, with beautiful, finely chiseled features.

She scrolled through several, male, female and some with children, families. The images made her chest tighten. Leeza had thought once before that Jorran could have been one of them, this proved it was so. There was a strong resemblance.

"Whoa, Jorran. Your ancestors. You never said," Azas teased, obviously noticing the same thing. "I wonder if this gives you claim to the ship?"

Vesar grunted in reply.

Leeza looked back over and found one of his ever present frowns on the man's face, but when he saw her looking it changed to a sneer. Leeza managed to ignore it and turned back to the screen. Pressing the next image, she brought up another screen. It was there she noticed the rows of symbols on the side changed each time. When she touched one of those, the screen changed again.

"It looks like we have a lot more recording to do," Esher said, as he leaned over Azas.

"Yes," Jorran agreed. "I think we are going to have to start a double team on recording, one early morning, the other later. I'll get a hold of Genis and see about another recorder and more storage memory. Let's start with the images next."

"What about diagrams?" Vesar objected. "Look at what we might learn."

Leeza figured Jorran was thinking what she was − what information the man could steal?

"We'll get to that. But the images will hopefully tell us more about their lives," Jorran countered smoothly.

Vesar looked like he wanted to argue but kept his mouth shut, where Norris would have blown up. It almost worried Leeza more that Vesar didn't react stronger, because looking at the man, she could practically see him planning something. She shuddered. She just didn't know what.

She glanced at Jorran, feeling a stab of fear for him. He must have picked up her tension because his eyes shifted to her, and he squeezed his hand down on her shoulder.

"Okay, we're done for the day," Jorran announced.

"The engine room. We still haven't gotten in," Vesar growled, his gaze going right to Leeza as if he knew it would bother her.

"It will wait." It was Jorran's turn to scowl.

When they got back to their quarters, Jorran insisted she rest while he contacted Genis to give a report and request the added supplies. Leeza fell asleep listening to the excitement in the men's voices.

C3&O

Jorran stood gazing down at his sleeping life-mate. Love swept over him so strong, he longed to pull her into his arms. He started to reach for her and froze. She needed rest. He'd seen it in her when he'd returned to the control room. Even with the excitement of the new discovery there was a weariness about her that couldn't be masked.

He was glad to see she'd been drinking the restorative drink Chel had prepared. They would have to stop by Chel's for an injection before they went to dinner. Leeza never complained, but his heart ached at the need.

Unable to stop himself, he lightly ran his knuckles across her cheek. Even with the barest touch he could feel the heat coming off her. She was running a slight fever again. He'd noticed it yesterday.

Tomorrow, he would insist she only spend half a day on the ship, the afternoon she would spend with Chel, resting. Leeza wouldn't be happy but maybe if he arranged for her to be able to go over the images they gathered in the morning, it would appease her. She could also continue her translating there under Chel's watchful eye.

At that thought, he found himself staring down into her captivating vivid green eyes. Love was evident in them as Leeza looked up at him. Even the sickness attacking her couldn't drain the vitality from those incredible eyes. A smile crested her lips, making his heart beat faster.

"Sorry, I didn't mean to wake you." The words rumbled from him.

"I'm not." Her words were soft and fluid. She lifted her arms and he slid into them.

Chapter Sixteen

Jorran looked at the scratches on the metal door and felt anger burn within him. He wanted to slam his fist into it but instead he pressed his hands to it and tried, with all his strength, to slide it open. Just like before, it refused to budge. Still, it was obvious someone had tried to force their way into the room.

He knew he shouldn't be surprised, that was why he checked it the first thing every day, before they started their investigation of the ship. The possibility that the engine room was behind that door was a strong pull to everyone because they all wanted to see it. That included him, but he had decided to leave it for last when he could concentrate fully on it, besides it gave him time to think how to handle details of the discovery.

Once in the room, it would be like walking a fine line of what to do with the discovery of advanced technology. Genis was already working with the governing council to have terms beyond existing regulations to protect whatever technology they found. That was another reason he was waiting. He wanted all the safeguards in place before they entered.

Running his finger over the gouges, his anger built to fury. Whoever had done this had to know he would notice, and he bet he knew who it was. Vesar. The man just didn't care because he figured he would have already gotten what he wanted, recording everything inside.

"Jorran," Rese called his name coming down the corridor. "Weren't we–," the young man trailed off as Jorran turned to him. "What's wrong?" He looked from Jorran to the door. A hiss escaped from him, and his own anger joined Jorran's. "Do you think they got in?"

"No," the words came out as a growl. "Not from lack of trying. Have you seen Vesar this morning?" He was thinking the man must have snuck in when Esher brought the early recording team in.

Rese wasn't at all surprised by the question but still his hands clenched. "Actually, yes. He was eating in the commons this morning when I went in. He was working on something over by storage when I came out."

Jorran understood the young man's reaction. Vesar never ate in the commons. He didn't like the coincidence behind it. "What about last night?"

"I don't know, but he left with us and you set the security shield."

"Where is he now?"

"By the storage hut. He was still finishing up on it when we headed to the ship. Said he'd join us shortly."

Jorran shoved his fingers through his hair. He didn't like it. It was out of character. Vesar was usually impatient to get on the ship each day. Jorran drew in a deep breath while he thought then let it out. "Okay, why don't you help me see if we can open this up?"

Jorran recorded the damages already done to the door while Rese retrieved the pry bar from his pack. They had never used the bar but always carried it in case of emergencies. Rese set the point at the edge of the door where the surface was already marred then both men put their weight on it. They groaned with exertion, but the door didn't move. After a second, they gave up.

"I don't think they made it in." Rese drew in a deep breath.

"Agreed." The knowledge didn't relieve his anxiety.

"Hey, what are you doing?" The voice of the man he was thinking about echoed down in sharp demand. "You said we weren't going to enter there until we finished the other exploration?"

Jorran turned to Vesar, barely locking his emotions down at seeing the man. "We aren't," he snapped. "We were just checking to make sure it was secure. It looks like someone's been trying to get in." He let the words hang as a challenge. When the man didn't react, he continued. "Where were you this morning?"

Open anger flashed over the man, but Jorran didn't care, he just waited.

"Had breakfast in the commons, then had to fix an attachment link on my belt." He reached down and shook the object around his waist as if proving it.

"What about last night?"

This time the man sneered along with his answer. "Spent the evening at Tash's. You can check if you don't believe me. Besides, I came out with you, and you secured the shield after us." He pointed out the same thing Rese did but this time a touch of something like glee slipped out.

Jorran knew the man's whereabouts would check out. He'd also bet the man knew about the attempt. So who was it? The thought hit him hard. None of his people would help Vesar, though Tranic controlled a lot of power. He needed to think. "Okay, we're done in here for the day."

"We just started." Vesar's expression dropped to one of fury.

"Someone tried to break in here. I need to report it and get a decision as to what the council wants to be done. This is a very high-profile excavation, if you didn't know. The significance of it is great and has to be handled with their guidance." Jorran pulled a justification he knew Vesar couldn't argue with.

Still, Vesar glared at him for several moments before he turned and stormed away.

"You really going to close down the ship?" Rese looked back at him after Vesar disappeared up the stairs.

Jorran nodded. "We'll keep the recording teams going, but I'm putting a guard on watch. Only those recording will be allowed on the ship today. Let's go."

◌◦

"Where's your life-mate?" There was no missing the accentuated disdain in 'life-mate'. It matched the rest of Vesar persona.

Leeza jerked, startled by the interruption. She was still annoyed about sleeping in and being left behind that morning. Jorran could have wakened her.

She didn't like seeing the man standing there, but was not about to be stressed out by him either. She met his irritated look with one of her own. "I believe since you should have been with him, you should know he is on the ship."

"He called a halt for the day and left before I could speak with him. I have some questions I want answered. Not that I expect him to listen to me, but Mr. Atrose wants the answer also." He glared down.

"Well, as you can see, Jorran has not returned yet." She motioned around Jorran's office, which she had appropriated so she wasn't in Chel's way. She'd hoped Vesar would take the hint and leave but there was no such luck.

He stood, looking down at her over the desk.

"What are you doing here?" His voice softened but it didn't fool Leeza, he just changed his tactics.

"Working," she answered in one word, shifting so her arm covered the screen.

He obviously didn't like her answer. "This is the site commander's office."

"And as you pointed out, he is my life-mate." This time she couldn't help but add sweetness to her tone to irritate him.

He scowled. "What are you working on?"

"Translating." She went back to a one word answer.

He leaned forward, and she resisted the urge to pull back. She didn't want him seeing the diagram and absolutely didn't want to tell him it had anything to do with the engines, even if it was on shutting them down.

After a minute, he pulled back slightly and spoke again, his voice low, which Leeza found more threatening.

"You have gotten quite good at our language, though you still use the translator." He nodded to the machine.

Leeza felt a second of panic and pushed it down. "I use the translator to look for word patterns. It catches possible root matches in other languages that I might miss." She tried to make her answer sound reasonable and keep the fear from overrunning her. She was not going to let the man panic her.

"People said you relied heavily on it when you first arrived here."

"It might have seemed so, but sometimes when I'm working on deciphering a new language, I get locked on it and have to think more when switching between languages." She tried to let the truth in the sentence overshadow the falsehood. She really did lock into a new language and had to think about switching. She was doing it now with Lannish, it was what her mind was thinking in.

"They said that you couldn't speak normal." He wasn't letting up on his challenge.

"I was exhausted and running translations in my mind. I was slipping into others while adapting the links. Is there anything else?"

"A check reveals no life info on you." He leaned forward over the desk. "Nothing at all."

"I have no answer for you on that. Now, Jorran is not here."

"There is no record on how you arrived here." He ignored her, placing his hands on the desk so he was now looming over her.

Leeza tried to calm the panic starting to rise in her. "You think I just walked out of the jungle?" The sarcasm she added came through, not that it did any good on Vesar.

"I don't believe that at all." He stared at her.

Leeza forced herself not to shift in her seat. "You want to believe that I came from the ship." She arched an eyebrow. "Which is even more unbelievable. You've seen the pictures yourself. You look closer than I do."

"Pictures, you conveniently brought up."

"The ship has been here for close to seven hundred years." She waved her hands accentuating the fact.

"Maybe."

"There is no maybe. If I came from the ship, how do you explain that there is only me? You've been all over the ship. I haven't, but from what I have seen, does it look like it has been sustaining life. That someone has been living in it recently?" She waited but there was no answer coming.

"Vesar?" His name cracked out in an angry snap from Jorran.

Leeza felt a flood of relief wash over her.

"What are you doing here?"

There was a tightening around Vesar's eyes before he turned to Jorran.

"I wanted to talk to you about closing off the ship. I talked to Atrose. He said if you are going to close off the ship, he is going to quit funding the expedition." The man went straight for his attack but Jorran showed no signs of concern.

"Work in the ship hasn't stopped. The recording teams are still active. I just pulled out the other teams until I complete my report of the incident on the ship and get the council's guidance. We do everything by the book here so we don't ruin the integrity of the excavation. I'm sure I don't need to remind you of the importance of this find. It will be investigated for the next century. There is no reason to go too fast and make a mistake now."

Leeza looked back and forth between the two men. Each stood rigid in challenge. It seemed a repetition of what went on with Norris, except something about Vesar scared her more. Norris was outright volatile. Tension boiled deep within Vesar. She wasn't sure what to do. Then suddenly, Vesar pulled back, nodded and strode from the room.

It took several seconds before she managed a swallow and looked back at Jorran. Corded muscles bunched on his arms and chest. His back was rigid. Heat burned in his eyes as he stared after where Vesar had disappeared.

When he turned back to her, his fury snapped out. "What are you doing here alone?" Immediately his countenance softened. "Sorry," he apologized before she could answer then took another steadying breath. "I didn't like finding him here with you. He's dangerous."

"I know, but I was expecting him to be with you. I was in Chel's way and came here to work. I figured it was okay."

He nodded, then as if he couldn't help himself, he came around the desk, pulled her up out of the chair and into his arms.

"I'm sorry, my heart. I worry about you. Especially with him around."

Leeza lifted her hands to frame his face. "I feel the same." She pressed her lips to his. The kiss ignited something in him. For a moment, she thought he would devour her right there. When he did get hold of himself and pull back, they were both breathing hard. Jorran raised one hand and ran his fingers over her cheek.

"My heart. How are you today?" He brushed a kiss on the end of her nose.

She smiled at his action. "I'm fine. I missed seeing you this morning." She arched an eyebrow at him but couldn't muster any of the annoyance she was feeling earlier about being left.

"I missed you, too, but you were sleeping so deep and peaceful, I couldn't wake you. You seemed to need the sleep." He kissed her again.

"I did," she conceded, finally admitting the truth to herself. "I slept very well and feel wonderful."

"Good enough to go on a picnic with me, since we will not be working on the ship this afternoon." He grinned.

Excitement burst through her. "Oh, yes. Then you did call a halt on the work?"

"Just the exploration, and only while I send a message to Genis, and he gets an answer from the council. Why don't you go see if you can get the food crew to fix us some lunch, while I get that done and we can go?"

"Okay." She stretched to brush a brief kiss over his lips then stepped away only to be pulled right back.

"Watch out for Vesar." He kissed her with barely controlled explosive passion then gave her a slight push down the hall.

Leeza's ears were still ringing from the aftereffects of the kiss when she stepped outside. One of the daily rains had ended not long before, leaving the ground wet, and the air refreshed but still muggy.

Leeza drew in a deep breath that didn't do much to calm her heart. She liked the way Jorran kissed, the way he made her feel. She headed for the commons, but only made it about halfway there when the tingling running over her body changed to one of alarm.

She froze and looked around. No one seemed to be paying any particular attention to her, but she could almost feel eyes on her. After a moment, she brushed the thought away. She was just reacting to Jorran's concern about

Vesar. Still, she sighed in relief when she stepped into the shelter of the commons.

ϑ

Jorran watched Leeza go, wanting to pull her back, wrap her in his arms where he knew she would be safe, but he didn't want her to hear his discussion with Genis. Sitting at his console, it was only a few seconds before Genis's image filled the screen.

"We have trouble," Jorran said without preamble.

The man's jovial expression turned serious. "What's wrong?"

"Someone tried to break into the engine room."

"Tried? Didn't get in?"

"No. The door's holding secure."

Genis looked thoughtful. "Tranic's pressing for you to get in there. Atrose has been to the council twice but not for the last couple days that I've heard." He didn't need to add he would have heard if he had. "He contacted me directly already today."

That surprised Jorran. He let it run through his mind, finding it interesting. "Maybe he got word whoever tried to get in couldn't," Jorran let the thought come out.

"So they called him to put more pressure on us?"

"I'd say a strong possibility."

"Have you made any headway?" Genis asked.

"Actually, I found what I think is the control panel."

"Can you open it then?" Genis's excitement showed through on the screen.

"I haven't tried. I want Leeza to look at it first, see if she can decipher any of it."

"When?"

Jorran felt his stomach muscles tighten. He knew it would upset her and understood why. "I need to break it to her."

"Today," Genis pressed.

Jorran sighed. He knew he needed to do it and had put it off as long as he could. "All right, I'll do it today and have her look at it tomorrow."

"Can you change that to this afternoon?" Genis leaned closer to the screen like he was trying to come through it.

Jorran hesitated. "We'll see. Do you want to be on hand?"

Longing flashed on the man's face. "I might see what I can arrange but don't wait for me. If I can, I will be there by mid-day."

"I'll need at least that long. It won't be easy for Leeza."

"How is she doing?"

Genis was the one person Jorran had told the full story. Genis was working discreetly with a trusted member of the council to get her papers and keep her from becoming a test subject. The woman was understanding about their dilemma, but was dying to meet Leeza as soon as possible.

"She is actually doing better than Chel feared. Chel's continuing to keep a close eye on her. For a while, I could see her failing quite rapidly." The knowledge ate at him. "But it seems she's been doing better the last couple days, though she's extremely tried and a touch nauseated. I don't know, maybe she's hiding it better from me or it's my own wishful thinking." He broke off, not able to continue.

After a moment of silence, Genis spoke again. "I will be there this afternoon to go in the control room with you and meet your life-mate." With that he closed off.

Jorran stared at the blank screen a moment before he pushed back and stood. Not able to contemplate the thought of losing Leeza any longer, he went to find her.

⋙⋘

A group of botanists were working not far from the pond when Jorran and Leeza arrived. After talking a few minutes, the group dismissed themselves to return to camp.

"I understand they have plenty back at the compound to work on, but that was nice of them," Leeza commented after they left.

"Yes," Jorran agreed as he slid his arms around her from behind, pulling her back into him. "Would you like to start with a swim?" he said, against her neck. The next couple hours passed quickly. They ate then both napped, cuddled in each other's arms.

Jorran came awake to a feeling of being utterly content. One of Leeza's small hands rested in the center of his chest. Every once in a while, her hand would make a little caress as if even in sleep, she savored the feel of him. He knew the feeling. He would never get enough of her and her soft touches on his skin. He closed his eyes letting the moment soak into his memory for the days when he had only those to hold.

Involuntarily, his muscles tensed, and her movements increased, trying to calm him. He forced himself to relax. She stilled, then after a second, shifted in his arms. He felt the feathery brush of her lips on his chest and couldn't keep from sucking in a breath, which rewarded him with another kiss. He buried his hands in her hair and tipped her head up to meet his gaze as he rose over her.

Her eyes were open, still looking a touch sleepy, but her smile was radiant. He lowered his head and kissed her. "I'm sorry I woke you," he said when he pulled back.

"I'm not." She raised the hand from his chest to caress his cheek in the same loving motion, before sliding her fingers back into his hair. Pulling him back down as she whispered, "You didn't wake me this morning, you owe me."

♋

Later, after another swim they ate the remainder of the food. Leeza was so in tune with Jorran she knew the instant the tension that had been plaguing him on the way to the pool returned. She laid her hand over his. Automatically, his fingers interlocked with hers.

"What's wrong?" she probed gently.

He didn't try to deny anything but took a moment before he looked to her. He sighed heavily. "I found a panel that I think will open the door to the engine room."

She couldn't help it, she sucked in a breath.

"I would like you to look at it and decipher what it says before I try to open it."

Ringing rose in her ears, cutting out his voice.

"Leeza."

He called her name but it sounded like it was from a long way off. Engine and open, were the only words she could seem to concentrate on. And with every beat of her heart, they pounded in her head.

Destruction to all. The words burst through her mind, wiping away her ability to breathe. Her stomach muscles tightened. The ringing in her head crescendo. She knew she was going to be sick as visions of long dead friends flashed through her head.

She pulled away and made it off the blanket they'd been sitting on before she was ill. Jorran was with her, holding back her hair. Her head had cleared when her stomach finally settled. "So much for lunch." She looked up and gave him a weak smile.

"I'm sorry. I should have waited to tell you." He helped her back to the blanket and started to pack their stuff up. "I'll get you to Chel." He didn't look at her.

"That is not necessary. Jorran." She laid a hand on his arm when he didn't look at her.

Slowly he turned. Pain filled his eyes.

"I am all right," she said firmly. "I–"

He cut her off. "I understand. I've been putting off asking you, but I'd feel better if I knew what it said before I tried. Genis is coming in this afternoon to go in with us."

Leeza felt her stomach muscles clench again and took a quick steadying breath.

"We are not going to try to start the engines, ever." Jorran rushed to get the words out, reaching for her. "The council already decreed it's too dangerous."

"But it is too important of a discovery to ignore." She finished for him, understanding.

She had worked on several explorations in her past. Funny, she hadn't thought about it, but as far as she knew, the people in her time had not even found the engine room. They had been too excited about activating the systems they found on the ship, which included the main power source, which was, the engines. So foolish, she shook her head. "We should get back so I can get ready to meet Genis."

Leeza pasted a smile on her face, though she knew it probably was as weak as she felt. Jorran helped her stand, not commenting on her need to steady herself against him. He folded the blanket and stuffed it in the pack with their other things, then wrapped his arm around her. Keeping their pace slow, Leeza leaned into him, absorbing his strength and comfort as much as using him for balance.

A shuttle already rested at the far end of the clearing. There was no need to go looking for the man that arrived on it as he was talking with a group in the quad. When Genis saw them, he excused himself and headed their way, bypassing Jorran to greet her.

"Leeza Jaeff. It is an honor." He stretched out both his hands, taking hers and bowing over them. "I should correct myself. Leeza Carrell."

Leeza bowed back. "I do not know how to address you."

"It is Director Pravail, but I think you can just use Genis."

"An honor. You are here to go on the ship?" She felt her stomach muscles clench again.

"Yes. Jorran has told you?"

"Yes." Leeza said through the tightness that moved up in her throat.

"Can we go now? I'm most excited."

"Leeza needs a rest first." Jorran cut him off, edging closer to her.

"I will be all right." Leeza looked up to find him already shaking his head at her.

"Rest first. We can go after we eat."

"That would be fine." Genis accepted readily, bringing relief to Leeza.

She honestly could use time to fortify herself both physically and emotionally. "Thank you. I actually would like to lie down."

"I'll walk her in then be right back."

This time, Leeza stopped him. "That's not necessary. I can make it myself."

"I'll walk her." Chel stepped up beside the trio, sliding her arm around Leeza and turning her before anything else could be said. They were out of hearing range when Chel spoke again. "So you were sick."

Leeza nodded. "I was doing fine until Jorran told me about opening the engine room. That is what they are planning on doing." She glanced at Chel. It was the medic's turn to nod. "I started to get upset, and I got sick."

"Well, we'll have you rest and eat then I'll give you a boost before we go to the ship."

"We?" She looked at Chel in surprise. She'd never known Chel to go.

"Yes. I want to be there to monitor stress levels on you."

Leeza wondered if she was also going in case anything happened.

"I also will check safety levels," the woman answered her unspoken question as they reached the door.

Leeza opened it and after a moment of silence said, "I napped by the pond."

"Good, still see if you can rest."

೦೪೦

Jorran spent a while with Genis going over with the director all that was happening. They were finishing up when Genis handed him a sealed folder. "Here."

Jorran arched his brow and opened it as he asked, "What's this?"

"Documentation for Leeza. It is under the name of Leeza Carrell, as you are already life-mates. It made it easier to put through as a name change because of bonding.

Jorran was astounded. "How?"

"It was felt by those I brought in on it that it was wiser to – expedite it, especially with Atrose prying about her. She's protected now. But, those of the council that know of her, wish to speak with her at the first possible opportunity."

He held up a hand forestalling Jorran from any reaction. "They assured she will not be made into a specimen but, as you yourself know, there is a lot we can learn about history from her, especially knowledge of before The Great Deluge. Now, it is time to eat. Why do you not go get your beautiful life-mate?"

Chapter Seventeen

Leeza stood in front of the hidden panel Jorran had found and her heart pounded. Her fingers trembled slightly as she reached out. She hoped the screen wouldn't respond, but it started to glow the instant she touched it.

Someone gasped in excitement behind her. She wished she could feel that way but her dread was too strong. She closed her eyes to steady herself then opened them. Studying the words, only about half of them were recognizable to her right off. Still, she had no trouble understanding. It was basically locked or unlocked.

"Leeza?" Jorran said over her shoulder, after she'd stared at it for a moment.

"You are right. It is to the power generator and drives, as well as the engine room. There is no request for a code or combination. I can open it."

To unlock was a series of three steps. She pushed one then the next, confirming the first request. She hesitated. "I don't know if there is enough power to activate the door."

She felt Jorran's hand rest on her waist.

"It's all right," Genis said. "Just try it." There was anticipation in his voice.

She glanced back at the people behind her. Besides Jorran, Genis and Chel, there were Esher, Rese, and Catlin, who was another older professor who was over the team working on the outside of the ship, and Vesar. All but Vesar and Jorran stared at the door.

Vesar watched her, and she knew he was trying to see what she was doing. Jorran placed his body in the man's line of sight, and as Vesar shifted, so did Jorran so Vesar couldn't see. With Jorran blocking the way, she touched the last button.

After a second, the door sluggishly slid back into the wall.

"Wow!" Rese exclaimed, startling her.

She looked into the room. Interest pushed her fear back. She'd never guessed it would've been so huge. An array of pipes, some bigger around than she was, stretched and curved to the ceiling at least two stories up from a massive maze of machinery a story below them. Metal walkways with stairs and ladders running between them, spanned the area to give access. Her gasp joined several others.

Unconsciously, she moved forward with the group.

"Wait until I finish the scan!" Chel's warning stopped them. They shifted trying to see through the room as they waited anxiously.

"We look good. No unsafe levels detected," Chel said after a minute.

"All right," Jorran spoke up, taking the lead, as always, even though Genis was there. "Recorders on, we stay together in one group. Everyone behind me, space out a little, but still together." Jorran looked directly at Vesar. "I'll go first to check the stability of the walkways. We'll do an initial loop around on this level then a sweep below."

Leeza's fear took another jump at Jorran's first step on the walkway, but there was no need to worry. The structure was completely sound. She didn't hear even a groan with the weight of the whole group on it. Leeza stayed next to Chel, holding one of Chel's scanners while Chel carried the other but kept an eye on both. They were directly behind Esher and Genis, who followed Jorran.

Leeza wanted to go to him, but his attention was fixed on the room around them. She could understand it was fascinating, though she knew nothing about machines or engineering. It all seemed amazing that what was around her could have propelled the craft through space.

She almost stumbled. She hadn't thought much about it, but what they were in, had actually traveled in space. If she was translating right, which she was sure she was, this ship had come from another planet, brought people here that stayed and integrated with existing inhabitants.

She looked ahead to Jorran. Was he one of their descendants? He definitely had the look from the images, though it was so long ago most of the people probably had some of the ship's occupant's blood. Looking around the group, she was the oddity with her pure Athurian looks. Norris's, and now Vesar's hang up on her being from the ship fit, if you looked at it like that.

The thought of the man had her glancing over her shoulder. She stumbled again as she met his gaze staring back at her. He didn't flinch at being caught and continued to stare at her with cold, calculating eyes. This time Leeza refused to turn away.

It was Vesar who finally broke contact. He raised his recorder, focusing on the big engines below them. His lips crested in a sneer that made her shiver.

For comfort, she turned to watch Jorran, though she was continually aware of Vesar. He'd linger in an area, dividing his time between watching her and studying the ship until Rese, who was bringing up the rear, commented to get him to move forward.

ଓଃଡ

Jorran completed the full circle and waited at the stairs for the others to reach him. Leeza stepped to his side. He caught her hand. Her fingers were chilled but she showed no signs of the panic that he'd detected in her earlier. Still, she pressed against him.

The temptation to pull her into his arms was strong but he held off. His concentration had to be on the room. It was fascinating. Engineering wasn't his field but he could admire what it took to develop something like it. It was amazing. He knew, once it was opened, the scientists would be studying it for years.

He pushed down his intrigue and glanced at his life-mate. She was stiff, staring behind him. He looked back and saw Vesar watching her so intently that for a moment the man didn't notice him. When he did, he just looked away.

"Let's go down." Jorran forced the words out. Keeping Leeza's hand firmly in his, he drew her with him down the stairs. Panning his recorder to the side as he descended, he caught sight of an object that made his heart jump. One wall was a whole panel of dials and gauges. Several feet in front of it centered in the area, was a console much like the one up in the command room. The computer screen was dark on this one.

"Do you think you can activate it?" Genis asked hopefully, as he stepped off the last rung.

Jorran saw her swallow and cut her off as she reached out her hand. "I'll do it."

"It's okay," Leeza said. "I probably know the console better."

"Wait." Chel halted her. "Let me do a scan first." After a minute she said, "It looks clear. Not even any signs of energy."

Leeza's hand was only a centimeter from the console when a voice stopped her action.

"Why is she doing it? She doesn't belong here." Vesar looked challengingly at Jorran. "Isn't that what you're saying?"

"I suppose you want to do it?" Jorran asked.

In way of answer, Vesar pressed his hand against the screen.

Jorran wished it would have shocked him but instead like the other, a faint glow filled the screen then words and small images.

"Leeza?" This time Jorran said her name, edging Vesar aside with his body so she could get close. "Can you figure out what it says?"

There were so many different things. "It will take some time to go over it all."

"What can you tell me now?" He pressed his hand to her back, giving her support.

"Everything is inactive," she said after a minute.

"We knew that," Vesar muttered sarcastically.

Leeza glared at him instead of showing signs of fear. "The instruments are not registering anything. Total shutdown to what they monitor."

"So activating the console did not activate any engine systems." For the first time that day, Jorran caught her pause and looked at the translator attached to her waist. She used it so seldom now, he almost forgot about it. It amazed him that just over three weeks ago she'd started learning his language.

"No. No systems were activated." Leeza didn't try to keep the relief from her voice.

He nodded. "Okay, one quick pass through then we're done here for the night."

Quick was a relative term when there was so much to see. Jorran, along with Rese, kept an eye on Vesar, who tried to hang back and stopped several times. Jorran had to caution him continually not to touch anything. Jorran was relieved when they made it all around the main corridor back to where they started.

"Let's go." Jorran motioned everyone up the stairs before him and Leeza. Out in the hallway, he turned back to her. "Will you close it, please?"

"What?" Vesar snapped.

"It needs to be closed up until a team of qualified engineers can be brought in to look at it. We have sufficient recordings for now. This is beyond the archeological field."

"Absolutely right," Genis added, backing him up. "If you would." He motioned to Leeza. She stepped to the panel and again Jorran positioned himself between her and the others so only he could see what she did. It only took a brush of her fingertip and the door slid closed. Two more and she stepped back so he knew it was locked.

He could almost feel the tension leave her body. He wondered if he hadn't been watching her so closely if he would have picked up her slight stagger. It must have been visible to Chel, because she sidled up on Leeza's other side, taking her arm.

"I think it is time we all return to the complex. You can fill out your reports and observations then get some sleep. We can go over everything in detail tomorrow." The medic's authoritative tone was so heavy it left no option for objection.

Not that Jorran planned on anything different because Leeza needed her rest. She'd held her stress in but it had taken a visible toll on her.

"You're right." Jorran slid one arm around Leeza while motioning down the hall to the others. "Rese will you help me set the recorders to download the data when we get back. I would like fully written observations to add to the data, and we'll go over it tomorrow."

cs80

Leeza woke the next morning with Jorran stroking her cheek. He smiled and kissed her. "Wake up, my heart," he said when she sighed and closed her eyes, basking in the feel of him beside her.

She breathed in. Jorran filled her senses. "I like this." She practically hummed the words.

"As do I. Unfortunately, we must meet Genis for a late morning meal before he leaves." His lips caressed her cheek.

She sighed again, then the words he said sank in. She opened her eyes and looked at him. "Late morning?"

"Yes. We have already finished our other meetings."

It was then she realized he was dressed and looked at the time. The morning was mostly gone. "I can't believe I slept so long." She sat up.

"Yesterday was a highly emotional strain for you." He stood and helped her up.

She went from feeling fine to the room spinning around her and nauseated in an instant. When it passed, she found herself pressed against Jorran's body, and he was talking softly to her.

"Jorran, I'm all right," she whispered back. "I just stood too fast."

He loosened his hold, easing back to look down at her as if to satisfy himself of her condition.

"I'll get ready to go." She stretched up and kissed him. She pulled back, and he released her, but she was conscious of his attention until she shut the door to the changing room. Looking at her reflection, she found it pale even for her. Feeling sick, she lowered her head to her hands resting on the counter.

After a moment, the feeling passed, and she quickly cleaned up and dressed. When she opened the door, Jorran was waiting for her. He reached for her hand drawing her into him. His need to hold her came through without a word.

Leeza ran her hands up and down his back to give him comfort. The thought of losing Jorran was more painful than the thought of dying. "I love you." She ran her fingers up into his hair, leaned back and tilted his head down to meet her kiss. Need exploded between them, and for a long moment, they gave over to it before Jorran finally pulled back resting his forehead against hers.

"We need to meet Genis." Regret then promise blazed in his eyes. He didn't say anything else just took her hand and led her out.

Instead of going to the commons, they went to Chel's chambers. Food was waiting for them on the table. Genis was conversing amicably with Chel when they entered.

"How are you?" Chel asked immediately on seeing her.

Leeza didn't want to admit she felt shaky in front of Genis, though, she figured he'd been told of her condition. "Fine," she said quietly.

Chel cocked an eyebrow. "Let's eat."

After the first few bites, the food helped steady her.

Genis took up the conversation. "I hope you don't mind, but I asked Jorran for this opportunity to ask you some questions. You must understand how extraordinary your situation is?"

He leaned forward over the table. "If there are answers you feel like not giving, you may feel free to tell me. I'm afraid Jorran has not given me many details, and I tend to be pushy. Before I went into administrative, I greatly enjoyed my time in the field."

"I will try to answer all your questions."

"Jorran gave me the time you lived. So many things have changed since then. Can you tell me what this region was like?"

"Around the ship was a dessert, though I know," she typed something in the translator, "geologists said it wasn't always so. They figured just a couple hundred years before it was a fertile region but something caused a shift in it."

"Maybe when the ship crashed," Genis said aloud what she'd been wondering. "So if it was a desert, how was the ship found?"

"Quite by accident, as I understand. The ship was totally buried but there was an odd distortion in the sand that was noticed by someone passing over, and it was investigated. They didn't know it was a ship. They thought it was a city left by an ancient, advanced civilization. I'm afraid there were people in the group hungrier for the technology then they were for finding answers. They were already trying to activate systems before I got here."

"So you came here as a linguist?"

"Yes, to try to translate the writing they found. It was supposed to have been my father." She swallowed hard as the pain surfaced. "But he was killed." She felt Jorran's hand close over hers.

"How long had you been working on the translation?" Jorran asked.

Leeza realized Jorran hadn't probed much into her past and now he was as curious as Genis. "Not long, only a couple months. I had just made a breakthrough in deciphering, and had figured out it was a ship, but I didn't have time to report what I found or the warning about the engines. Zareck, who was a powerful man in my time, wanted the technology. He caught me on the ship and locked me away so I couldn't stop the startup of the engines. He planned for me to die, instead ..." She couldn't go on.

"Instead, when they started the engines, everyone else did." Jorran finished for her.

She nodded.

"Most fascinating. I want to thank you for staying and helping. I know you are not feeling well, and want you to know we have some of our best medics looking at how to help you. We will do all we can."

"Thank you." Leeza choked up at the sincerity in his tone. She wanted to hope they could find something in time.

"You're welcome. I am afraid I must leave. I have so much more I'd love to ask you, but it will have to wait. Maybe we can talk over the communications link." Genis stood, taking her hand. He bowed over it then said his farewell and left.

Leeza didn't even see the hypodermic in Chel's hand until she felt the prick on her arm. "Just your booster for the day," Chel said when she jumped. "I would suggest you take it easy today." Chel looked to Jorran. "What do you have planned?"

"Going over the recordings and writing up observations and recollections."

"So not going back in?"

"In the engine room, not for a couple days, then it will just be me and Leeza. I have the recording teams continuing double shifts, and we have exploration teams logging other areas." Jorran drew Leeza out the door, "If you'll excuse us, we left something uncompleted when we came over here."

挃指

Three days later, Leeza was working on translation with Azar in her and Jorran's chambers when Troth, one of the younger team members, tapped on the door.

"Leeza, Jorran wants you to meet him at the ship."

The surprise Leeza felt turned to tension when she realized it meant Jorran wanted to go back into the engine room. Several times they talked about him wanting to investigate without anyone else around. "Now?" She looked at the time. She was surprised. As late as it was the work would be ending for the day, but that made sense if Jorran wanted to be alone.

"I guess. I was just given the message."

She nodded. "Thank you." Her legs didn't feel very steady when she stood.

"Azas, do you want to join me to go eat?" Troth looked hopeful.

Leeza caught the light of pleasure in the woman's eyes, but Azas looked at her. "Do you want me to walk with you?"

Leeza was warmed by her concern. "I'm fine. If you'll close off that," she motioned to the computer, "I'd appreciate it."

"Sure, I'll see you later."

Normal for late afternoon, when it wasn't raining, there were more people in the quad as teams finished their work and congregated to visit. Several people waved to her, and she returned the motion. It felt good. She knew everyone by name now. She really felt like she belonged. Belonged here more than she did in her own time, the thought hit her.

She walked down the jungle path taking in the beauty of it. One of the many colorful birds took flight catching her attention. It really was amazing that in her time this had been a desert.

She went quickly through the ready hut, not stopping to get anything because she knew Jorran would already have what he wanted. When she came around the bend to the entry, there was no one in sight, which was odd because Jorran usually had someone assigned to watch the site when the security pillars were not activated.

Tendrils of unease hit Leeza. She stopped, looking around. Fear spiked in her. She tried to tell herself that it was foolish.

"Jorran." Her voice shook.

"Afraid not." Vesar stepped out from the foliage.

Chapter Eighteen

Leeza spun around to run and smacked into the hard, muscled body of Norris. One huge hand clamped on her arm, the other over her mouth cutting off her scream before it could make it out.

"She's alone," Norris said over her to Vesar. "Have any trouble?"

"The old fellow had no idea what hit him," Vesar snickered. "He won't be causing us trouble even if he wakes up."

Leeza's fear blossomed as she thought they were talking about Jorran. Vesar moved to the side, and she caught sight of Esher tied up on the ground, barely visible under a massive fern.

Leeza struggled to break free to help Esher, but Norris just jerked her around, giving her a rough shake that made her vision blur.

"Don't hurt her. We need her," Vesar ordered.

"Let's get going then before her life-mate gets here," Norris growled back as he dragged her into the ship.

"Thought you wanted to get your hands on him?" Vesar said.

Leeza didn't have to see the man to know he was sneering.

"I do." Norris snapped. "And when I do, he won't have any life left."

Panic speared Leeza to action. She dug her feet in and tried to throw herself back into Norris. More by accident than plan the back of her head connected with his nose. The man howled and released her. Freed, Leeza fell but was right back on her feet and running. She heard what she figured was a curse then Norris roared, "Broke my nose again."

The sound of heavy footfalls filled the corridor behind her. Once more, she was being chased through the ship but this time she knew it better. Unfortunately, they were too close for her to hide.

She tried to put on more speed. Leeza bypassed the control room taking the hall to the stairs without slowing. She took the steps on a run. She wasn't off the bottom step before she felt one of the men on the top. She didn't look back to see which one, she knew they both were there.

Farther back, she heard wheezing, and the curse, so she knew it must be Vesar directly behind her, and he was gaining. She tried for more speed but her body didn't have anything more to give. At the next corner, she slipped, sliding into the wall, hitting hard.

Vesar reached for her. Leeza kicked out. He caught her foot before it could make contact. His other hand locked the front of her shirt, hauling her up. She struck out, but he knocked her arm away easily, grabbing it to get control of her just as Norris came barreling around the corner and ran right into them.

Vesar lost his grip on her as he tried to keep from going down. Released, Leeza stumbled back, almost going down herself, but kept her footing. Turning with the momentum, she was running again.

She reached the next intersection before she heard them after her once more, and turned down the hallway. She had no idea where she was, she just wanted to get away. Catching a glimpse of an opening in the ceiling, she ran for it hardly slowing before she grabbed the rung and started to climb. It was her chance to make it out.

In her haste, she almost slipped off, sheer desperation kept her on and climbing. Making it through the opening, she sagged onto the floor, chest heaving. She fought to be still as she heard the sound of footsteps enter the hallway below her. The pounding kept coming. Leeza pressed her hand over her mouth to hold any sound from making it out. The first set of footsteps went past. She waited for the next.

"Hey, down there." Norris's sounded right below her.

There was a dull clunk of boots on a rung, but she couldn't tell if he was going up or down. There were two more of the thuds and her hopes started to rise when Norris's head popped up through the hole. Leeza screamed. The orange glow glistened off the blood still flowing from his swollen nose to make it look like he was wearing a grotesque mask.

Leeza screamed again as his hand reached out for her. She kicked out, this time aiming for his nose.

He caught her ankle in a crushing grip, pulling her toward the opening. "Not this time," he growled. "You're going to pay for that."

Terror overtook her. She kicked with the other foot, not aiming, just trying to get free.

With one hand on her ankle and the other on the rung, Norris had no way to defend himself. Her first strike hit his shoulder. The next caught him in the side of the head as he turned his face to the side at the last second. He cursed as Leeza kicked out again. He tried to duck and lost his grip on her ankle. He disappeared through the hole.

Leeza stumbled her way to her feet, not looking to see if he fell. Her ankle protested with pain as her weight came down on it, but she ignored it. Catching the edge of the next corner, she swung around it right into the taller, muscled wall of Vesar.

Brutally powerful arms locked around her before she even had a chance to fight. Leeza tried ramming her head into him as she did with Norris but this time it didn't work as her head only reached the top his chest.

He shoved her back, releasing one arm. Before she could try to pull away, his palm stuck her cheek hard enough that everything went hazy. Her ears rang. She was aware of him hauling her off the floor and being slung partially over his shoulder.

Her mind registered them going around the corner then down the stairs. Through the fog that wanted to sweep over her, she heard Norris's voice grumble something, but couldn't focus enough on it to understand. Everything slipped into a blur as they continued down the stairs and corridors to the depths of the ship.

They stopped. Vesar dropped her feet to the floor and pushed her face against the wall. The world cleared enough for her to realize she was staring at the access panel to get into the engine room.

"Open it." The order was growled into her ear.

Leeza shook her head, setting off the ringing in her ears again. "No."

A hand burrowed into her hair at the base of her neck, clamping on, yanking her head back.

"Open it." Hot breath swept over her face.

Leeza tried to turn from it but couldn't.

"Open it." Vesar jerked her head back farther.

Leeza cried out. Tears flooded into her eyes. "No."

"Maybe this will change your mind." He forced her head around.

She saw Norris coming down the hall toward them. She had to blink to see what he carried over his shoulder. Esher came into view.

"Looks like we are going to need him." Vesar's voice rumbled behind her.

Norris just grunted, dropped Esher to the floor, and kicked him.

CB&O

Jorran finished his report to Genis, anxious to be done so he could see Leeza.

"In a hurry?" The man arched an eyebrow and smiled.

"I thought I'd take Leeza to the pool and have dinner there tonight. It's her favorite place."

"I talked to Chel. She said Leeza is still doing well. Much better than she figured."

Jorran nodded, pain still hit him. "She plans on running another series of tests tomorrow." Jorran wasn't sure if he wanted to know. Leeza seemed so alive when she lay in his arms. He was just thankful for every moment he got with her.

"Let me know what Chel finds out. Enjoy your evening."

Jorran nodded again, disconnecting, the need to go find his Leeza was stronger than ever.

When he entered their chambers, he was surprised not to find her there. He headed for Chel's, and once again found the place empty. Jorran broke into a jog on the way to the commons, stopping just inside the door to scan the room for her. She wasn't there but both Chel and Azas were. He reached Chel first.

"Have you seen Leeza?" he asked without greeting. Unexplainable tension rose in his body.

"Not since this morning."

Jorran was already turning to the next table where Azas sat before Chel finished the answer.

"Azas, do you know where Leeza is?"

The woman looked surprised then concerned. "She went to meet you."

"Meet me, where?"

"The ship. She left immediately after she got your message."

"What message?"

"That you wanted her to meet you." Azas glanced at the man sitting next to her.

Troth spoke up, "Vesar said he wasn't coming directly back and asked me to deliver a message, that you wanted her to meet you at the entry to the ship."

Jorran went cold inside.

"You didn't send the message?" Chel asked over his shoulder.

He shook his head and turned, dodging around tables and people. He was at a run by the time he burst out of the entry. Picking up speed, he crossed the yard and headed down the jungle path. Behind him, he heard the compound alarm ring, but ignored it as the thought that Vesar had lured Leeza to the ship burned in his mind.

There was only one reason for it. He wanted her to open the engine room for him. He would use any means to do it, including force. There was no way around it because Leeza would never open it willingly. He couldn't imagine that Vesar thought that she would, then again Vesar wouldn't care.

On a full out sprint Jorran burst through the ready hut, and out the other side. He came to a halt before the final bend to the ship. Cautiously, looking around the foliage, he found the way was clear. There were no signs of anyone. Fear had him wanting to rush forward, but common sense held him in check.

He eased up to the opening then looked around the area behind him before entering. The corridor was clear. Moving stealthily down the hall, he checked each room as he passed. When no one was in the control room, it reinforced that they had to be in the engine room. Jorran went right to the stairs, taking the most direct course below.

CB&O

"No," Leeza cried as Norris kicked Esher a second time. This time the man moved slightly.

"Open it, or we'll kill him."

Tears streamed down her face. She couldn't do it. She couldn't open the doors. She looked down at Esher. Bile rose in her. "You can't," she whispered out.

In the way of answer, Norris grabbed a fist full of Esher's hair. Esher stirred and groaned as Norris hauled him up. Then, to Leeza horror, Norris pulled a knife and laid it on the side of the semi-conscious man's face. "Where shall I start?"

"Please? You don't know what you're do–" Leeza's plea ended up in a whimper as a tickle of blood appeared on Esher's cheek as Norris pressed down on the knife. "No," Leeza cried again.

"Open it then." Vesar caught her wrist, raising her hand to the panel.

Leeza shuddered. She couldn't let them into the engine room, but she couldn't let them torture and kill Esher either. She wanted Jorran. His name gave her the only hope she could hold on to. He would come looking for her. She just had to give him time to find her.

"Now," Vesar ordered, and she flinched. "Norris–"

"No!" Leeza cut him off. Swiping at the tears on her face, she placed her trembled fingers over the panel, bringing it to life. She kept her motions slow and hidden, wishing there was a way to eat up more time. Was Jorran even looking for her yet? The question ate at her as she touched the next place. The hand at the back of her neck tightened as she hesitated.

Another groan of pain came from Esher prompting her to press the last spot. The door slid open, the motion smoother than the first time.

"Let's go." Vesar pulled her away from the wall, forcing her through the opening. Norris followed them dragging Esher with him. Once over the threshold, Vesar turned her to the wall where another panel was clearly visible. "Close it," he barked, making her jump and startling her back to the reality that neither her, nor Esher were going to make it off the ship alive.

This time Leeza didn't hesitate. Stepping in front of the panel, she quickly ran her fingers over it. The door whooshed closed, cutting off the world and all aid. She was trapped again on the ship, but this time, those who would do harm were just as trapped as she was.

Leeza wasn't surprise when Vesar gripped her arm and propelled her to the metal stairs. Norris was right behind them dragging Esher. More groans came from the older archeologist. When Leeza glanced back, she saw he was fully conscious. Blood was smeared over the side of his face and down his neck. Pain showed on his face.

"I'm sorry," Leeza said looking at him.

Esher nodded back.

Looking in his eyes, she knew he understood what she was saying. No matter what, she wasn't going to help them. That meant they were going to die. Pain of her own hit her. She wasn't ready to leave Jorran yet. She wanted more time. Wanted to tell him she loved him, just once more. She pushed it back. Whatever happened, Jorran would be safe. His world would be safe. She would make it so with the last breath she took.

"I want to see how the machines work. Activate it," Vesar demanded.

"I cannot," she said firmly.

"Don't tell me that. You did it the other day."

"You do not understand. You do not know what you are trying to use here." She tried to explain.

"Activate it," he repeated.

"The engines are damaged. It happened when the ship crashed."

"She's lying," Norris snapped.

"I am not. You cannot mess with the systems on the ship. If the engines were to start, they would cause great devastation. That is what the first message is – a warning about the engines bringing destruction."

"You want to see the old man suffer?" Norris reached for Esher.

Leeza rushed at Norris, throwing herself at him. She pounded his head with her fist.

He shoved her away.

Leeza hit the wall and dropped on the floor, stunned. Her mind cleared as she looked up and saw Vesar place his hand on the screen. "No!" she cried out as the computer came to life.

He turned to her and glared. "I'd say it works just fine."

She started to shake her head. "The computer, yes. But the engines are damaged. That is why the people remained here on this planet. They had no choice."

Norris reached down to haul her up. "She lies. She's from their ship. One of them," he spat.

Leeza tried to pull back but couldn't. "No. You want the truth? I was on the ship. It was found four hundred years ago. I was trying to translate the language. But, there was a man like you. He locked me away, and they started the ship. It caused The Great Deluge. The one in your history."

"You expect us to believe that?" Norris snapped out again.

But Vesar at least looked thoughtful. He eyed her over. "You say you're four hundred years old?"

Norris snorted.

"Over. The ship put me to sleep until the day Jorran found me." She looked at Norris. "You were right. I did not know your language. I had to learn it."

"You learned it awful fast." Vesar looked her up and down.

"I'm a linguist. I have an affinity for languages. I was trained from the time I was little."

"So you can read what's here." Norris shoved her toward the computer. "You can activate this so we can get the information we want." He pushed her again. Leeza fell against the console, catching the edge of it to keep from sinking to the floor.

"Bring up the information on the engines," Norris demanded.

Leeza flinched, but shook her head.

"Do−" Norris broke off as Esher rammed into the two men, his arms stretched out wide, taking them both to the floor as he went down.

"Hide." Esher grunted as Vesar slammed a fist into his stomach then one to his jaw.

Leeza didn't wait. She sprinted down the aisle between the machinery, dodging around huge metal pipes. She wove a chaotic pattern, turning on a whim before hunkering down in a small recess.

A full minute passed before she heard the sound of heavy boots on the floor. Her heartbeat increased as they came closer. She caught her breath, then to her relief, the sound faded as the man moved away in the other direction. Leeza chanced a glance, leaning forward, seeing Norris as he disappeared around a bend.

She caught sight of him several times coming close before she realized she had yet to see Vesar searching for her. The thought came to her mind an instant before an alarm burst out, echoing off the walls.

"No," Leeza gasped out. Panic flooded her. Vesar was trying to activate the engine. She couldn't let that happened.

Chapter Nineteen

Jorran reached the door, surprised to find it closed. Fear speared through him as he thought he'd figured wrong, and Vesar hadn't brought Leeza here. Before he could debate further an alarm started to resonate overhead. He glared at the door. The significance of the sound settled in him.

Ignoring the impulse to throw his weight against the door, he stepped to the panel and fought to remember what he had seen Leeza do. He went over each step in his mind, knowing he couldn't afford to do it wrong. He groaned in relief when he touched the last image and the door slid open.

He stared into the enormous expanse and stealthily headed for the most logical place for them to be. He was half way down the ladder when, he caught sight of Esher lying on the floor. At first, he thought his friend was dead then Jorran caught the faint rise of breath in his chest.

Jorran went down another step before he could see someone standing by the control console. Cautiously, he took several more steps. Vesar came into full view, his back to him working on the console. Jorran hesitated. He didn't see any sign of Leeza.

As if sensing his presence, Vesar turned, his hand going to the holster on his waist. Jorran recognized the weapon and dove from the stairs at him before Vesar had a chance to pull it free. They crashed down on the console, the force of the impact rolling over it.

Locked together, they dropped to the floor. Vesar ended up on the bottom.

Their hands wrapped around each other's neck as they struggled for supremacy. Vesar gouged a thumb under Jorran's neck and things began to blur. Jorran released one hand and sent his fists repeatedly into Vesar's side. The pressure in his neck faded just before Jorran thought he would pass-out. Still, his reactions felt sluggish as he tried to block a blow Vesar sent at him.

Vesar's knuckles glanced off his ribs. The man shifted under him, rolling to the side, throwing Jorran off.

Jorran rolled away, using the space to draw in several deep breaths to clear his mind before pushing off the floor to meet Vesar's charge. They locked together again, the muscles in their arms and legs bulging. Groans erupted from both as they struggled for control.

They staggered back into the panel of gauges. Vesar shifted, forcing Jorran up against the bottom of the stairs. Jorran shoved him back into the wall. They crashed their way around the room, getting blows in where they could, but neither gaining the upper hand.

Vesar pulled back suddenly, ramming Jorran's head into the wall. Pain spiked in Jorran's mind but he ignored it, swinging Vesar around so he was now pressed up under the stairs. Jorran released Vesar, slamming a fist into Vesar's abdomen followed by a blow to his jaw. Vesar staggered back then dropped his head and plowed into Jorran.

Jorran clamped down on Vesar's shoulders as he was crushed into the wall. Locking his fists together, Jorran smashed them down on Vesar's shoulders and the back of his head. Vesar broke away and came right back in, wrapping his arms around Jorran, once again trying to squeeze the life out of him.

ೞ

Leeza used the scaffolding overhead as a guide back toward the control console. She heard groans and sounds of fighting before she emerged from around the machinery.

Esher was crumbled on the floor. Her attention bypassed him, caught by the two men locked in battle. Each had one hand wrapped around the other's neck while they lashed out with the other fist.

Leeza barely kept back the cry that wanted to slip out. Only her fear of distracting Jorran kept her quiet. She glanced at the lights flashing on the control panel and knew there was no time to help Jorran or worry about where Norris was. The engines were trying to power up.

She rushed to the controls, studying what was there. Large letters flashed a warning, and the rise in the tone of the alarm added to her need to hurry. Leeza forced in a breath and fought her own battle for calm. She brought up the memory of the diagram for shutting down the engines. Her fingers trembled as she touched the screen, one spot after another following the sequence, step by step.

A groan of pain caused her to glance at the men. She gasped when she saw Vesar slam Jorran's head against the wall. Blood tricked down the side of his head. Tears burned in her eyes, but she forced her attention back to the console.

She glanced at the gauges on the wall, feeling a wave of despair when the reading didn't seem to be decreasing. She concentrated again, continuing on to the next series of commands. Suddenly, the warning ceased to flash and the blaring overhead stopped as the engines went dormant.

Leeza raised her head in time to see Vesar charge Jorran, shove him into the wall, up off his feet. Jorran countered, ramming his elbow repeatedly into the man's neck until Vesar dropped him. Jorran gripped Vesar, forcing him back against the stairs then slammed his head into one of the metal posts. Vesar dropped to the ground, not moving.

Jorran reached down and pulled the weapon from Vesar's belt then looked at her.

Tears burned Leeza's eyes, and she rushed for him at the same time he started toward her.

His whispered name turned into a scream when, out of the corner of her eye, she saw Norris come out from behind the machinery. The long bladed knife he'd held on Esher earlier was raised and ready to throw.

"No!" Leeza screamed as Norris's arm came forward. She dove at the man. Leeza cried out as pain burned into her shoulder. Her momentum carried her forward but she was spun to the side. She was falling and could do nothing to stop herself. She hit the ground and everything faded away.

Jorran swung around when Leeza's gaze shifted to the side and she screamed. His shock at seeing Norris changed to terror as Norris released the knife in his hand just as Leeza moved between them. Jorran fired the weapon in his hand but it was too late. Norris hit the floor an instant after Leeza, but all Jorran's attention was focused on her.

He ignored the sound of running up above as he dropped down beside her. His first instinct was to scoop her up in his arms, but the knife protruding from her shoulder stopped him. He reached out and brushed back her hair.

Her eyes fluttered open at his touch. "You're … safe."

"Shh, be still. I'll get you to Chel."

"Not important. Just wanted … love you."

Tears pooled in his eyes. "And I love you, my heart." He glanced up as Rese and Troth reached the bottom of the stairs followed by two other men.

A hiss escaped Rese as he looked down at her. "Chel is right behind us."

"Esh …" Leeza gasped.

"Rese will see to him." Jorran assured her, stoking back her hair. The pain clouding her eyes ate at him. He pulled off his shirt and tried to use it to staunch the blood seeping around the blade.

Behind him, Rese and Troth went to Esher while the other men split between Norris and Vesar. "He's alive," Rese announced. "What happened?"

"Esher tried … save me," Leeza said between small gasps.

"Shh." Jorran brushed his finger over her lips to quiet her. "I don't know except Norris tried to kill me and Leeza got in the way." He wanted to yell at her for the foolish action but emotion tightened his throat.

Above them, Chel called Rese's name.

"We're here," Rese answered back.

"Hurry, Leeza's …" Jorran couldn't say it.

A second later, Chel reached them. She eased the shirt away to look underneath. Blood still oozed. She opened the small bag she carried and pulled out a hypodermic. "I'm going to give you something for the pain. It's going to make you sleep," she said to Leeza, but Jorran knew it was meant more for him.

"Jorran," Leeza gasped his name as Chel pressed the syringe to her.

"Shh, my heart." He stroked her cheek as she slid into unconsciousness.

Chel raised her head to look at him. "Can you carry her back to the lab without jostling her too much? I'd rather remove the knife there. It's helping control her blood loss."

"I can carry her," Jorran said firmly.

"Good." Chel helped ease Leeza up so Jorran could get his arms under to lift her. Once he had her cradled in his arms, Chel looked at him. "I'll see to the others and be right behind you."

"Norris is dead," one of the men announced.

"It must have been set to kill." Jorran glanced at the man, then the weapon, and dismissed them as he headed up the stairs.

Jorran moved, careful of every step, conscious of Leeza in his arms. Her breath was just a faint stirring on his neck. He wanted to hold her tight against him, to feel her heartbeat with his, but couldn't with the knife still between them. He wanted to yell his anger at the offensive weapon, though he knew it wasn't the knife's fault, but the man who wielded it, but Norris was dead.

He felt no remorse for Norris as he glanced down at his life-mate, though he wondered how the man got back into the camp. Obviously, he and Vesar had been working together trying to get information off the ship. He'd known they were both underhanded enough to steal it. He just had never considered they'd go so far as to kidnap and kill.

It was his miscalculation, and Leeza and Esher were the ones paying for it. He wondered how his friend was. He hadn't trusted Vesar, that's why he'd warned Leeza about being around him, but he never foresaw this. He should have taken more precautions.

He looked down at Leeza and felt like he was tearing apart. He could not lose her. It was not time. "Not yet," he ground out.

"It'll be okay."

He heard Chel say over his shoulder. He hadn't even heard the woman come up behind him. He swallowed hard. "How is Esher?"

"He is unconscious but will be all right. Rese is making arrangements for him and Vesar to be brought to the lab then he'll contact Genis about what to do. They will keep Vesar under guard until you can tell them what happened."

They emerged into the clearing. People were still clustered from the alarm. There was open shock on their faces at the sight of blood on his face and soaking Leeza's shoulder. One of the women ran ahead to clear the opening for them. Jorran didn't slow, heading straight for Chel's lab.

239

Jorran suppressed a shudder. Crossing the quad like this was becoming common, but never before had it felt this dooming.

"The back room," Chel directed him to the table where he eased Leeza down. "Now go."

Jorran looked at her, shocked at the order.

"Out. I have work to do, and it will be easier without tripping over you."

Jorran was torn. He knew Chel was right but every thread of him screamed to remain with Leeza. Leaning down, he brushed his lips across her forehead. "My heart."

"She will be all right." Chel tried to give him comfort as he straightened himself, but he could see the worry on her face. It took all his effort to force himself out the door which closed firmly behind him.

Jorran paced the lab back and forth. The fury and pain in him barely caged.

When they brought Esher in a few minutes later, he helped settle him on one of the tables in the outer room.

"Where's Vesar?" Jorran asked. Fortunately, they didn't bring Vesar in. Jorran wasn't sure what he'd do if he saw the man.

"We locked him in one of the small storage rooms. Troth and Abams are on guard," Rese told him. "Catlin went to contact Genis."

Jorran nodded and turned his attention to tending Esher. After cleaning the cut on his cheek, which wasn't as deep as he first thought, Jorran found a bump on the back of his head. Other than that, and some bruises, the man seemed to be okay. As if to prove it, Esher started to stir.

"Easy. Just stay still." Jorran placed a hand on Esher's chest when the man tried to sit up.

"What?" the man said confused and blinked his eyes several times. "Where?"

"You're in the med-lab."

"Where's Leeza?" He looked around and groaned.

"Chel's tending her." The image of her bleeding came to his mind. He returned his focus to Esher. "Can you tell me what happened?"

"I don't remember much. I was talking to Vesar then there was a sharp pain. The next thing I was in the ship. Vesar threatened to kill me if Leeza didn't open the door. Vesar wanted her to activate the engines. When she refused, Norris cut me."

Esher met Jorran's eyes becoming more focused. "Leeza looked at me, said she was sorry. I knew she was saying we were going to die because she would never do it, no matter what they did to her."

Jorran felt his chest tighten.

"They were focused on her, so I rushed them. I lost consciousness again after that."

Jorran placed a hand on Esher's shoulder and squeezed lightly. "You saved her." He looked at the door where Leeza lay beyond. He wanted to go to her. He jerked when the door opened and Chel came out. Her face gave nothing away. He stepped to her.

"You can go in but don't try to wake her," she said forcefully. "I have her asleep."

"Chel?"

"The knife didn't do as much damage as I feared. I've mended and sealed the wound but she lost quite a bit of blood. Even though we experimented with giving her blood to activate her immune system, I am leery of giving her any now. I don't know how she will react to it. She's very weak. We will just have to see if her body can recover. It's already weak from fighting off just normal stuff around her."

Jorran wanted to deny the words. Instead, he nodded and went in to see his life-mate, leaving all silent behind him.

Leeza was so pale she almost blended into the white sheets wrapped around her. Her hair was a luminescent cloud around her head. Jorran caught a strand and let it run through his fingers, bringing it to his lips.

He placed his cheek next to hers. "Rest, my heart. Heal." Jorran willed the words into her. Tears burned his eyes. He turned his head enough to press his lips to her smooth skin. For once, she was slightly chilled.

He went to the shelf and pulled down a blanket, unfolding it over her, then slid a chair over, settling in it. Reaching under the blanket, he found her hand and interlocked their fingers. He laid his head on the edge of the bed, suddenly bone weary.

He didn't know how much time had passed when Chel came in to check Leeza then insisted on tending him. Later, she brought in food and stood over him until he ate. He fell asleep in the chair at some time. When he woke, Chel was checking Leeza again. Leeza was still so pale it hurt.

Chel caught him moving and turned to him. "Go clean up and eat," she ordered in a hushed voice. "You don't want her to wake and see you like that. It will scare her."

"Will she?" He choked on the words.

"Yes, it will still be a while though. So go, and don't come back until you've eaten."

Jorran stood. His muscles were stiff. He didn't want to go but a touch to his face affirmed the need. He kissed Leeza's cheek and left.

Esher was no longer in the outer room. Jorran took that as a good sign as he hurried to his chambers to clean up. The commons was packed with people when he entered. All attention turned to him as he stepped into the area. He nodded to everyone and went directly for the food.

Nothing looked good to him, but he loaded the plate because he needed to eat. He would be no good to Leeza if he got sick. There was a possibility Chel wouldn't even let him near her if he became ill.

He saw Esher sitting among the packed tables and went to join him, the others at the table slid over to make room for him.

"How are you?" he asked his friend as he settled down.

"Better. Sore, but my head has finally stopped pounding thanks to something Chcl gave me. She told us Leeza is doing well."

Jorran nodded.

"Genis and the authorities will be here any time," Esher said.

"Tell him I will be with Leeza when he needs me," Jorran said between bites. "I want to be with her when she wakes." He took another bite of food then unable to be away from Leeza any longer, picked up his plate. "I'm going back over."

Esher nodded.

"I'm glad you're all right. Thank you for helping Leeza."

"She saved me as much as I her. For that matter, she saved us all."

"She did." Jorran headed for the med-lab. He knew there were things he would have to handle, there was no option about it, but Leeza was his only concern at the moment.

⊗≈∞

Pain hovered on the edges of Leeza's mind as she drifted into consciousness. *Jorran.* Leeza forced open her eyes needing to see him. "Jorran?"

"Right here, my heart." He leaned over her. His hand came up to brush the side of her cheek.

"You're all right. The engines ..." Her throat was too dry to continue.

"You shut them down."

She watched his eyes drift over her face like he was drinking her in. She tried to raise a hand to cup his face and the pain hit her. She groaned.

"Lay still." It was a cross between an order and a plea.

She felt confused for a moment then the image of Norris with a knife in his hand flashed through her mind. "Norris. He was going to kill you." Fear crested in her then dissipated under Jorran's gentle touch.

"He's gone. He'll never try to hurt either of us again." He leaned down and brushed his lips to hers.

She savored the taste of him.

"You scared me to death when you moved between us. What were you thinking?" This time, he kissed her fiercely.

"I couldn't let you be hurt."

"And what about me, when you ..." Pain burned in his eyes.

With care, she raised her hand to touch his cheek. "I am going to die anyway. We both know that, but now, I know you'll live. I had to save you."

"You saved everyone."

His words brought her a rush of comfort. "That was what was important."

He caught her hand holding it against his face. "You're what is important to me."

"I love you. I think I was born to love you. I am thankful for every day I have had with you." The tears that escaped her were more happy than sad.

"I'm not ready to let you go."

"That's good to hear," Chel said from the doorway, "because you may be stuck with her for a very long time. How are you feeling?"

"Tired," Leeza's answered automatically, trying to go over what the woman had just said.

"That's to be expected. Let me know if the pain gets bad."

"Chel, what are you not saying?" Jorran pulled back looking at the medic as she calmly walked over to them.

"Hmm."

Jorran was not fooled by her nonchalant attitude. "Chel!"

"Oh, that you two will probably be together for a very long time. Though, of course, there are no guarantees."

Leeza met Jorran's glance, feeling just as confused as he looked. She still didn't get what the woman was hinting at.

"It seems your immune system is kicking in." Chel lifted the corner of Leeza's bandage to check under it.

"You said nothing was working." Jorran watched Chel.

"Nothing I was trying was. I just never thought of this. Seems, whether or not they had birth control shots in Leeza's time, she'd never had one and you, not being married, hadn't worried about yours." Chel raised an eyebrow.

"Birth…" Jorran shifted his gaze to Leeza, a smile blossoming on his lips.

"I'm … pregnant?" Leeza couldn't believe the possibility. "I'm …"

"Yes, several weeks I'd say, possibly your wedding night. I haven't been checking for that. It seems that, though your body doesn't have the natural antibodies, Jorran's does, and since the baby is made up of Jorran, too, it appears to be feeding your body the immunity from the inside, and your body is not rejecting it. I will have to run some more tests but I am quite certain it will hold."

"I'm not going to die," Leeza gasped.

The woman grinned, her face vibrant with the news. "By the way it looks, you're going to be fine."

"I'm going to have a baby." Leeza gasped, her eyes filling with tears of joy.

"It seems so. As I said, I'll have to run some more tests, but I've run that one three times." Chel looked at them and brushed a tear from her own cheek. "You are going to have a baby. Now, I'll give you a minute to celebrate then I want you to rest some more." She walked out.

Leeza turned her head to meet Jorran's gaze, all the pain was forgotten as joy floated through her. "I'm going to live. I'm going to have your baby."

"Our baby." He growled in pleasure and framed her face while lowering his head to kiss her. He raised his head just enough so he could look down at her. "Our miracle." He brushed his fingers over her face as he kissed her again.

"Am I dreaming?" she whispered the words between kisses.

Jorran pulled back, his eyes burning with intensity as he looked down. "None of my dreams have ever been this good. This is destiny."

"Destiny," she agreed, just before they sealed it with a kiss for all time.

About the Author

I grew up in a small town in Wyoming loving the outdoors, sports, art, and reading Hardy Boys books. After reading them all at least a half dozen times, I started writing my own stories.

Thirty years ago I married a wonderful, honorable man. I'm mother of five children and grandmother of six boys. I love traveling. Through my husband's work and vacations, I have visited much of the United States, all over Eastern Europe, Canada, Mexico, China, Thailand, Cambodia and Australia, giving me many intriguing locations and experiences for my stories.

I am a storyteller. I write the classic hero story because I think there's a need for more heroes, love, and adventure in our lives. I'm not out to change the world with my writing; I'm just hoping to make your day a little better.

Hope you enjoy.
Alysia S. Knight

Please feel free to visit me through my website:
www.alysiasknight.com

www.ingramcontent.com/pod-product-compliance
Lightning Source LLC
Chambersburg PA
CBHW031720170626
46808CB00005B/1820